DEMON DAYS

Book Three

DEMON DAYS
BOOK THREE
By Richard Finney
D.L. Snell

Copyright © Richard Finney
Published by Lono Publishing

This is a work of fiction. All characters and events portrayed in this book are either products of the author's imagination or are used fictitiously. Any similarity to real persons, living or dead, is coincidental and not intended by the author.

ISBN 978-1-938457-11-1
FIRST EDITION 2013

Original publication 2011
as DEMON DAYS – Angel of Light

Printed in the United States of America

PRAISE FOR DEMON DAYS

"*Demon Days* by Richard Finney and D.L. Snell is a fresh and rich approach to the age-old battle between good and evil. It's a gripping, visual, pulse-racing read."

—Andrew Neiderman, Author of *The Devil's Advocate*

"*Demon Days* is, by far and away, the best damned horror novel I've read in ages. It's been awhile since anyone has written compelling religious horror, the kind that harks back to *The Exorcist* and *The Omen*. *Demon Days* brings back elements that, for the most part, have been missing from horror novels for a while—compelling characters, and a sense of mystery and suspense. I hope to read anything Finney and Snell write in the future, whether individually or together. Their arrival in the genre is a welcome event!"

—Ray Garton, author of *Live Girls*

"*Demon Days* delivers suspense and pacing that rivals a James Rollins thriller, with stabs of visceral horror worthy of Douglas Clegg and Brian Keene."

—John Kirk, author of *The Talion Moth*

"Inevitably, somebody will try to tell you this book is part *The Da Vinci Code*, part *The Exorcist*, but they will be doing *Demon Days* a grave disservice. Yes, it's a high octane Church-centered conspiracy thriller. Yes, it's a terrifying account of demonic possession. But Finney and Snell have reached beyond those beginnings and have given us a truly important modern horror story. Like the best of T.E.D. Klein, *Demon Days* builds to an awe-inspiring confrontation between our thoroughly modern sensibilities and the supernatural. Finney and Snell will have your full attention right up to the last word."

—Joe McKinney, author of *Apocalypse of the Dead*

Demon Days offers up a hearty serving of end-of-the-world conspiracies, Biblical prophecy to the End Times, a clever spin on near-death experiences and plenty of political intrigue. And after reading *Demon Days* cover-to-cover in one sitting, I was asking for seconds. The end boasts a mind-numbing twist that I did not see coming and sets up for the sequel, *Demon Days: Angel of Light*, which I eagerly await! I wholeheartedly recommend *Demon Days*!

—*FatallyYours.com*

Demon Days is one of the best books of its kind to come along in quite some time. *Demon Days* was something fresh and entirely different. Finney and Snell took a chance... and it works. The idea of Satan using near-death experiences as a way to take control of people is a great idea. I think readers will agree after giving this book the chance that it deserves. The writers are working on a sequel and I know I will be the first in line to pick up a copy.

—*Horror News.net*

Demon Days delivers paranoid thrills into an end-of the-world scenario. This is a race against time for a young woman who must prevent the apocalyptic prophecy from coming true. Authors Richard Finney and D.L. Snell crafted a spell-binding tale... a nail-biting page turner... with a plot twist I was not expecting. *Demon Days* is a good, fast read.

—*Fangoria.com*

Demon Days is an easy recommend. The book is near flawless. Prepare for many sleepless nights!

—*28dayslateranalysis.com*

DEMON DAYS
BOOK THREE

BY

RICHARD FINNEY

D.L. SNELL

LONO PUBLISHING
Encino / California

RICHARD FINNEY

For Brooke, who's had to learn over the years how to live with a Demon.

D.L. SNELL

For my brothers, Andy and Zach, who over the years have done a commendable job curbing their urges to kill me.

The Story Thus Far...

In *DEMON DAYS* we met Sandy Travis, a news producer for a network TV show. She and her fiancé, Tom Hansen, are involved in a tragic helicopter crash while vacationing in Hawaii.

Tom dies as a result of the accident... but returns to the living after a Near-Death Experience. However, Tom is a changed man, his N.D.E. serving as the conduit for a demonic spirit to possess his body and control his future actions.

Father Alan Olsen approaches Sandy soliciting her support in helping him investigate supernatural incidents he believes are part of a worldwide conspiracy to usher in the End Days.

Their investigation uncovers proof of a deadly strategy, hundreds of years in the making, with an assassination plot as the most recent machination.

And at the centerpiece of the scheme is Sandy's fiancé Tom.

At a peaceful, celebratory gathering, viewed by millions on TV all over the world, the plan to usher in the End Days is enacted. But it turns out to be Sandy, not Tom, who shockingly ends up carrying out a violent act enabling Satan to possess the body of the influential diplo-mat, John Wolfenson.

Satan is here and is walking amongst us.

DEMON DAYS – BOOK TWO introduces Jenna Grant, an American Archeologist who specializes in Paleography, who is currently living in Cambridge, England.

Seemingly out of the blue, Neal Grant contacts his younger sister to request her return to Washington D.C. He needs her expertise in au-thenticating an artifact known throughout history as "the Black Pages."

Jenna returns back to the states. While fulfilling her sibling obliga-tion to Neal, she discovers two secrets -- the artifact she ends up verify-ing might be the key to a worldwide conspiracy to usher in the *End Days;* and her brother Neal, is not himself.

After Neal purchases the artifact, the two siblings are driving back to the city when she learns her brother's recent cycling accident led to a Near-Death Experience, which allowed Neal's actions to be in com-plete servitude to the agenda of an apocalyptic cabal known as the "Red Veil."

His final act, on behalf of the doomsday group, is to steer their car toward a collision course with a speeding commuter train that will not only kill them both, but destroy the recently acquired artifact.

Jenna fights back, and escapes the vehicle seconds before the impact with the train. She also manages to save the artifact from destruction.

Etan Vlessal has been in pursuit of the Black Pages for years, a hunt which has left in its wake a series of violent ritualistic murders. His chase has taken him all over Europe and more recently, to the United States.

As Jenna lay in the weeds recovering from the train derailment caused by her brother, Etan appears on the scene. He assaults her in an attempt to ascertain the whereabouts of the Black Pages. Seconds away from succumbing to Etan's attack, an unlikely source intervenes -- a passenger on the commuter train, who has miraculously survived the collision.

For months George Wyatt has been sleep walking through life, his almost trance-like state caused by the tragic accidental death of his wife, Carri.

After his latest visit to his wife's gravesite, George boards a commuter train, which turns out to be the same train that eventually collides with Neal's car.

Somehow George survives the collision, and comes to Jenna's aid, fighting off Etan until the killer is forced to ignobly retreat.

With the Black Pages in their possession, George scurries Jenna away from the scene of the accident and spends the next few days nursing her back to health.

Thus begins what can only be described as a mismatched partnership in search of the truth. One of the many problems challenging their working relationship is George's dawning realization that only paranormal reasons can explain the fact that they are both still alive. This is in deep contrast to Jenna's scientific background, and her general skepticism about anything that might be classified as supernatural.

But they are unified in discovering the truth behind events that have affected them both. Their quest takes them to London, Jenna's adopted home turf. She calls on the help of a co-worker, Raymond Chappell, in sorting out the hidden meaning contained in the text of "the Black Pages."

The dire situation ends up drawing Jenna and Raymond closer. During a break, the two share a romantic kiss while standing together on the hotel room balcony.

Meanwhile, across the street from the hotel where the three are staying, a familiar face watches with binoculars. Etan checks in with his superior via text message, asking for a green light to finish the job.

CHAPTER 1

CARL SARACEN MARVELED at the pristine condition of the Luftwaffe flight jacket.

"Look at it, sir," the Nazi memorabilia dealer said. "Not a mark on it." He held the coat near the window of the hotel suite, twenty-five floors above Paris. The lights from the city reflected on the re-conditioned coat's black leather.

"And yet I can verify that the owner wore this on at least two dozen sorties before he was grounded."

Carl caressed the jacket's shoulder, soft as butter. He traced the zipper down to the little buckle at the waist.

"Why don't you try it on?" the dealer said, peeling it off of the coat's padded hanger.

Carl held up his hand. "That's not necessary."

And it was probably impossible. The jacket, tailored to fit a slim German pilot in the cockpit of a Messerschmitt BF 109, was too small for Carl. For a fifty-five-year-old who travelled much of the year, he thought he was more than adequately fit. Even if his physique did fall short of his own expectations, it was the best he could manage under the circumstances; there was only so much exercise one could get in at international hotel gymnasiums. But the true issue he had with trying on the jacket was his height. Carl stood six-foot-two in his bare feet.

"I'll take it," he said, "along with the sketches by Speer." Carl consulted his wristwatch and realized he needed to call for his car to the airport, to catch his private jet to Tel Aviv. "Just leave everything and I'll have my people collect it. Payment in the usual way?"

"Yes, sir, thank you."

Carl dismissed the dealer and turned to Albert Speer's architectural design for the Volkshalle, a great hall, greater than the Pantheon in Rome. The impressive dome was meant to be the crowning monument of Hitler's Germania, his new Berlin. Carl loved Speer's concept that a city should be built to maintain aesthetic, even as ruins, or fossils. Throughout history, Carl believed the mark of a great man had always been to build upon the ruin of others. If you can predict how things will fall apart, you can work them into long-term strategy. Which, as he knew, was why some civilizations had been built upon age-old faults.

"Sir," the memorabilia dealer said.

Carl looked up in surprise; he had assumed the merchant had left.

"I must ask you. Did you ever acquire the Black Pages you were seeking?"

Carl hid his shock well. "No, I'm afraid the pages are either a myth or no longer attainable."

The dealer nodded. "I only inquire because I recently renewed my efforts on your behalf. I have made some headway in locating them."

Carl set down the phone, which was still ringing his driver. He approached the memorabilia dealer casually, as if headed for a towel after a dip in the pool.

Back in his early thirties, one of Carl's employees, a poker player, had told him something important after witnessing one of his nasty business disputes. "Your showdown walk is a total tell. I knew that guy was dead just by your swagger."

In the twenty-odd years since, Carl had perfected his game. He put his hand affectionately on the shoulder of the Nazi memorabilia dealer. "Unfortunately," he said, "I sincerely believe the Black Pages to be unattainable. However, I do plan to tell my accountant to add another zero to your deal, as a way of saying thank you; thanks for being more human than businessman."

"Thanks," the dealer said, practically in tears. Another zero meant a lot. "Thank you."

Carl smiled and said, "Allow me to see you out."

As he and the dealer rode the elevator to the lobby, Carl texted one of his employees concerning the fate of the man standing next to him. The message read, *Liquidate SS$$*

———

FROM A YOUNG AGE, Carl had intuited a simple concept: neither those who raised him nor his peers held the answers to the questions that most troubled him. Even his teachers ended up providing the same pat answers to questions that strayed beyond math, history, and science. Gradually the realization led to a huge change in his life.

In his adolescence, Carl left home to follow a guru through India, firmly convinced the holy man held some insight to humanity's salvation. But after just a few months, Carl became hopelessly disillusioned: his guru was no more immune to the lust for money and his more attractive followers than any other common man who had achieved, or was granted, a position of power.

Much later in his life, when Carl had long surpassed the need to be a sheep in another man's flock, he became aware of a secret group known as the Red Veil. Within time he insinuated himself into the group, not as a follower, but as one of its main benefactors, and then, later, one of its chief architects. From that position he spent years building something that could stand the test of time and, more importantly, the effect of turbulent events. Not future seismic upheavals based on readings from tarot cards or crystal balls, or even the Bible, but apocalyptic changes he himself was engineering—to ensure that when they did occur, he would be in control.

Then everything changed.

His son Ami was hit by a car.

He died.

After the paramedics revived him, the boy spoke of a bright tunnel, and an angel of light. He said that he had been sent back... because he still had work to do.

Immediately Carl knew his son was no longer his son. And he began to question all of his plans and efforts for the last two decades.

Later, when the Angel of Light finally possessed John Wolfenson, Carl and the rest of the Red Veil travelled to his hospital bed. The angel revealed his plans to them, and demonstrated his powers. But while the others may have departed his bedside convinced of their allegiance,

Carl left with only unanswered questions. At the top of his list: why had the Angel of Light possessed the loved ones of his devout followers? To control the Red Veil's loyalty? Because that's certainly how it seemed.

When the envoy called him to an impromptu lunch at The Oval Room in Washington D.C., Carl showed up believing that the opportunity had arrived to express his struggles in private. But things between them only got worse.

Wolfenson pushed across the table a napkin he had been doodling on while they waited for their food. Next to some sketches of dandelions and butterflies, he had written a list of names. Carl knew each and every one of them.

"These are the people who might not be with the program," Wolfenson said. "Potential weak links. We need to keep an eye on them. A jaundiced eye is what I recommend."

Carl saw the list of names as a slap in the face. Every "weak link" had been working for the Red Veil for the last decade, some for the last two decades. Each one of them had helped make the Angel of Light's transition to Earth smooth and successful.

After everything the Veil had accomplished, and everything they had sacrificed—everything and everyone—the angel intended to swat them like flies.

That's all Carl could think as he stared at the names Wolfenson had written with a red crayon, which he had borrowed from a child doodling under the umbrella next to theirs.

———

WHEN CARL TOUCHED DOWN at Ben Gurion International, Tel Aviv, his man on the ground, Randy Reitz, greeted him right off the plane.

Reitz had known his employer long enough to skip the small talk and launch directly into a status report.

"We have three hours before Wolfenson is scheduled to arrive," he said. "We have secured the perimeter around the airport with over four dozen of your best men."

"Excellent," Carl said. "Let's do lunch."

After eating in the King David Lounge for VIPs and running several security checks, it was time. Carl went out and waited on the tarmac. He wanted to be the first to greet the Quartet's Envoy to the Middle East as he stepped off his Boeing 777. Accompanying the diplomat was his wife, Patricia, and the psychologist, Dr. Fincher.

"Mr. Envoy," Carl said with a brief nod and handshake; like Reitz, he knew to be short with the pleasantries. "Just to warn you, sir, I need my men to immediately intervene."

Reitz, taking his boss's cue, outfitted the envoy with a bulletproof vest. Wolfenson clearly expected the extra security precautions, but Patricia did not take it so well.

"My God, Carl, is this necessary?" she said, yelling over the noise of airport traffic. "Have you received any specific threats?"

Carl leaned close to her so he didn't have to shout. "No specific threats. We just want to do everything we can to make sure the envoy is safe. He's a very special man."

Patricia nodded, but still frowned and crossed her arms as Reitz injected a tiny homing beacon underneath the skin of her husband's wrist.

Watching Wolfenson, Carl couldn't help but think of his own wife and son, their trips to the beach. Like the security personnel surrounding the envoy, his wife had always stood in front of Ami so that he could change from his wet bathing suit into dry clothes—as if she were shielding him, not just from view, but from any attack while he was at his most vulnerable.

————

"I UNDERSTAND, IMAD," Wolfenson said, "but is this really the time to let your differences with Israel affect your decisions?"

Six passengers filled the Mercedes SUV to its recommended capacity. They all sat in respectful silence while the envoy spoke via satellite phone with the Syrian Ambassador to the United States.

"People in your country are dying by the minute, Imad. Without more help, more people will perish!"

Patricia glanced around the vehicle. Two armed body guards had accompanied them on the ride into the city. One sat in the front passenger seat, and the other sat in the far back between Carl and Dr. Fincher. Patricia and her husband occupied the two seats in the middle of the Mercedes, and on the road ahead of them, Reitz drove another SUV full of guards.

"I'm sorry, Imad," Wolfenson was saying, "but that's not an acceptable answer. We both know they are the best at this type of rescue."

Patricia couldn't overhear what the Syrian ambassador was saying, but judging by her husband's side of the conversation, Imad was refusing any Israeli rescue teams into Aleppo.

"They've had years of experience..." Wolfenson said, trailing off as the ambassador cut in. "No, I wasn't implying anything by that last remark. Please, Imad, don't be that way. I'm just trying to help. So are they."

The Syrian said something, and though the sound of the SUV still obscured his exact words, Patricia could hear his voice.

"That's bullshit!" Wolfenson replied, leaning forward so sharply that his seat belt locked and strained against his chest. The scar on his neck had turned pink. "No dying man cares who is reaching out to save his life!"

As the ambassador replied, Wolfenson covered his mouthpiece to update everyone in the car. "He says his people would rather die an honorable death than owe their life to a Jew."

"Don't argue with him," Patricia said, putting a hand on her husband's arm. "Just find a way to save his people."

Wolfenson thought for a second, then nodded and spoke into the phone. "Okay, Imad, no Israeli will be personally part of the earthquake aid. Yes, yes, I understand. But we must certainly take advantage of their search-and-rescue equipment. It's state of the art...

"Come on, Imad, do you really want to be the one to explain why you're trying to get people's loved ones out of the rubble with a farm tractor?"

This time Imad said something that made the envoy grin. "Very good decision, Mr. Ambassador. So, just to be sure that nothing's lost in translation: I have your permission to load up our planes with as much Israeli search-and-rescue gear as we can carry? Okay, good... No, of course not. Why would I need to mention it at my press conference? I won't mention it to the media at all. You have my promise. Okay, we'll see you in less than forty-eight hours."

Wolfenson handed the phone back to Carl, who clicked a button and terminated the connection.

From the back seat, Dr. Fincher said, "Very good, sir," but the envoy's attention was totally on his wife, as if he were waiting for her approval.

"You handled that beautifully, John," she said.

He smiled. "Having you with me has already made a difference."

"No, this was all you. Don't take anything away from your moment."

Wolfenson raised his wife's hand to his lips and kissed it. "Together, we'll make a difference in this tragedy."

Patricia, blushing from the public display, glanced again at Carl and Dr. Fincher in the back seat.

Carl, who had been watching the envoy intently, turned to look out the window. He knew Wolfenson was acting and didn't want his eyes to reveal the charade.

———

AS THE CONVOY APPROACHED the Melody Hotel just outside downtown Tel Aviv, traffic began to slow to a crawl. A horde of picketers, marching, clogged the streets around the hotel. Carl called Reitz in the SUV ahead of them.

"I want you to surround the vehicle after we stop," he said, surveying the angry parade. Most of the picketers seemed to be in their twenties, but Carl saw many who looked younger. "And if one of those protestors gets within ten feet of us... take him down."

Patricia stared out her window as they waited to make the turn into the hotel's front driveway. "Oh my God," she said, "what's going on?"

"Nothing to worry about," Dr. Fincher called out from the back seat. "Just protestors marching toward the Wailing Wall."

Patricia tried to read some of the pickets, but couldn't understand the Arabic. "What are they protesting?" she asked Carl.

"They're Palestinians," he said, keeping his eye on the crowd—especially on the pedestrians within a dozen yards of the convoy. "And also some Muslims standing up for the Palestinian cause."

"Is this about the Temple Mount then?" Patricia asked. She had begun to recognize a few of the more common Arabic symbols.

"Hey, good eye, Patricia. Yes, they're protesting the heavy-handed security at the Al-Aqsa holy compound. It's the latest skirmish in the war for control of East Jerusalem."

"Have any of these protests led to violence?" she asked.

Dr. Fincher answered before Carl. "Not really. For the past week, the Israeli military has been responding to the protestors with tear gas and rubber bullets. But again, nothing to worry about. These protests have become annual events, like the bulls running in Pamplona... or the protests of the bulls running in Pamplona."

Carl shook his head and looked at Patricia. "I know Dr. Fincher is trying to ease your fears, but the situation in the Old City is extremely tense. We need to behave and act accordingly." He could feel Fincher's eyes burning into him, but ignored it. He had more pressing concerns.

Once their convoy finally pulled up and parked in front of the hotel, Carl waited until his security team was in place before he threw open the passenger door and emerged first. After a look around, he turned and helped the envoy out of the Mercedes. Patricia went to exit the vehicle, too, but Carl put a hand on her shoulder.

"Just a minute," he said, and he waited while Reitz and three security guards escorted Wolfenson into the hotel. Once they were safe inside, Carl helped the envoy's wife step out.

"Let's go together," he said. Patricia nodded, and they moved toward the hotel, with Carl's arm wrapped around her shoulders as if he were protecting her from a rain that had just begun.

———

WITH THE ENVOY AND HIS WIFE securely lodged, and the Arab protestors long gone for the Wailing Wall, Carl Saracen went to a cold place to meet with Dr. Fincher. "To pick each other's brains," as Fincher had put it.

Carl had bribed the hotel's restaurant manager for use of the chef's freezer. Surrounded by shelves of frozen vegetables and quality cuts of meat, the two men spoke of recent events.

"Your security measures since we've landed have been impressive," said Dr. Fincher, intoning as evenly as he smiled.

Carl nodded. "The envoy's wearing a human suit. That makes him as vulnerable as you and I are."

"Ah, this is why we are all blessed to have you as an asset, Carl. Because you're a man who thinks. It's why I've called you here. To ask a question, and your opinion."

"Yes, of course."

"How's your son?"

Carl didn't react to the question. For one, he wasn't sure who was asking it, Fincher or Wolfenson. Worse, he didn't know why. He certainly had his ideas. One was a napkin of red names.

"I have seen a definite improvement," Carl said. "Only the people closest to him could tell that he's... not really Ami."

"Yes, exactly. It seems each day the envoy is with us, his demons get a stronger grip on their hosts. Before, outsiders could notice a difference. The stretched skin, the shift in personality. But now *seamless* is the word, I think."

Carl nodded. "*Seamless* is the perfect word."

Fincher sighed, and his breath turned to a cloud of frost. "Forgive me, but there's something I don't understand..."

Carl had known Dr. Fincher long enough to understand the deception in his words. The reality was that the doctor was never at a loss for words or confused about anything.

"We agreed at our last conference that I would be the one to obtain the Black Pages, correct?"

Carl did not hesitate to respond. "Yes, of course."

"And did you hear about the train wreck in the States?"

"Yes," Carl said, "I saw the news. Of course I assumed it had to do with the pages. Was my assumption in error?"

"No, the only error you may have committed was in your decision to intervene." Fincher stepped toward him, and Carl could see it now, what the poker player had once observed in Carl's own swagger. He saw how naked body language betrayed the hand you were about to play.

"I want to know the truth," Fincher said, no longer smiling. "Convince me that you followed our agreement, that I, and I alone, would handle acquiring the pages."

A long time ago in Africa, Carl had become fascinated with how hyenas chose their target, how they favored prey that displayed a limp or a slight flaw in its gait. He had asked a zookeeper about it once, and the keeper confirmed it: he said he could never show the slightest flaw or vulnerability when entering the hyena cage, else the animals would pounce.

Carl handled Fincher the same way. He didn't step back, but nor did he march forward. He simply stood his ground.

"When the Red Veil listens to the entire group, they always end up speaking as one," Carl said. "No single member, including myself, can run counter to its aim. I've left it to you to acquire the pages."

His words, and his performance, must have swayed Fincher, for the doctor nodded and stepped back.

"So, did you retrieve them?" Carl asked.

Fincher let out a short, cathartic sigh, what Carl believed to be a genuine one. "I'm afraid not. The two assets I activated to obtain them have failed and are dead."

His words hung in the air of the walk-in freezer, where everything smelled of ice. By admitting failure, Fincher was also admitting that he was telling the truth. Carl was positive of that. And he couldn't be more elated.

He looked down at the floor to appear humble, and to hide his face. "Do you want my aid in retrieving them?"

Fincher stared at him for several seconds, with no evident hesitation or embarrassment or any feeling at all except objectivity. Carl had grown accustomed to the doctor's socially unacceptable stares. He suspected that Fincher, over the years, had become so used to visually evaluating patients that he could no longer measure the rate of his own blinks. The cold distance in his eyes had always unnerved some members of the Red Veil, so much so that Fincher had earned a nickname, Medusa.

"Yes," Fincher said, this time with a genuine sigh, and a shudder, which, Carl thought, was an encouraging sign that the cold could get to him. "If I'm right, and the pages are still floating around, I will call on you."

Without any sentiment or closing line at all, Fincher turned to leave.

Carl put a hand on his shoulder. "Colin, wait. Will you allow me to speak the unspeakable?"

"Yes," Dr. Fincher said. "In fact I encourage it."

Carl nodded. "Without knowing their actual contents, we seek to have the Black Pages destroyed. Have you thought about why?"

"No doubt I have given it some thought."

"And?"

"And I have decided that those thoughts could get me killed, Carl. Both of us killed."

Fincher's admonition, blunt as it was, meant nothing to Carl. The only thing he cared about now was Ami and the demonic tapeworm controlling his son's actions—an uninvited visitor sent by the Angel of Light. The possession had driven Carl to hate the sight of his own son. His boy's face, indeed his entire body, had become just a skin-deep semblance of who Ami once was.

So Carl, heedless of the warning, decided to speak the rest of his mind, hoping Dr. Fincher had arrived at the same conclusion somehow, by another path unique and personal to him.

"If our thoughts could get us killed," Carl said, "then you, me, or any one of us would probably be gone by now. We're only human. That was not the point I was trying to make."

He took a few small steps toward Fincher, keeping his hands at his side and his gaze fixed on the doctor. As a psychologist, Fincher had studied the eyes of a hundred psychopaths—hopefully he would see that Carl's intention was not to lead him into a trap. It was to enlist his aid in getting out of one.

"Colin, listen to me. I believe there are some restrictions to his... abilities. Restrictions that make him vulnerable. That's why he wants those pages. Rather than seeing his directive as a task, let's explore the possibilities that it may be a way for us to achieve some leverage—"

Unexpectedly, Fincher stepped forward and embraced Carl, held him tight. "You are instrumental in making all of our dreams come true," he said. "But you are *instrumental*, not essential. Is that clear?"

Carl nodded, knowing that the doctor could feel the gesture against his shoulder.

Fincher pulled him into a tighter hug, then released him and walked away.

Despite the doctor's display of emotions, Carl knew it was just a shortcut to where Fincher wanted the road between them to dead-end.

Business as usual.

Near the freezer exit, the doctor stopped, and after a considerable pause, he turned his head. "For me, this has never been about an altruistic pattern of choices. I've done what I've done for purely selfish reasons. And I see no reason to change course now. Helping the envoy build an empire upon the backs of the lost and misguided, watching them suffer as they lift us up—that's what I'm looking forward to. Carl, I do hope you appreciate that I took the time to share this with you, this private and guarded ambition I've never shared with anyone else."

Fincher's last words hung in the air, lingered there even after he had slammed the door. Carl watched the mist float until it disappeared.

As he was opening the freezer door to leave as well, his phone vibrated, a text message from his employee, Etan: *I have eyes on our target. There's another player involved. What are my instructions?*

Carl decided to stay in the cold a second longer to reply, and found that he, too, had begun to shiver.

CHAPTER 2

THE MOMENT JENNA AND RAYMOND stepped in from the hotel balcony, they smelled smoke. George no longer sat in the easy chair, and the Codex Gigas pages and translations had vanished from the bed.

"The loo," Raymond said, detecting thicker smoke around the bathroom door. He knocked. "You in there, mate?!"

Jenna tried the knob and found it unlocked. "George, we're coming in." No one answered. So she let herself in. Raymond wished she had allowed him to take the lead.

The sight in the bathroom caused them both to gasp. Raymond froze, and Jenna choked on smoke. She rushed to the toilet and threw up. She had expected George's body, but she hadn't expected this.

In the bathtub, just a few feet from where she knelt, they had found the charred remains of the Codex Gigas pages. All eight of them. Jenna's translations floated up as embers.

"Are you all right?" Raymond asked, stepping up to help her. Jenna wiped her mouth and stood before he could reach out.

"Excuse me," she said, and she went to the sink to rinse out her mouth. Afterward, she took a deep breath and turned to face the bathtub.

All that work. And everything that depended on it. Gone. That's why she had vomited.

Jenna scanned the rest of the bathroom, this time with a clear head. Throwing up had helped.

She pointed out the smoke detector, which someone had disconnected.

"Whoever burned the pages didn't want to set off any alarms," Raymond said.

Jenna nodded. "Yeah. But if you were a third party, why even take the chance of burning the pages here? Why not just take them and destroy them at your leisure?"

"It scares me," Raymond said, without a shred of humor. "You're starting to think like a bad guy."

Jenna didn't respond to the observation; something else had distracted her. A theory.

"George burned the pages," she said, and Raymond saw a look on her face that he didn't think she was capable of.

Jenna barged out of the bathroom, and he followed, but not too close behind.

"There's no sign of forced entry," she said, glancing around the room. "No sign of a struggle."

"He looked pretty beat-up already," Raymond said. "Maybe he was easy prey."

"No, not George," Jenna said, looking for any clues her friend might have left behind. "No matter how weak he was getting, he would've put up some sort of a fight."

"You sound as if you've known him for ages," Raymond said.

Jenna gave him a look, because that's all the hint he needed. He had the knack of saying just the wrong thing at exactly the wrong time.

On the bed, where the eight pages had laid, there sat Jenna's purse. But she hadn't left it on the bed. She had left it by the table.

George's accidental clue.

"He took my passport," Jenna said after rummaging through her personal belongings. "Damn it!" She hurled the handbag against the headboard. "I thought we *had* this discussion!"

Raymond stood a safe distance from her, too scared to say a word. She was no longer a woman, but a whirlwind, tearing up the room. She snatched up all of her loose belongings and stuffed them in her purse, then yanked open the closet door and threw on her coat, which billowed up around her. One of the sleeves wadded up and caught her arm as she tried to stuff it inside, so that she had to punch and struggle and build up her aggravation. She was still struggling with it as she blew out the front door.

Raymond flinched as it slammed shut behind her. He stood there alone, trying to process everything.

There was a knock on the door, and he was so clueless at the moment, he actually wondered who it was.

"It's me," Jenna said.

Even more confused, Raymond opened the door for her. "What—"

She kissed him, right on the lips. He tried to kiss her back, but she had already pulled away.

"I don't want you to think I regret making out with you on the balcony," she said. "Even if it did cost us the archeological find of the year."

Raymond stammered, but Jenna was already saying goodbye and racing down the hall toward the elevator.

"What do you want me to do now?" he yelled after her.

"Just stay here until I call you! And don't answer the door for anyone!"

Raymond watched her disappear into the elevator and she was gone, leaving an eerie calm.

———

ON THE ELEVATOR RIDE DOWN, Jenna scolded herself for breaking the golden rule of science: never let your emotions persuade you. Because if you did, you would start to see only what you wanted to see.

Or want to believe, she had told Raymond earlier when they were analyzing the quatrains.

Jenna had broken that rule with George. He had saved her life—twice. He had protected her, when she needed someone to protect her. After the train collision, she felt emotionally dead. Not now.

George had become the conduit for all of her deferred grief, someone she could feel sorry for, because of everything he had lost. Someone weak that she could protect in return. Someone who could feel her feelings for her, so that all she had to feel was empathy. That's what she had wanted to believe.

And this belief had led her to rationalize some pretty inexplicable events simply to justify her trust in George. But Raymond was right:

she didn't know him from Adam. And she certainly didn't know what he had become since the train wreck.

The elevator doors dinged and opened to the lobby, where a line of people waited at the check-in desk. Jenna cut to the front of the line, ignoring the protests from behind her. She got the attention of a young Englishman, one of two clerks working the desk.

"Excuse me," she said, "my friend left our room. I'm wondering if you've seen him? He's mentally ill."

"I'm sorry, ma'am," the first clerk said, "but I've been a bit preoccupied." He was the only one tending the line and was clearly busy.

The other clerk, a man of Asian descent, was tied up on the telephone at the moment, listening to someone who sounded angry. But Jenna's inquiry had caught his ear, and he looked like he was trying to get off the phone. Meanwhile, Jenna was stuck with the Brit who didn't know anything.

"Maybe we should call security?" the Englishman said.

"No," Jenna replied, perhaps too hastily. "That isn't necessary."

She glanced at the Asian clerk, who kept covering the mouthpiece as if he meant to say something. But then the person on the other line would shout, and the clerk would have to say, "Sorry, sir. Yes, sir. I understand."

Speaking to his manager, Jenna thought. She couldn't wait. And she didn't want security involved.

She knocked on the counter and said, "I'll just go find him, thanks." She started to walk away.

"Wait!" the Asian desk clerk said, covering the mouthpiece. He was holding the phone away from his ear while his manager screamed on the other end. "This man you're looking for... is he in his thirties?"

"Yes," Jenna said.

"Sickly looking, wearing a buttoned-down dress shirt?"

The English clerk perked up. "Oh yeah, *that* guy. I just thought he was pissed."

Jenna had lived in England and had known guys like Raymond long enough to know that *pissed* was proper English for shit-faced drunk.

"Which way did he go?"

The Asian clerk held up a finger and put the phone to his ear. "Sir, I think I have someone here who can help us."

"Help you with what?" Jenna asked. "What happened?"

"Your friend passed out in the lobby," the Englishman said.

Covering the mouthpiece, the Asian added, "It was just a few minutes ago. One of our hotel guests helped him up. I asked him if I should call a doctor, and he just kept walking toward the station—"

Jenna broke away from the desk and hurried through the crowd toward Paddington Station.

George meant to catch a train.

———

PADDINGTON STATION RESEMBLED a giant airplane hangar with skylights running down the center of the vault. The station served as a terminus for several different railways branching throughout London. Multiple sets of tracks, divided by platforms, lined the massive train shed.

George had been sitting for almost ten minutes on a steel bench in the station, catching his breath. His sweat had begun to pool. Dozens of commuters walked by him, giving him a healthy berth.

Tourists and businessmen alike waited on the platform for the Heathrow Express, about fifty travelers in all. Everyone waited silently, checking city maps or texting on phones.

George's breath sounded loud in the silence. Louder and louder, until he realized part of the sound was just the oncoming train.

The express docked, and he stood up to board with the others. The train ran every fifteen minutes to the Heathrow Airport.

Suddenly, across the station platform, a horse went galloping; a blazing stallion with golden fire for a mane, its hooves echoing off the tiles like a dozen horses running at once. George's vision exploded with light—daylight from a long time ago, shining on a horseracing track; and he could feel Carri's warmth right beside him. The horse was on the track, burning so fast it seemed no darkness would ever catch up.

But then the horse passed behind a crowd of people on the platform, and when it came out the other side, it was just part of a logo on some tourist's t-shirt from the Epsom Downs.

"England's most famous horse racing venue," the shirt said. The fabric rippled as the tourist boarded the train, so that the horse appeared to gallop down the aisle.

The flash was gone, and Carri with it. It had faded to the harsh fluorescence of the station.

Something in George had faded too. His energy. He felt as if his lungs were a balloon and someone had let all the air rush out of it. He could do nothing but stand there while everyone else boarded the train. Stand there, and try to catch his second wind.

As a photographer, Carri had always contemplated the concept of someone's life flashing before their eyes. "Our whole life's like one big photo shoot," she once said. "Right before you die, all the important images flip past you." George never bought into Carri's beliefs. He knew how the brain worked and seriously doubted the hippocampus would access information stored over someone's lifetime at the moment of death. Sadly, he was sure Carri had discovered he was right as she lay on the side of the snow-covered highway, drawing her last breath.

But ever since the train wreck, memories had been creeping in like the bruises. Each snapshot seemed to slowly scintillate until it was blindingly bright, and George had come to understand that these were the flashes. His life was just hitting him in slow motion, like his death.

This last flash with the horse had been faster than the others before it. So fast he had barely registered it. And he had noticed that, in general, the flashes were getting closer and closer together.

Time was catching up.

George lifted his eyes to look for the horse again, hoping to get a deeper impression of the flash, or at least to feel the glowing presence of his wife again, however brief. But something else caught his attention. This time, it was more than a memory.

Carri was on the train.

George stumbled forward, trying to run. "Carri..."

A buzzer sounded.

"Wait!"

He reached the train doors just as they shut. "Carri!" he said, pounding on the glass, leaning on it, too, for support.

"George!" a woman shouted. Her voice came from everywhere, and all at once. He looked up and around, trying to find the source—and then the train lurched forward, and George collapsed.

The express pulled out, and Carri was gone.

"George!" Jenna cried again, her voice echoing in the giant tunnel. She had seen him faint and was running across the platform toward him. His fall had drawn the attention of bystanders, but no one moved to help.

Jenna, distracted, ran smack into a black teenager wearing a backpack and headphones. They both sprawled out on the ground in opposite directions.

The teenager, a Jamaican, sat up and removed an audio bud from his left ear; the right bud had fallen out. "Girl, are you all right?"

Jenna ignored him and looked across the platform. Twenty-five yards away, a man in a gray sweatshirt and black gloves made a beeline for George's body.

Her head was still spinning from the collision, but Jenna swore the man in the leather gloves was the same person who had tried to strangle her after the train accident in Virginia. The stranger with the one green eye.

A shot of adrenaline got her on her feet and running, so fast she hardly noticed when one of the teenager's ear buds crunched underfoot.

The strangler had arrived at George's body. Jenna ran faster and almost called out.

Kneeling, reaching out for George, the strangler hesitated—but only because an older man had come out of nowhere and had set a hand on his shoulder. The strangler looked up, stood up, and the two men exchanged a few words.

The older man wore a wool cap and a long cashmere coat. He kept his hand on the strangler's shoulder. After a moment, the two men headed up a stairwell and disappeared to the street.

Jenna arrived breathlessly at George's side and dropped to her knees. He lay flat on his back, eyes shut, chalky lips trembling. He was saying something, mumbling. Jenna couldn't hear him over the noise of the train station and the murmur of the good Samaritans who had gathered around. She leaned closer and tipped her ear toward his mouth.

"No magic," he said, "no magic." She could feel his ragged breath on her cheek and in her hair; she could smell it. "No magic," he said again.

She pulled back, frowning. The words made no sense. And the smell: she had expected something bad, something dead, but it didn't even smell like breath. It smelled like... air.

Jenna looked down at George's blue sports shirt, transparent with sweat. The harsh lighting of the train station might have exaggerated his condition, but the bruising seemed to have spread across his entire chest, purple and green. Nothing on his upper body resembled the color of human skin.

"Shall I call for help?" someone in the crowd said.

"No!" George shouted. His eyes had snapped open, as if he had awakened from a nightmare. "No, I think I'm just winded," he said, much quieter now. "I'll be all right."

The group of good Samaritans looked to Jenna, who nodded, and then they slowly dispersed, relieved that someone else had taken on the burden.

"I'm sorry," George said, raspy and barely audible over the sound of another train pulling into the station. "I'm sorry I ran out like that."

"Jesus, George, what were you thinking?"

"Please," he said, "tell Raymond I'm sorry."

"Tell him yourself."

"I'm not sure that's going to happen."

Again, she looked at his wounds. She understood better now how deeply they hurt. "It *will* happen," she said. "Even if I have to call him right now."

"No, you don't understand. I'm not—" George tried to sit up, but couldn't move an inch without convulsing in pain. After a few more attempts, he lay back down, winded.

"Hey, girl," the Jamaican teenager said, holding his ruined ear bud a few inches from Jenna's face. "You broke my headphones."

"Oh, sorry," she said, "let me make this good." She took some cash out of her purse and gave it to him.

The kid stuffed the money in his pocket. "Want me to help you get your friend up?"

Jenna looked around. For whatever reason, subway security had not shown up. More importantly, she saw no sign of the strangler from Virginia.

"That would be great, thanks—"

George's coughing fit interrupted her. It sounded deep and wet, and disturbingly weak.

After a minute, when George still hadn't stopped, Jenna dismissed the teenager. "Thanks," she said, "I've got this."

The kid nodded and walked away.

No sooner did George begin to cough up blood.

"Oh God, George!" Jenna turned him on his side so he wouldn't choke to death. His next cough shot blood onto the concrete in stipples and high-velocity streaks.

He's going to die, Jenna thought. *Right here in my lap, he's going to die.* She tried to comfort him as best she could. Tried to comfort herself.

The coughing eventually stopped, and George lay back, catching his breath. His lungs didn't sound quite as wet anymore. "Can you help me up?" he asked.

Jenna was so stunned by the request she just sat there until George tried to get up by himself.

"Here..." She reached her arm around his back and helped him sit up. Then, kneeling behind him, she put her arms under his armpits and hurt her back lifting him to his feet.

George looked around the station, almost as if he were seeing the place for the first time. "I'm feeling much better," he said.

"Really?"

"Yeah, I think so. Can you help me to that bench over there?" He threw an arm over her shoulders and she curled an arm behind his back. Earlier in Occoquan, after he had saved her life, Jenna had helped George walk out of the New Age shop the same way, with him using her as a human crutch. Here across the pond, they were doing it all over again—stumbling forward together.

They fell onto the steel bench in a heap of tired limbs. Both of them, resting, stared silently at their surroundings, never once looking at each other.

"Why?" Jenna finally asked. "Why did you burn everything?"

"Because. Carri told me to."

"What?"

"She told me to burn the pages. It's the first time I've heard her since she told me to kill Dr. Fincher."

"Why didn't you tell me?" Jenna asked. It was the first time she had really yelled at him. Not that any passersby would have noticed, over the constant influx of trains. "Your dead wife's talking to you, and you never say a word?"

George shrugged. "I thought I did."

Jenna shook her head, then stood up from the bench and dug her phone out of her purse.

"What are you doing?"

"I'm calling Raymond. He's going to come take you to a hospital."

"No," George said, trying to get up. He fell back onto the bench. "You can't... you need my help."

"Your help?!" Jenna cried. "You just burned the pages!"

"Yes, because it's what made sense."

"I thought Carri told you to burn them."

"She did."

"And how does that make sense?"

"Her words made sense."

"Yeah, maybe if you're working for the same person as my brother it makes sense. They *wanted* the pages destroyed, George." Jenna was pacing in front of him now, like a school principal lecturing a student who had set fire to the chemistry lab. "Don't you understand? We're all just... loose ends now. You, me, and... oh God, Raymond!"

"I was trying to save you."

Jenna stopped pacing to stare at him. Slumped on the bench, he looked cowed, meek. He wouldn't meet her eyes.

She opened her mouth to say something, but an announcement over the station speakers interrupted her: the next train to Heathrow Airport was arriving.

"What are you talking about?" Jenna asked once the announcement had finished.

"I saw you and Raymond on the hotel balcony," George said. "I wanted you to stay with him."

He glanced up at Jenna and noticed she was trying not to cry. Out of respect, he looked down at his body, his wounds.

"I know I look like a mess," he said. "But I still wanted to take care of everything. I figured, maybe only one of us had to play this out to the end."

Jenna wiped her face with the back of her hand, surprised to find it soaking wet. *What the hell!* She was never this weepy. It had to be the alcohol, or the lack of sleep.

"George, I appreciate everything you've done. I really do. And I think you're right—only one of us has to play this out to the end." She started typing a number into her cell phone. "That's why I'm flying to Tel Aviv. If you can come, great. Love to have you. But if you can't, then I'm calling Raymond this instant, and the two of you will spend the next few weeks fishing for trout in the Thames."

She tapped in the last few digits, confident that her challenge to him would settle the matter. George could not possibly stand, so she would be off on her own, and he would get the medical attention he desperately needed.

But the moment she waved her phone in his face, in what George perceived as a call to arms, he closed his eyes and took a moment to center himself. Then he leaned forward and, hands braced against the edge of the bench, started the initial push.

Blood rushed to his head, leaving his knees to tremble. Jenna reached out to brace him.

"No," he said, waving her away.

Slowly, feebly, doggedly, he stood by himself. For the first time since he had collapsed on the platform, he felt in control of his lower body.

"Okay," he said. "I'm ready if you are." He tried to sound casual but knew he wasn't fooling her.

It was almost impossible to fool Jenna.

CHAPTER 3

THE PRIEST WAS SWEATING as he stood at the visitors entrance to the Israel Prison Service Medical Center. His perspiration was not a direct result of the heat, as he had taken a taxi from Jerusalem to Ramla where the facility was located. He had spent much time in Israel, and under any other circumstances he found the temperate climate hospitable. But after several weeks of not wearing his cassock, he had apparently lost the ability to moderate his body temperature to compensate for the stuffy clerical uniform.

The visitors door to the medical center buzzed, and when he opened it, he was immediately greeted by an IPS guard who smelled as if he had bathed in cologne.

"You must be Father Alan Olsen."

"Yes," he said. "I was wondering if you would be so kind to lead me to the check in."

The IPS guard had first noticed the priest's garb as he stepped out of the taxi. Only as Olsen drew in closer did the guard also see his milky eyes and graying hair. The briefing had said nothing about the priest being blind. The guard rested a hand on Father Olsen's shoulder and guided him to the front desk to check in.

Olsen hadn't worn the cassock since his expulsion from the parish in New York City, not even to Sandy Travis's funeral. He had worn it today hoping to elicit better treatment. He was trying to avoid a repeat of his dreadful experience weeks ago at the detention facility in Jerusalem, where they had mistaken him for a lawyer.

After about a dozen steps into the facility, the guard gently pulled Father Olsen to a stop, and a woman with a thick Hebrew accent said, "Please sign your name. Also put the prisoner you wish to see, and the time."

She slid the sign-in book across the table to the priest, who didn't move to accept it.

Like the cassock, his blindness often earned a fair amount of respect. He had almost brought his white cane to really sell the act, but decided it would be one prop too many.

"Be so kind to write it for me?" Father Olsen asked. "And help me to my signature, child?"

The guard nodded to the woman, and she humored the old man. His hand shook beneath hers as she guided his pen.

Writing a legible autograph had become harder for him, year after year; that part was not an act.

Just when he thought he was going to be escorted back to the prison's medical ward, the guard said, "There's someone who wants to see you first." He led Father Olsen down several hallways before giving him a gentle pat on the shoulder to guide him into a room. Olsen followed the guard's direction and walked half a dozen steps forward. The door he walked through shut behind him.

Immediately he felt the temperature drop well below the heat in the outer hallway. The room was comfortable, clearly air-conditioned. He took several steps in each direction, so he could feel the cool air bouncing off the walls and get a feeling for the size of the space: it was not too large, not too small; oblong, like a conference room. It was also silent. Probably soundproof. This was a place where people met. People who made important decisions for others.

"Hello, Mr. Olsen," a man said. "Please, have a seat."

"Aluf Ginsberg?"

He posed his statement as a question out of modesty. But Father Olsen was fairly certain the voice belonged to the Shin Bet agent he had met the night before the assassination attempt on Envoy John Wolfenson.

"If you just take about four medium steps to your right," Ginsberg said, "then a few small steps forward, I think you'll be able to grab a chair at the table. Then we'll be sitting opposite each other."

"I appreciate your specific directions, sir, but I'm here to see Tom Hansen."

"I know, Mr. Olsen. I also know this is not your first attempt. So if you don't want today to end up being another fruitless effort, you will follow my directions and take a seat."

Olsen followed the agent's directions.

As the priest settled in his chair, he said, "Are you admitting then that you had a hand in rejecting my repeated requests to see Tom Hansen?"

"I neither deny nor admit any involvement regarding your visitation requests. I hope my response to your question demonstrates how very careful I've become while dealing with a blind man. I have learned the hard way that people tend to trust a handicapped person's version of events as more trustworthy than the account of a government agent."

"And it would probably not help that I'm a priest."

"Ah, but the way I understand things, you really aren't a priest anymore. Or did I screw that up as well?"

"No, Mr. Ginsberg, you got that part correct."

"Please, Mr. Olsen, refer to me as Agent Ginsberg. At least one of us has managed to retain his title through all of this."

"Well then, Agent Ginsberg... are we finished here? Because I believe I have finally been granted permission to see Tom Hansen."

"You've been granted permission because I've arranged it. So let's be clear about that."

"So, sir, shall I assume there is a reason behind your change of heart?"

In one corner of the room, a small combo television/DVD player sat on a cart. The priest didn't know it was there until Ginsberg turned it on. Its speakers blared, but the sound of the footage was even more nerve-racking—if not for the deranged ravings, Father Olsen could have believed he was listening to the howls of a savage animal.

"I know you can't see this, Alan, but I'm sure you can guess who's screaming. I assure you, the video is every bit as distasteful as the audio. While in isolation, your good friend Tom Hansen refused to eat or drink, which wasn't too much of a worry. Believe me, we often get our share of prisoners opting for the starvation diet. But then at one point he bashed his head against the wall. He banged himself up pretty good before the guards could restrain him."

In between the screams, Father Olsen could clearly identify Tom's voice. He heard the guards on the video shuffling in and cursing, wrestling with Tom, then administering physical measures to put him under restraint.

"Please turn it off," Olsen said. "Please, Agent Ginsberg..."

After the second plea, the agent complied. "Hansen was moved to this facility after he continued to exhibit signs of a complete mental breakdown. Normally I would ask the opinion of a man like yourself, who is also a mental health professional. But we both know you have a checkered past judging the mental stability of people with whom you are associated."

"Disparage my credibility all you wish, but I previously admitted Mr. Hansen under my authority to a mental hospital while back in the United States."

"That's what the records indicate. But somehow he wound up here in our country shortly after his admittance. And so did his fiancée. And together they attempted to assassinate Envoy John Wolfenson."

"I assure you, they were not working together—"

Ginsberg pounded on the table.

Father Olsen jumped.

The vibrations had shot through his knees, which had been pressed against the lip of the table. He tried not to wince.

"If they weren't working together, then why was he a decoy while that bitch almost killed the man we were protecting?!"

Father Olsen didn't respond to the outburst. He felt sure if he did, it would only incite a tirade.

He heard a small, hollow pop and rattle from the other side of the table. Father Olsen had heard the noise so many times he felt sure what it was.

"Agent Ginsberg, are you taking medication? Perhaps something for your heart? Or something to relieve stress?"

The agent answered as he was capping the pill bottle. "So observant and intelligent. I've always thought of myself as possessing both qualities as well. Yet here we both sit in disgrace. Tell me, Alan, how did this occur?"

Father Olsen leaned forward, he hoped in the direction of Agent Ginsberg, because he wanted to add special emphasis to what he was about to say.

"I've come to learn there are mysteries in this world, Agent Ginsberg. Mysteries that neither you nor I can fully comprehend. And that's why, despite our best efforts... shit happens."

The agent had to stifle the urge to laugh.

"But that does not excuse the part I unknowingly played in the attempt on John Wolfenson's life. I assure you, my own heart grieves every day for my actions."

There was silence.

The priest had always been a man full of hope. So he entertained the possibility that Agent Ginsberg was weighing his words.

"Well said, Mr. Olsen. I would tell you to memorize that speech for the witness stand at Tom Hansen's trial, but the fact is, there probably won't be a trial. It doesn't look like your friend will make it long enough to prosecute him."

"So that's why I've been finally allowed to see him."

"Whether or not your church is officially allowing you to do such things, Tom looks like he needs to hear the same departing words you recently gave his fiancée."

The agent had stood up. Olsen could tell because his last words changed in pitch and echo. Ginsberg walked around the table as he continued to speak.

"Wherever they both end up in the afterlife, I'm sure Sandy Travis and Tom Hansen will discuss how your voice was the last they both heard at the end of their miserable lives."

Olsen wanted to flee the room. Agent Ginsberg had enough bitterness in his belly that he could spew for hours, if not ages. Only time would heal the reflux. But the priest knew he could not leave without apologizing for his own shortcomings.

"Before I go, Agent Ginsberg, I want to express my regret and sorrow that my actions led to any... disgrace that you have suffered."

"I don't want your apology. And even if I did, it's wasted on me. Because of my exemplary record, my career suffered very little damage from my failure. I will get a few negative comments in my file. And, of course, I will never again be assigned to protect high-value individuals in the future. Who you *should* apologize to are Agents Spielman and Levi. You may not have known their names, but they were the ones who allowed you to approach the assassin and perform the last rites. What they did was deemed by their superiors as irresponsible and a total violation of Shabak procedure. They have been suspended, which may not sound like a big deal, but I assure you, the careers of those two agents have been completely derailed. All because you wanted to save some killer's soul."

Father Olsen was about to respond, but then the door to the room opened, and he smelled cologne.

"Father," the guard who had been escorting him said, "if you will follow me, I'll take you to the inmate now."

Olsen ignored him. "Agent Ginsberg," he said, "if those two men suffered professionally because I was trying to give Sandy Travis comfort in the last seconds of her life... please, I deeply apologize."

"Father, sir," said the guard, "Agent Ginsberg has left the room."

————

THE IPS GUARD LED FATHER OLSEN down the corridor to the infirmary. Medical equipment hummed and beeped in the background, and the priest's shoes echoed on tile. He could tell from the acoustics and the slightest shift in the air that they had entered a large room, which smelled at once sterile and polluted. He heard coughing and soft chatter and legs restless beneath the covers, as the guard guided him down an aisle between a dozen beds.

Father felt the patients' eyes tracking him, watching him. He heard leather creaking, metal clinking, and knew without knowing that these men, these prisoners, were either strapped down or handcuffed to their cots. To their deathbeds, some of them.

At the far end of the infirmary, the guard unlocked the door to a small hospital cell. Father Olsen stepped into it, into a stench so tangible it stopped him, surely as a wall. Not even the guard's cologne could overpower the vomit and rot and excrement—a smell to which Father Olsen should have been acclimated. The boy Ami, during his possession, had smelled worse.

The guard said, "His cot is about a dozen feet in front of you. He's the only one in here, and he's to stay in his restraints. Would you like me to take you to him?"

"No, I can manage from here," said the priest. "Thank you."

"Just knock when you need out." The guard shut the door behind him.

Slowly, Father Olsen *swam* through the stench, through the thick of it.

"Tom," he called out.

No answer, except for his own voice resounding off the dimensions and contents of the room: the single bed; the medical equipment keeping the patient alive—at least the meat of him.

Father Olsen felt his way to the head of the bed. He heard labored breathing, rumbling with phlegm.

"Tom..."

At first, no one answered. But then Father Olsen heard the creak of bedsprings as Sandy's fiancé turned his head.

"The one inside me..." Tom whispered. "He says they have her."

"Lies," Father Olsen replied with a wave of his hand. "Sandy is with the Lord, I'm sure of it. They will tell you anything to keep you in their grips."

By some audio trick, the humming of the machines had become just another texture of Tom's unhealthy respiration. Together, the sounds swelled like the ocean: long in, longer out; low tide.

Tom said, "He says he doesn't need me anymore."

Father knew enough to pay little credence to the forked tongues of demons and their lies. Even their occasional half-truths served only to keep everyone, especially their host, off balance.

"If that is true," Father Olsen said, "he will leave you now."

From his pocket, he pulled out a wooden cross. The guards had confiscated everything else: his rosary beads; the chain and crucifix around his neck. He held the cross toward the prisoner's face.

Tom took a deep, congested breath. "I'm not worth saving."

"Tom, that's the biggest lie they tell. We're all worth saving..."

"What I did to Sandy... and now they've got her..."

Father Olsen moved closer to him, so close he could whisper yet be heard, and be heard well. "You need to live so that her death means something."

Tom's breath slowed and weakened, distant as the sound in a seashell. Father Olsen had heard this type of breathing before, those times he performed the last rites. He thought about saying something more, to relieve some of Tom's guilt. But he didn't know what else he could possibly say. Sandy had been innocent in spirit but guilty in flesh, and now the world had condemned her as a terrorist, all while elevating John Wolfenson to the status of martyr, savior, beyond mere politician.

"He says he will leave now," Tom finally whispered. "He is finished."

Usually, sounds guided Father Olsen well, but he missed several times before bringing his hand to rest atop Tom's head, finding hair that was dank and soaked with sweat.

He said, "It is but God who will liberate you from this evil spirit—it is but God who commands it to leave..."

Beneath the priest's hand, Tom started to vibrate, and then convulse. Thick slime bubbled between Father Olsen's fingers, warm from the body and smelling worse than the stench before it, now raw and wet.

Tom hacked up more of the foul waste—gagged and vomited it. His very pores excreted it. And globs of it overflowed his cot and splattered the tile.

"God commands you to leave this body!" Father Olsen shouted, feeling golden strength surging through him, as if he had collected all the light from the sun and was shining it bright.

With terrible suddenness, Tom fell still.

Cardiac arrest, Father Olsen thought, feeling the stillness, and the cold.

But then Tom let out a sigh from deep in his gut, and his breathing stabilized, free of phlegm.

"Father..." he said, followed by something else, spoken so quietly the priest missed the last half. So he leaned closer, and Tom said, "The Angel of Light has come..."

CHAPTER 4

RAYMOND HAD SENT ELEVEN text messages during Jenna's train ride with George. Cellular reception on the express had been weak, so all of his messages pinged her phone at Heathrow Airport.

George noticed Jenna reading them as they walked to the ticket counter of El Al Israel Airlines.

Do you know Bernard Rose? Raymond's first message said.

How about Sandy Travis?

Her fiancé Tom Hansen?

Jenna, I know the questions are rhetorical. You do your homework. But let me refresh your memory. Both Rose and Travis were shot trying to kill John Wolfenson.

Here we go, Jenna thought. The lecture.

Rose was the first failed assassin in Tel Aviv. He was gunned down by the Secret Service... on the very day Travis and her fiancé were in a helicopter accident!

Again, you probably know that. But do you know Helen Myers?

How about Terry Zernke?

Jenna definitely had heard both names. As Raymond suspected, she had researched the topic on her smartphone during some unbearable airport waits.

Both Myers and Zernke worked with Sandy Travis, Raymond explained. *Myers was attacked by a dog, and Zernke died in a car accident...*

Please!!! Really?!!! A dog attack and a car accident, all within days of a helicopter crash and two attempts on Wolfenson's life?!!! You've got to be kidding me—

—!!!!

Jenna almost laughed at the last message, despite everything. It was just, Raymond had gone so wild with exclamation points, he couldn't even fit them all into the character limits of a single text.

She noticed, too, that he had sent some of his messages minutes apart. She could picture him, switching back and forth between his phone's Internet browser and text messenger, sending her second-by-second updates of his search results.

The dictionary defines 'coincidence' as 'something that happens by chance in a surprising or remarkable way'. But the definition of the word doesn't mention any—

—thing about frequency.

I think another 'C' word better defines what I've been reading about, and what's been happening to you since the States: 'CONSPIRACY'.

For the first time, Raymond's messages actually surprised her, and it had nothing to do with his British treatment of punctuation. Jenna had been running so fast and so hard she hadn't seen the full truth, that all these little details represented the strands of a very large and very sticky web. As if it all had been *spun*.

Don't just hit 'erase' on your phone, Jenna. I'm perfectly sober as I write this... Call me!!!!

Jenna's thumb was already hovering over the delete button. Raymond's texts weren't meant to help her. They were arrows to puncture her bubble. Maybe he had fired so many because she had become a moving target since last they talked.

"I'm going with George to Syria," she had told him back at Paddington Station, back when she still had some semblance of cellular reception. "We're catching a plane to Tel Aviv."

The connection had been sketchy and full of static, but Raymond's reaction had cut through the noise without a problem. "If you do that, Jenna, it's clear evidence you damaged your brain whilst in the States."

"You know, Raymond, it's funny how your accent can be sexy on the balcony of a hotel, but when it comes time to castigate me for something, it makes you sound like a baton-carrying Bobby."

His response had been broken up by the bad connection, and dampened by the sound of the arriving Heathrow Express. Jenna caught only a few words: *stubborn*, *foolish*, and, much to her surprise, *dysphoria*. Later, on the ride to the airport, she would puzzle over the context in which Raymond might have used that final word.

"I can't hear anything you're saying," she had told him, plugging her other ear. "Just stay low, do you hear me? You're right about everything... but that only means you could be in danger too. So stay out of sight, okay, Raymond? Raymond?!"

A dead silence had muted even the static on the line. "Damn it," Jenna said, clapping her phone shut. She had forgotten to tell him about the man with the one green eye, who was possibly loitering about the hotel.

During the train ride, she had tried several times to call Raymond back, but hadn't gotten reception until now, here at the Heathrow Airport. Except now, she had decided against calling him. It was something her brother had said: "We can't leave a cyber-trail. Too easy to trace." The statement reminded her too much of webs, purposefully spun.

Not only had Jenna physically involved Raymond in her problems, she had left records of her previous calls and texts to his number.

Against his wishes, she started deleting every last one of his messages. She planned to delete her call history after that, and all of her contacts—any information at all that could be used to hurt someone else. She knew the really important numbers by heart anyway.

As she and George joined the line for the ticket counter of El Al Israel Airlines, he said. "Checking cricket scores?"

Distractedly, Jenna looked up. "Huh? No. Sorry. Just... reading some texts."

"From whom?"

Jenna smiled, but George could see her jaw muscles clenching. He couldn't tell whether she was reacting to him, or to the messages.

"They're from Raymond," he guessed.

Jenna lowered her phone and looked up at him. "How are you, George?"

"You know... every time you ask me that, I think I'm getting a little better."

She thought he was being sarcastic. "Sorry, didn't realize I'd said it so much."

"No, please, it's a legitimate question. So tell me, what are the messages you're erasing?"

"George, I'm sorry but—"

"You keep saying that too."

"Yeah," she said, "I do. It's just..." She thought about what Raymond had said, that Jenna didn't really know George. But that wasn't entirely true. "I'm just not sure how much I should be telling you."

George nodded and looked ahead. "Well, I certainly haven't given you any reason to. I know that."

"George..."

"Just know, Jenna... I've told you everything."

"Except what's really happening to you."

Jenna must have thought George looked troubled, because she seemed vindicated by his response.

She turned back to her phone and continued to delete Raymond's messages.

George didn't ask why she was getting rid of the evidence. He knew why. Jenna was deleting the messages for the same reason George had tried to flee the Hilton alone: to protect someone she cared about.

He also knew her precautions wouldn't matter. All of his certainly hadn't. Otherwise he would have been standing in Heathrow Airport by himself. He could barely comprehend how Jenna had shoehorned her way into his plans. In fact, everything in the past few hours had fallen into a thickening fog.

"George..." Jenna said, nudging him toward the ticket counter. It was their turn.

He smiled weakly at the attendant. "Two tickets on the next flight to Tel Aviv please. First class, if you have it."

The attendant checked her computer. "I'm sorry, sir, but the only seats left are in coach."

George sighed. He had wanted to expose himself to as few passengers as possible. "Oh well," he said, handing her a credit card. "We'll take what you have."

The attendant charged the card and printed out their boarding passes. She handed them both to George with a smile. "Your plane boards in approximately thirty-five minutes, sir. Enjoy your flight."

———

JENNA WENT AHEAD OF GEORGE through the security checkpoint, purposefully moving quicker than he was able to. She made it through the magnetometers, the wand, and the carry-on X-ray, and then, while collecting her shoes, jacket, and cell phone on the other side, she watched George make his way through the same inspection gauntlet.

His sickly appearance only made the guard with the wand more uncomfortable as she scanned him from his damp socks to his damp, matted hair. The wand didn't detect anything unusual, but the guard still signaled the senior inspector to conduct a full body search.

Jenna hadn't expected the pat-down. Still, she let it happen. They were no longer carrying the Codex Gigas pages, so neither of them should have had anything to hide.

Having found nothing on George, the senior inspector took the other guard aside to deliberate. They still seemed concerned.

"You know..." Jenna finally said, "he's with me..."

The words sounded distant and removed, as if someone behind her was impersonating her and throwing her voice. All the security guards turned to stare at this ventriloquist behind her, and it took Jenna a second to realize they were really staring at her.

"You're the one!" the senior inspector exclaimed.

Jenna almost flinched, she was so taken aback. Paranoia instantly set in. Had her name ended up on some watch list? Was her photo being circulated to security personnel that very instant?

No, she thought, that couldn't be it. They had issued her a ticket and had checked her identification without raising any alarms.

The inspector certainly recognized her though. "*Stripped and Exposed*," he said, as if he had just lit on it. "That's what you are, right? Am I right?!"

Jenna chuckled, hoping she didn't sound nervous, or too relieved.

"Tell me I'm right!"

"Actually, sir, you're spot on if you're talking about my radio show. But if you're referring to my present state of dress... well... let's just say I avoided the strip search."

All the guards laughed, even the one who had flagged George for the body search.

"What happened to your face?" the senior inspector asked Jenna, still in good spirits.

"Fell down on a dig," she said, and again everyone laughed. They all shook her hand and asked for her autograph, and took a couple of photos with her. As the cameras flashed, she felt even more self-conscious about the bruises. Fortunately she had used makeup to conceal how deep they really were. And at the very least, she had sorted out her hair.

As Jenna smiled for the last picture with the senior inspector, she glanced at George, who had made it through to his carry-on bins, fresh out of the X-ray. He had passed this test, if not the one before it. And Jenna was comforted by that, despite all the peeved looks from the other passengers who had been delayed by her celebrity.

———

THEY BOTH WALKED SWIFTLY from the security maze with George still holding his wallet, shoes, belt, and keys. They hadn't waited for him to get dressed in case the inspectors changed their minds.

"Here," George said, handing his belt and car keys to Jenna. He pulled most of the cash from his wallet and said, "I want you to take this."

She waved it away.

"Jenna, don't be ridiculous. We both know you must've maxed out your credit card with the hotel room in London." When she didn't correct him, George shoved the cash into her purse. "And here..." He pulled out his ATM card.

Jenna stopped walking and wheeled around to face him. "I thought we were doing this together, George."

"We most definitely are." He stuck the plastic card into her purse and took back his belt and keys. "I'm going to tell you the ATM code. Think you can remember it?"

He grinned lightheartedly. Over all the miles they had travelled together, Jenna had never seen such a sight. It only worried her. Sometimes George seemed to be ahead of the curve, but right now a curve ball probably would have hit him square in the head.

Jenna's phone rang, and she almost jumped. She hadn't had time to delete all of her contacts yet, but she had definitely deleted Raymond's, so only his number registered on the caller ID.

Jenna thought about ignoring his call. But he had already initiated the cyber-trail. *Damned if you don't*, she thought, and pressed *Talk*. "Hello?"

George could hear Raymond's voice over the little speaker, but couldn't hear what he was saying. He waited for Jenna's reaction to see what the call was about.

"Yes, Raymond, I'm going through with this. Yes, yes, of course I got your texts. I appreciate the information. Did you get the text messages I sent you? Yes, the man with the green eye. Just watch out for him, okay? Promise me."

George wanted to step away and give her some space, but he thought if he did, she would only panic.

"Raymond, it sounds like you're upset that we didn't thank you for all your help. I promise you an acknowledgment when I submit the article to *Archeology Review*."

"He was a lot of help," George said, touching Jenna's elbow. "Please, let him know how much we both appreciate it."

Jenna turned from George and rolled her eyes, astounded that her obvious stab at sarcasm was lost on him.

"Look, I'm sorry," Jenna told Raymond, "I was kidding. What you're saying makes perfect sense. But as you've seen for yourself, none of what's happened up to this point makes any sense at all unless it's been orchestrated."

She fell silent again as she listened to whatever Raymond had to say. George still couldn't understand him, but knew that Raymond was attempting in every way to stop Jenna from moving forward. And Jenna was hanging on every last one of his words.

Back at the hotel, George had seen something on the hotel balcony. He was seeing it again as Jenna listened to Raymond.

What these two had together was special.

"SO," JENNA SAID, "any dreams about Carri?"

Their plane had just landed in Tel Aviv, and the touchdown had jarred George from a deep sleep. Immediately he sat up and checked his pillow. Then, from his nostrils, he pulled out two plugs of Kleenex, which he had gotten from Jenna before takeoff. The little wads came out perfectly white.

George closed his eyes and settled back in his seat. "No," he said, "no dreams at all, in fact."

The plane parked, and the other passengers crowded the aisle.

"Seriously, George," Jenna said, "I wouldn't worry too much about the dreams."

"And yet it was the first thing you asked me when we landed."

"Actually, I set aside the first question I had because you fell asleep so quickly after takeoff."

A man in a suit opened the compartment above Jenna, and she leaned into George, who sat in the window seat. She didn't want to get hit in the head by someone's carry-on.

Normally, she was the first person on her feet when the plane landed. She would always race forward and see how many rows she could pass before anyone else emerged from their seats.

Not today. She knew George was too weak to stand with everyone else in the aisle. So they waited. It was just as well. Jenna wanted the opportunity to talk with him after he had gotten some sleep.

"'No magic,'" Jenna said. "What does that mean?"

"What? Where did you—"

"That's what you kept saying on the train platform when you were... pretending to be dead."

"Hmm," George said, "you know, that might be the first time I've heard you crack a joke."

"Actually, George..." Jenna began. She had planned to cite her recent attempt at sarcasm on the phone with Raymond, but changed her mind. "Quit dodging my question."

"I'm not dodging." He turned to look out the window and said nothing more.

After a few minutes of silence, they unfastened their seatbelts and walked down the empty center aisle and left the plane.

———

FROM THE BOARDING GATE, they walked across Ben Gurion International toward the car rental companies near one of the exits. As Jenna mentally weighed which company to choose, George coughed, cleared his throat, and picked up where they left off on the plane.

"Do you know anything about horseracing?"

"No," Jenna said, "not really."

"Yeah, Carri and I were never that big into it either. But a few years ago there was this one horse named Zen."

"Oh yeah, the horse with the perfect record."

"So you know the horse?"

"Kind of."

"Well, in a sport dominated by males, Zen was a mare with a perfect record, including victories over some of the best colts ever."

"Actually," Jenna chimed in, "her perfect record might have been a tad suspect. Since she ran mostly on synthetic surfaces rather than genuine dirt."

"I thought you didn't follow horseracing."

"Zen was huge. I guess I picked up a few things and didn't realize it."

George shook his head. He couldn't believe it was just now hitting him: Jenna's brain seemed to be a giant repository of acquired facts. If he had recognized that sooner, he never would have questioned her ability to memorize the quatrains and the exorcism.

"Well," George said, "Carri and I both got caught up in the hysteria of this horse, and so we flew to Kentucky for her final race. There were more than seventy-two thousand people at the track that day. I think all of them, certainly Carri and I, were hoping Zen would remain perfect before retiring."

Jenna winced. She knew exactly how this story ended.

"The race started out like all her others: Zen immediately fell behind. But then, in the homestretch, she made her move. And like in all her previous races, it appeared as if she was going to come from behind and win. But..."

George couldn't utter the words, so Jenna finished the sentence for him.

"The horse lost."

"By a nose," George said. "Her attempt at perfection was spoiled by a colt who was also running his final race."

The moment they had landed, Jenna had pulled her smartphone out of her coat pocket. Now it suddenly lit up in her hand. The clock had readjusted for the time zone change, and, she noticed, she had a signal, but only a few bars.

George fell silent as he watched Jenna peruse the screen on her phone.

"Sorry," she said, turning back to him. "Go on."

George nodded. "After the horserace, I saw Carri crying. Bawling like a baby. When I was able to get her to talk to me, she said there's no magic left in this world. She said it over and over as I hugged her. 'No magic. No magic...'"

George's words drifted off and his eyes glossed over as he stared at some tacky sign for a rental car agency.

Jenna touched his shoulder and kneaded it, hoping to bring him back from memory lane. "No disrespect to your wife," she said, "but Carri was wrong. You standing here beside me... that's magic."

George's eyes eventually focused, and Jenna said, "Now come on." She started toward one of the rental car establishments.

"No, I'm not finished," he said.

Jenna stopped to listen, but then her phone beeped, distracting her. She had received a message. A message with an attachment. She didn't recognize the number, but the subject line read "Raymond." She hit the button to download the file, then turned her attention back to George. "I'm listening."

"The day after the race, I made a point about reading in the newspaper about the jockey who beat Zen. I wanted to know what he thought about stopping her from achieving something people all over the world could admire for decades. The jockey admitted he had mixed emotions about winning. He said he wished Zen had gone out with a perfect record, but only at someone else's expense."

Jenna's phone beeped again as the download completed. She barely heard it, too intrigued by George's story, and perplexed about the point he was trying to make.

"It's what the jockey said that you and I need to believe in now, Jenna. He was fully aware that, even though he was running against perfection, maybe even magic, he wasn't going to give in. Don't you see? He beat Zen because he would not allow fate to dictate his role in history."

Now it was Jenna's eyes that glossed over as she digested his story. The moral was easy enough to understand. What stumped her were two little voices in her head arguing over whether she believed in fate.

Out of the corner of his eye, George noticed moving video on the screen of Jenna's phone. "What is that?" he asked, pointing.

She looked at the screen, and at first she didn't understand what she was looking at. Her eyes took a few seconds to adjust to the fuzzy quality, and even then she had to play the ten-second clip again to confirm what she had seen.

"It's... Raymond," she said. "Sitting at Gerry's."

"Who's Gerry?" George asked.

"No, it's... a pub we go to. In Cambridge." She squinted and brought the phone closer to her eyes. "He's watching a... soccer game, I think." She started tapping the buttons to play it again, but someone behind them interrupted.

"This time when you play it back," the man said, "look at the teams that are playing."

Jenna and George both turned, confronted by a trim, deeply tanned man with salt-and-pepper hair, wearing tan slacks and a white linen shirt beneath a beige blazer. He held a cell phone in his hand and a newspaper in the other.

"Or perhaps the teams would be clearer if you watched the video of Raymond on my phone," he said. "I think I might have the better picture." He held up the newspaper in his hand. "Today's sports page should confirm that the two teams he's watching are playing at this very moment."

For the second time in less than six hours, Jenna wanted to throw up. This time she controlled herself. "What do you want?"

The man smiled before he responded, and Jenna thought he meant it to be a comforting, reassuring smile.

"Oh, I'm quite confident you know exactly what I want."

CHAPTER 5

TRYING NOT TO BLINK OR FLINCH, or show any sign of fear, Jenna took a step toward the man with the salt-and-pepper hair. She couldn't stop thinking about what might have happened to Raymond. And what might happen to her and George.

"We don't know who you are," she said, "or why you're threatening my colleague Raymond, but I want to assure you our visit to this country is purely for humanitarian reasons. My friend here, as you can clearly see, is very sick. He's actually been diagnosed with a terminal illness and his... last wish was to see this part of the Middle East. That's it. That's why we're here. If you believe otherwise, then I suggest you review the sources of your information."

George watched the man as Jenna spoke. Watched him shake his head, not out of frustration, but out of admiration.

"That was beautiful," the man said. "I bet you would have beaten a lie-detector test. But now, if you'll indulge me, I'll appropriate your story as a guide for my response..."

Jenna tried not to make it obvious, but as the man spoke, she averted her eyes in an attempt to locate airport security. A pair of uniformed Israeli soldiers stood just fifty feet away near one of the main entrances. Both of them toted rifles.

"My name is Carl Saracen," the man said, "and that's my real name. When we're finished together, you can confirm my identity through the Internet. I only ask that you ignore some of the embarrassing photos your search will pull up. Unfortunately when I was younger, a fashion guru sold me on the concept of blending Western and Mideastern clothing styles. I followed his advice because he was my brother-in-law."

Jenna was not impressed. The self-effacing comedy actually terrified her. Carl, as he called himself, was in no hurry to make his point, and wasn't afraid at all that anyone around them, including the guards, would interrupt. And worse, Jenna was absolutely certain the joke had been crafted to make her underestimate him.

"So," Carl said, "let's talk about your friend Raymond. I know it'll be very hard for you to believe this, but my surveillance is for his own protection. There are some very dangerous people determined to kill the both of you, and everyone you've involved over the last couple of days."

He stopped to let that soak in. Jenna let him have his dramatic pause. She knew he wouldn't quit talking anyway. His type liked to hear his own voice.

"Now, I most certainly will put my information-gathering system under review if the following facts are incorrect: your name is Jenna

Grant. Your brother, Neal, was killed while trying to murder you. He missed. And as a result of his action, dozens of innocent people were killed on a train in Virginia."

Jenna couldn't help but facially react: a frown, an involuntarily twitch of the eyelid. Hearing the cold hard facts of what her brother had done, and not some euphemism they used on the news... it made her acutely aware of how much the hand-shaped bruise on her arm still hurt.

"And you, George Wyatt, your wife recently died in a car accident."

An image of Carri, clutching her camera and leaning out of the car window, flashed into George's brain. He shook his head, trying to concentrate on what Carl was saying.

"You, too, were involved in the train collision caused by Jenna's brother."

Again, Carri popped into George's mind, this time sitting on the commuter train with her back to him. Then the impact of the train collision, his muscle memory of it, shook George back to reality; back to Carl's version of it anyway.

"I'm going to bet that the two of you, after everything you've been through together, have developed quite a close bond, maybe even a symbiotic relationship."

Jenna had never thought of it as a symbiosis, but she and George certainly had been keeping each other alive.

"So I'm here to challenge a notion that I'm sure you've never thought twice about: your assumption that running into each other as a result of the train collision was mere happenstance."

Another dramatic pause. The way Carl watched Jenna's face and eyes with anticipation, she knew he was waiting for the moment his revelation hit home.

"Are you saying this has all been orchestrated?" she asked, feeling that it was time to interrupt.

Carl took his own step toward Jenna and George but never lowered his voice, displaying no fear of inquiring ears or cameras.

He said, "By acquiring the Black Pages, you've put yourselves in the middle of a seismic event, the gravity of which you may be aware of, but which I doubt you truly comprehend."

It was the first time Jenna had heard the phrase "Black Pages." Under different circumstances, she would have beaten herself up that the words had not once crossed her radar.

"The purpose of introducing myself today," Carl said, "is to convince you that the artifact in your possession will only get you killed, along with everyone you care about. I'm here to convince you to accept my help."

Jenna marveled at how smooth Carl's delivery was, and she decided to comment on it. "My mother, she used to point out how victims of a conman always say something like 'I don't understand, he seemed so sincere.' She said of course conmen come off that way, otherwise they wouldn't be able to steal your money." Jenna injected her own dramatic pause, glad to see she had Carl's full attention.

"You seem pretty sincere," she said.

George glanced at her, admiring Jenna's show of strength.

"Now I understand your suspicion," Carl said. "Any paranoia you have has undoubtedly been well earned. But this is not a con. If you don't help me, someone I love will die. As will so many others I care deeply about. And if you don't accept *my* help... then you will discover the problem with symbiotic relationships is that the two organisms usually end up sharing the same fate."

His declaration moved Jenna to modify her original assessment. Carl wasn't a con man. He was an extremely talented con man. Probably gifted. He used truth as camouflage for lies.

And he knew that to properly market the "product" he was selling, he had to throw in concern for his loved ones and the omen of certain death. But obviously he benefited the most from his proposal, or he wouldn't be talking to them.

"Let's say for a moment we're interested in buying what you're selling," Jenna said. "Why don't you go ahead and make your point? Tell us how you can help."

Carl looked disappointed. "Unfortunately, the rest of my proposal includes a... presentation. And for that, you must come with me, to another location."

A sardonic grin spread across Jenna's face. "How'd I guess?"

"I absolutely guarantee your safety. And as an extra incentive for you, Ms. Grant, you might be excited to know the presentation includes an artifact created at the same time as the Black Pages."

Jenna saw his attempt to manipulate her as an obvious weakness, often one that led many intelligent people to disaster. Carl obviously thought that, because he was so brilliant, everyone around him was stupid.

"We accept your invitation," George suddenly announced. Jenna turned to look at him in complete shock. "How long will your presentation take?"

"I promise to have you back in less than three hours," Carl replied.

Before Jenna could contradict what George had said, he was already opening his big mouth again.

"That sounds fine. But you should know, we no longer have the Black Pages. We destroyed them—but not before memorizing their contents. So if your intention is to kill Raymond, and then the both of us, you should know the contents of the Black Pages will be lost forever."

George refused to blink his eyes as he spoke, taking in every moment of Carl's reaction. His discipline was rewarded when Carl's pupils instantly dilated. It was a recessive trait the human species had passed on from one generation to the next.

Enlarged pupils were a sign of panic.

———

A FEW YEARS AGO, Jenna had been part of a supervisory team on a dig near Cairo. The Egyptian government had run the dig like a spy operation, complete with surveillance cameras and full body searches of the workers at the end of each day.

On one occasion that year, Jenna had accepted a ride with Cairo's cultural minister. It was her first time in a bulletproof vehicle, which excited the minister. In a big booming voice, he had described in great detail the bullet-resistant glass and steel-reinforced doors; the tubeless tires that could function even when full of lead.

Jenna recognized these same fortifications in Carl's vehicle idling at the curb outside arrivals. The black Hummer had completely black windows.

Carl opened the back passenger door and helped Jenna and George inside. Then he climbed into the front passenger seat and motioned to his driver, a short, muscular woman wearing a bulletproof vest over a casual khaki top. She began to drive, and Carl turned in his seat to address Jenna and George.

"Do you normally travel in a bulletproof vehicle?" Jenna asked. "Or is this just part of your presentation?"

"Well, unfortunately these measures are necessary based on the threat I outlined in the airport. I only wish we were making the entire trip in this vehicle."

"We're not?" Jenna asked.

"I promised I would take three hours of your time. The only way I can accomplish that is to fly."

He turned back to his driver as she steered the Hummer onto an access street leading to a different part of the airport.

With Carl's attention diverted, Jenna turned to George and whispered, "I hope you know what you're doing."

He looked at Jenna but didn't respond. Despite the perspiration covering his face, he looked calm, even serene.

George lowered his eyes to Jenna's chest. He had never shown a hint of sexual interest before, so his fixation confused her. When he looked up, he saw her furrowed brow, and once again directed his attention to her chest.

This time Jenna realized he was focused on her jacket, specifically the interior breast pocket. She touched it quickly with her hand and felt the contours of her smartphone. George nodded, then turned to look out the Hummer's tinted window.

Okay, Jenna thought, George was thinking of her phone. But why? Then it hit her.

Raymond.

He wanted her to contact Raymond.

The thought of her colleague flooded Jenna with contradictory emotions: fear that he would end up like Arnaud Tottone in Fairfax, or poor Kelli Langton in Occoquan, or any of the other victims over the last couple days; but also anger, because she had expressly told Raymond to stay out of sight, and had warned him about the strangler with the one green eye. Jenna couldn't fathom how, hours later, Raymond had ended up at their favorite Cambridge bar watching soccer.

Men, she thought.

Carl's Humvee approached a small concrete building, a security checkpoint into the airfield reserved for private planes.

Jenna noticed the beefed-up security. Dozens of fully armed, uniformed Israeli soldiers manned the checkpoint. On the other side of the wall, military vehicles waited on standby.

One of the soldiers approached the Hummer, and Carl's driver handed over some paperwork and her ID. The soldier checked the paperwork against a tablet computer. Meanwhile, his brothers in arms circled the vehicle with handheld bomb detectors.

The guard with the tablet dipped his head through the driver's window, catching sight of Jenna and George in back. The guard clearly recognized Carl, who held up a finger in acknowledgment. The guard nodded and withdrew his head.

Soon enough, the steel gate was rising, and the spikes in the pavement were retracting like claws.

The Hummer crossed the threshold and turned onto a service road parallel to the tarmac. They passed hundreds of small hangars and parked airplanes ranging from small Cessnas to Learjets.

About a half mile from the main gate, a helipad became visible in the short distance. A sleek black helicopter waited on the pad, its rotor blades already spinning.

Carl turned around again to address Jenna and George. "Okay, so here's our ride. I want to warn you, the windows in the cabin are completely blacked out."

Jenna could see that. Every window on the chopper, except those in the cockpit, looked blacker than the Humvee.

"The details of our destination need to be kept private," Carl explained. "I assure you, it's for your safety as well as mine. It's the one thing I require if you wish to continue."

"It sounds like you're giving us an option here," Jenna said. "Are you saying we could stop right now and go back to the airport?"

Carl nodded. "You say your memories are all that's left of the... artifact. I believe you."

Jenna noticed that he chose his words carefully around his driver, even though the woman clearly worked for him.

"By destroying that artifact, you've unwittingly helped the people who are out to kill you. You've done half their job for them. Don't make their other half easy. Let me help you."

Jenna looked over at George. "Looks like Carri was right about burning the pages," she said. She still wondered how George had known that destroying the document would maximize their leverage with Carl. "Is she telling you anything about helicopter rides?"

George shook his head. "Not a word."

Carl frowned. "Carri, your dead wife... she's talking to you?"

George stared at him, but didn't respond.

Not intimidated, Carl immediately followed up with another question. "Has Carri also memorized the contents of the artifact?"

"Maybe," George answered with a sly smile.

"And," Jenna said, "if she's right one more time about what she tells George, we're both leaving on the next plane to Vegas for the Black Jack tables."

Carl considered what they had said. The sound of the chopper was getting louder as they approached. "There are some guidelines we need to go over before boarding."

Jenna started buttoning her coat. "Let's do it."

"Okay, pay attention," he said, in the same rote tone as a flight attendant. "Jenna, I'm going to get out and open your door first. I want you to get out of the vehicle and stand next to me. When I touch you on the shoulder, we're going to move quickly to the helicopter.

"After we get in the vehicle, I want you, George, to do the same thing with my driver. And be sure that the both of you keep your heads down around the blades. Am I clear?"

Both Jenna and George nodded.

"Let's go." Carl opened his door and quickly exited the Hummer. He threw open the back passenger door and extended a hand for Jenna. She ignored it and got out all by herself. Then together, they ran through the choppy wind of the rotor blades.

At the helicopter, Carl threw open the cabin door. Jenna hopped onto the boarding step, then jumped on board. Carl slid into the leather back seat behind her, pulling the hatch shut. It barely muffled the *whoop-whoop-whoop* of the propeller.

Immediately, Jenna looked around the dark cabin interior, letting her eyes adjust. Not only were all the cabin windows completely black, but a solid black divider prevented her from seeing the cockpit.

Carl stared forward. Jenna could see him breathing heavily from their sprint across the tarmac, but couldn't hear him over the blades. The sound became background noise as they waited in uncomfortable silence for George.

After a few minutes, Carl checked his watch. For a split second, he looked up to a spot near the black privacy partition, and Jenna followed his line of sight. He was looking at a small, silver, lipstick-shaped device, which was attached to the wall of the cabin.

A camera, Jenna thought. It probably fed a shot of the cabin to the cockpit, so the pilot could see his passengers.

From his coat, Carl pulled out a small walkie-talkie. He hit the talk button. "What's going on?" he shouted and then held the speaker next to his ear.

Whatever was being shouted back at him, Jenna couldn't hear it over the engine and propeller.

Carl turned to her. "Apparently, George is having some kind of trouble."

Jenna immediately reached for the door.

"No," Carl said, "I'll handle this. Please, stay here." This time he didn't give her a choice. He just got out and slammed the cabin door behind him.

Jenna wondered what had happened to George. She hoped he was just creating a distraction so that she could use her phone.

Back in the Hummer, she had run through her mind how best to warn Raymond. She had come up with a quick suggestive message that hopefully he would interpret as an alert.

Her plan counted on the fact that Carl's employee in London was shadowing Raymond, not holding him captive. But it didn't account for a lipstick camera staring her in the face. If the pilot saw her using her phone, Carl would definitely find out, and who knew what would happen next.

Jenna stood up and started to take off her coat, purposely putting her back against the lens of the camera. Quickly she pulled out her smartphone and slid open the keyboard. She typed out a text message, just three words.

Unfortunately she had deleted Raymond's contact information and had to manually enter his number. She had to delete a few digits before getting it right.

Finally Jenna hit send and then finished taking off her coat. Her whole action took less than forty seconds, and then she was sitting down again, her phone tucked away.

Not long after, the hatch door flew open. Carl helped George up and into the passenger seat, and George collapsed next to Jenna as if he were a totally spent man. But Jenna had just seen him at his worst at Paddington Station, and right now he actually looked in pretty good shape.

After Carl shut the door behind him, Jenna put her hand on George's arm and gave him a worried look.

"Are you all right?" she asked, raising her voice over the sound of the chopper.

"Sorry," he said. "I was feeling like I couldn't get to my feet. I hope I didn't scare you."

"You did. But I'm actually feeling better now. George, are you sure you want to go on?"

"Oh, yes. I think we need to hear what this man has to say."

"Buckle your seatbelts," Carl shouted before putting on a headset. As Jenna and George followed his directions, he hit the talk button on the headset to alert the pilot.

"Okay, we're ready back here. Let's go..."

Then Carl tapped a button set into the armrest on his seat. As the helicopter began to rise from the landing pad, a soft yellow glow illuminated the cabin, and the three passengers could see each other clearly for the first time.

CHAPTER 6

RAYMOND CLAPPED HIS PHONE SHUT after his conversation with Jenna. He stood still for a moment in the hotel room, trying to gather his thoughts.

Jenna was determined to fly to Tel Aviv with George, despite the necrology Raymond had texted her, the list of people who had gotten caught up in this mess and then had either mysteriously died or were flat-out killed. If that hadn't convinced Jenna to stay far away from John Wolfenson, Raymond didn't know what would.

His mum was exactly the same way—stubborn like a cloud that refused to let the sun shine. How was it that all these years, Raymond had resented his mum's pigheadedness, but somehow in Jenna he found it charming?

At least before today.

Raymond started to gather up his things. He had intended to stay longer and lay low as Jenna suggested, but then he remembered: he had made previous arrangements to meet his brother and father at the family cottage on the beach. Their trip had been planned for months.

So Raymond would lay low, as told, but he'd do it on his way back to Cambridge. Of course, he would make absolutely certain no one was tailing him. The last thing he wanted was to end up as just one more search result when someone typed in "mysterious deaths related to John Wolfenson."

Raymond peered through the room's peephole, and then stuck his head out the door to have a look around. Nobody in the hallway. No man with one green eye. Raymond left the room and shut the door behind him.

As he made his way toward the lift, he rubbed at his nose, trying to wipe away the smell of burnt vellum. Not only did it remind him of a precious artifact that had been destroyed, it was revolting, the stink of burning animal flesh hundreds of years old.

And there was something worse, a smell he tried not to think about, but one that wouldn't go away. The smell of death.

As Raymond rode down in the hotel lift, he thought about Jenna and their kiss. Them... together... looking toward the city's horizon; and further, to the future. Not a future with marriage and kids, but the near future. At the very least, a few nights together.

As he had stared at her, with the taste of her wine still on his lips, he had begun to fantasize about sleeping with her, and then later going into the radio station together to answer listeners' questions about Roman hobnailed boots and bluestones at Stonehenge, all the while grinning at each other from behind their microphones. Grinning because they shared a new secret.

Raymond even thought there had been a point out on the balcony when, if he had been more aggressive, he could have gone a bit further than just kissing. But then he had remembered George sitting on the other side of the glass and had relented.

George.

Raymond stopped at the hotel's front desk. "I'm here to settle the bill for our room," he told the clerk. "It was my friend who checked in. But unfortunately something came up and she had to leave. Anyway, here are the keys."

Keys, he thought, grimacing. He had stayed in plenty of hotels in the last few years, and they all used key cards. But somehow he kept referring to them as *keys*. He sounded like his father, who still referred to a collection of music as an *album*.

Raymond couldn't help it though. When he was a kid, his parents had taken him all over the world, and hotel rooms always had come with keys. Somehow that term had stuck. Was it possible that everything he thought, and everything he believed, fell into a mindset that had formed ten years ago?

The front desk clerk, an Asian, took the key card and started the checkout process on the computer. When he saw the room number, he stopped and looked up at Raymond.

"Excuse me, I hope you don't mind but... I was wondering how it all worked out?"

Raymond stared at him. He couldn't decide whether it was a trick question.

"The woman who was looking for her friend?" the clerk explained. "He seemed seriously ill."

"Oh, that," Raymond said, smiling. He quickly realized it was nothing to smile at and put a dour look on his face. "That was... most unfortunate. Uh, they're fine now. On their way to meet trained medical professionals. So thank you, and... thanks to anyone who might've helped."

"I'm so happy to hear that everything worked out, sir." The Asian clerk turned back to his computer and continued with checkout.

As he waited, Raymond wondered why his first reaction to the clerk's question had been to smile. He quickly came to his answer: George. There was something weird about George.

Initially, when Raymond met him at the café, he had been suspicious of the guy. George had led him back to the hotel without a single word. At one of the traffic stops, a mentally ill man had slammed up against the hood of their cab, screaming something unintelligible in Cockney. No reaction from George. Not a blink.

Then at the hotel room, as the three of them deciphered the quatrains, Raymond had begun to change his mind about this terribly weakened, shy man, whose wife had tragically died. Raymond began to trust that George was completely looking out for Jenna, and that he would protect her from anything.

The newfound trust didn't last long. When George burned the Black Pages, along with Jenna's notes, Raymond's original suspicions resurfaced in force. He was still angry at himself for being fooled.

The Asian clerk looked up from his computer while the LaserJet printed out Jenna's invoice. "Thank you for your patience. Our system seems to be running a tad slow today."

"No worries."

When the print-out finished, the clerk slid it across the counter to Raymond. "I want to point out some charges to your room's mini-bar before approving the invoice on your friend's credit card."

Raymond quickly reviewed the printout and was impressed: not only had the hotel documented every beverage and snack removed from the mini-bar in the last several hours, but everything in the last few minutes too, including the bag of pretzels he had eaten during the last phone call with Jenna.

Modern technology! he thought.

"Only one problem," Raymond said. "I was the one who drank and ate like a bloody idiot. I need you to break off these fridge charges from the rest of the bill, if you can."

"Absolutely, sir." The clerk turned back to his computer.

"Wait! No. What am I thinking?" Raymond was talking to himself as much as he was addressing the hotel clerk. After a few seconds, he nodded, knowing exactly what he needed to do. "Actually..." he said, smiling broadly at his own word choice. "If it's no trouble, I'd very much like to pay for everything, including the room."

"Oh, no trouble at all."

Raymond took out his credit card, the one that gave him air miles, and he handed it to the clerk. *Yes*, he thought, it's what any proper Englishman would do.

———

AFTER LEAVING THE HOTEL, Raymond purposely strolled around the block a few times, pretending to window-shop. He even stopped at one of the coffee shops to buy a paper.

When he felt certain no one was following him, he slipped back through the hotel lobby, into Paddington Station. He waited for close to an hour, walking from one platform to another, again to see if anyone paid any interest. Satisfied, Raymond caught the underground circle line to the King's Cross St. Pancras station, a short ten-minute trip.

By the time he arrived, one of the faster cruiser trains to Cambridge was just pulling in. *Good timing*, he thought. He would be back at King's College in less than an hour.

After one final look around the platform, he hopped on board.

During the ride, Raymond pretended to look out the window, but was using the glass as a mirror to scan his fellow passengers: mostly college kids, taking the train back to school after a trip to the city; and some older couples too, husbands sitting just inches from their wives in complete silence.

There were also two sets of men.

One pair appeared to know each other, and when Raymond looked directly over, he saw them playing cards. The other two men seemed completely oblivious to each other. One was younger, and asleep, his head leaning and bouncing against the window. The older gent was reading the *London Times*, too old to be much of a threat. Raymond would only have to run, and the geezer would die of a heart attack giving chase.

He settled more comfortably into his seat and opened his newspaper. He couldn't focus enough to read. All he could think about was Jenna.

The first time they had met at the radio station, Raymond was impressed by how she would pause before speaking, carefully choosing her words, but then burst like a dam and let it all rush out. Was it possible that she could form complete, Godzilla-sized thoughts, then spit everything out in one breath, and all along expect her behavior to be considered normal? Yes. And somehow, Raymond accepted it. Not as normal, but as special.

He took out his phone and looked at its clock. Maybe he could still catch her before she and George got on the plane. And maybe this time she would take him more seriously, now that he wasn't slurring his words.

Slurred speech had always been a point of contention between Raymond's mum and dad. Sometimes, when his parents were having a row, his father would tell Raymond to take their mum to bed. "She's embarrassing herself," he would say. But Raymond thought his mum almost always made sense. Her words just had to circle a few times before landing on the runway.

Jenna's voicemail picked up. For some reason, she had deleted her outgoing message, so Raymond didn't even have the pleasure of hearing her recorded voice; just some cold automated one.

He folded up his phone. He would have to try again once he got back to his apartment, once she and George had landed in Tel Aviv.

————

"WILL YOU BE WANTING ANOTHER PINT, love?"

Mindy, one of the bartenders at Gerry's, asked Raymond the question while looking at the football game up on the big screen. She never looked at him directly anymore whenever he came into the pub.

"No, I really can't," he said, watching the game himself; it was West Africa vs. Cameroon, another African team, so Gerry's was only half filled with patrons. "I'm meeting my brother and my dad in a few hours. It would not be a good thing, showing up completely pissed."

"Suit yourself." Mindy moved down the bar before Raymond could ask for more chili. Earlier that night, bowls of it had been placed on the bar as the special attraction for football fans; it had gone quickly.

Down the bar a few stools, Mindy stopped to attend the next customer, giving him the courtesy of direct eye contact.

She had been treating Raymond like this ever since he had turned her down for a date about a month ago. Instead of just asking him out, she had tried to make it into some sort of contest. If she were to win at darts, he would pay for their date, but if he were to win, she'd pay. "I think I'm going to have to go for the third option," Raymond had said. He hadn't meant it as a joke, but a couple regulars at the pub had laughed.

Still wanting that chili, Raymond peered into the bar mirror, again to check out the people around him.

Though a few of the patrons were strangers, he knew everyone else. Some of them worked at the college, while the other three dozen were the same blokes who were there every evening. The match between West Africa and Cameroon wasn't about to attract the normal wrecking crew that filled Gerry's to capacity most nights. But any football match got the diehards to show. And, glimpsing himself in the bar mirror, Raymond had to admit: if he was sitting on a stool, tonight of all nights, then *he* was one of the diehards as well.

Raymond hadn't planned on stopping by Gerry's. After stepping off the cruiser from London, he had planned to catch a cab back to his flat. Normally he would have walked—it was only a couple miles—but

Jenna's words, "lying low," were stuck in his head like peanut butter in a dog's mouth.

His plans changed when he couldn't seem to get a cab. So he decided to do what he would normally do and hoof it. Except normally he wouldn't first have to make sure no one was keeping tabs on him.

Halfway from the train station to his flat, he came upon Gerry's Pub. By that time, having walked a mile or so, he was thirsty. He saw some of the lads smoking on the pavement outside, and he stopped to chat for a second. But then someone said something about Cameroon's assistant coach, a bloke Raymond had gone to school with, and so Raymond said, "Quick pint couldn't hurt. But just a quick one, and then I've got to run."

He had hoped his mates would hold him to it, but they just laughed and shoved him into the pub.

It was too noisy at this hour with the match going on, but Raymond called Jenna again anyway. After two rings, he got her voicemail. He folded up his phone without leaving a message.

Suddenly the whole pub erupted: Cameroon had scored! They were beating West Africa two to one.

Raymond remembered that West Africa was in the same bracket as England, so everyone in the pub was rooting for Cameroon. The enemy of your enemy is your friend.

"Here you go, mate!" one of the pub regulars, "Shanty" Bob, shouted. He stood several stools behind Raymond, talking to another man at the end of the bar.

They called him Shanty Bob because he lived in his mum's guesthouse a couple miles away, and one of their pub mates, upon seeing the guesthouse, had called it a "shanty." The nickname stuck.

"This is for you!" Shanty Bob said, slamming a glass of beer on the counter in front of the guy. The ale leapt in the cup, as if on a trampoline, then settled back to the bottom.

"You won a bet, and didn't even know it," Shanty Bob said to the startled customer. "Now all you got to do is drink it before the next score, and I'm coming over to give you another."

Shanty Bob laughed, slapped the customer on the back, and then walked back to his mates, who sat at a table a few feet away, laughing too. Raymond smiled. That's what he loved about this pub. Everyone was always up to some kind of shenanigans, but there was no real harm in it. He could only remember a few times when things had gotten out of hand. Not like up north.

As Raymond was turning back to the big-screen telly, he caught sight of the customer who had unwittingly won a pint from Shanty Bob. For some reason the guy was staring right at Raymond, but quickly turned away. Raymond did the same thing and focused on the game.

The expression on the guy's face—Raymond had only locked eyes with him for a second, and it could have been embarrassment, but his expression reminded Raymond of something different. His mum used to make a similar face whenever his dad discovered one of her liquor stashes.

Furtively, Raymond shifted his eyes from the telly to the mirror. At the end of the bar, the customer was wiping up around him with some napkins. Apparently, not all of the ale had bounced back into the glass.

The guy wore a grey sweatshirt, and looked to be in his thirties, with close-cropped hair. Something dangled around his neck, but Raymond couldn't make out what it was.

Some of the regulars started clapping. Raymond looked up and saw that the first half of the football game had ended. Cameroon was still ahead, two to one.

He turned back to the mirror to find that the guy in the grey sweatshirt had left his barstool.

"Want a free drink?"

Raymond practically jerked out of his seat. The guy with the necklace now sat in the stool next to him.

"For some reason, those guys just bought me a drink," he said. "I think they're having some fun."

"Don't take it personal," Raymond replied. "You do understand it's the football calling the shots. Wouldn't be surprised if they've already lost their minds."

"Okay, glad to hear it. But the problem is, I don't drink beer. I was wondering if you wanted it." He pushed the mug toward Raymond, whose eyes flicked from the drink to the guy's necklace. An animal claw of some sort.

"Very nice of you," Raymond said. "I'll drink it when I get another bowl of chili, thanks."

"Right, don't worry about it getting warm. It didn't start out cold."

Raymond smiled and pulled the drink closer. "Thanks again."

On the big screen, the football announcers were recapping the first half and talking over the highlights.

"So who are you rooting for?" the man asked Raymond.

"Don't really have a dog in this fight. How about you?"

"West Africa. I kind of grew up there. More accurately, one could say I grew up while living there, if you know what I mean."

Raymond shook his head as he turned to face the guy. "No, mate, what do you mean?"

"Tough times." He took a gulp from his drink. It was in a highball glass, and was red, with a cherry on top. Raymond knew that's why the lads were having a bit of fun with him.

The guy set down his glass. "But it made me into a man, you know what I'm talking about?"

"So is that where you got the, uh..." Raymond cocked his chin in the direction of the necklace.

"Rooster claw," the guy said.

"A rooster claw? So did you get that in West Africa?" Raymond knew that voodoo, or vodun, was a prevalent and traditional organized religion in that corner of the world. Oftentimes talismans incorporated dried animal parts for healing or spiritual rejuvenation.

"Nigeria to be specific," the man said. "But it has nothing to do with what you're thinking."

"How do you know what I'm thinking?"

"I can see it in your eyes. Most people assume it has something to do with voodoo, but it doesn't."

"Well, I wasn't thinking anything like that," Raymond said. "But I've had my pint, so let me have the back story. Right now I'll believe anything you tell me."

The man put down his drink and held up the rooster claw. "It came from the rooster that was with a clan warrior on the day he died. That's what makes this special."

"Hey, love," Mindy said. She had come back around to Raymond's side of the bar, but was talking to the guy with the cherry on top. She had no problems looking him straight in the eye. "How you doing with your drink?"

"I'll have another, thanks. And my friend here was interested in another bowl of chili." He turned to Raymond. "To go with his ale, right?"

Mindy turned to Raymond, finally meeting his eyes for the first time in weeks. "Oh, so you fancy another bowl of chili. Well, I'll be sure to get right on that." She wheeled around in her heels and left without another word.

The pub broke out in a loud cheer. On the telly, the announcers were interviewing the goaltender from the English team, which would be playing the next day in the tournament; he was giving his predictions for the upcoming match.

As the cheers died down, Raymond heard another noise: his smartphone, vibrating on the bar. He forgot he had set it down after his last call to Jenna.

She had just sent him a text message.

Raymond snatched up his phone and opened the text.

spot the fake

That's all it said.

He looked around the pub. Perhaps Jenna hadn't gone to Tel Aviv after all. Perhaps she was standing in the corner, having a laugh on his account. But he didn't see her.

"Is something wrong?" asked Mr. Cherry on Top.

Raymond closed his phone and put it in his pocket. "Just looking for that waitress with my chili."

As if on cue, Mindy appeared. She dropped off a bowl on the bar in front of Raymond, spilling some of its contents in the process. Then, more gently, she set down another glass of the red concoction with a cherry on top.

"Do you two have history together?" the stranger asked as Mindy walked away. "Because I'm sensing something. Or maybe that's just the way you Brits treat each other?"

Raymond shook his head. "No history. She wanted to create some history, but I wasn't interested." He looked down at the chili, then at the glass of ale.

Jenna had sent a text, but in Raymond's head, she always narrated her own messages—"Spot the fake."

He remembered another recent text, and Jenna's voice echoed again—"The guy who tried to strangle me, I think he's at the hotel! Watch out for him, Raymond. You'll know him because he's got one green eye."

Cherry on Top raised his drink, as if working some retirement party. "Since you don't have a dog in this fight, do you mind if we make a toast to West Africa?"

Raymond raised his old glass, which still had some beer in it.

"To West Africa," said Cherry on Top, "where my soul transformed into a fighter."

He went to clink glasses, but Raymond held his back.

"If you don't mind, I'm going to drink to something else. To having no dogs in this fight. Because I wouldn't want my dog to go up against your rooster."

Cherry on Top laughed, and they clinked glasses.

"Cheers," Raymond said.

All through the toasts, he stared at the other man's eyes. They seemed to twinkle. And it wasn't an effect of whatever red crap the cherry was bobbing in. This guy was amped up, ready for something. West Africa's victory over Cameroon perhaps.

Raymond also noticed that Cherry on Top's eyes were brown. Both of them.

"Now is the other beer the same thing you're drinking?" the guy asked.

"Doesn't matter, mate. I like it all." Raymond shoved a spoonful of chili into his mouth, and thought he probably had more to fear from Mindy poisoning his food than this bloke turning the ale into poison piss. "Mmm, now that's good chili. The wait was halfway worth it."

As Raymond was chewing, Cherry on Top turned his head just right, so that the lighting in the pub revealed his makeup. The skin-colored cream covered his forehead and the side of his face.

Back in the hotel room, Jenna had talked about George hitting one of her attackers with a rock. This had to be that guy. The only men who dared to come into this pub wearing makeup were frogs. So either this guy hid his French accent really well, or he was using makeup to conceal his failure to kill Jenna in the States.

"Don't forget about that drink with your chili," Cherry on Top said.

Raymond stood up and took a deep breath. If he was wrong, he would never forgive himself. But if he was right and did nothing about it, he knew he wouldn't have to worry about forgiving himself ever again.

"How dare you call him a nancy!" Raymond bellowed, as if he were speaking outdoors at one of the open-air classes at King's College. The whole pub seemed to grind to a halt around him.

Cherry on Top stared at Raymond, speechless, eyes no longer twinkling.

"I don't care if you are cheering for West Africa," Raymond said, "this is our goaltender, and we rather think the world of him. So stop calling him a nancy!"

Shanty Bob stood up like he had heard someone was buying a round. The rest of his mates joined him. But they weren't the only ones. The lads at half of the other tables, including the ones accompanying women, had gotten out of their chairs as well. In fact, Raymond thought, the men at those tables had been the first to stand.

Cherry on Top's reaction relieved Raymond of any doubt that he might be throwing an innocent man under a double-decker bus. The man grinned. He knew he had been exposed, and for some crazy reason Raymond couldn't fathom, he looked excited for what was to come.

"You're dead. You know that, right? You and your two friends. Dead."

That's exactly what Raymond was hoping Cherry on Top would do. Talk to him quietly enough that Raymond could play word alchemist.

"Nancy boy?!" he said. "I can't believe you keep calling him that. Well then, let's take this outside. Because I certainly don't want to hear any more of this crap from some foreigner—especially from one who's been talking down to me and my Queen for the entire half of football!"

Cherry on Top didn't respond, but it wasn't as if he had a chance. Shanty Bob was like a violin, stepping up until he was practically planted underneath the man's chin.

"We all saw it when you first stepped in," Shanty Bob said, "wallowing in your own self-importance. But if it's a broken nose you be wanting, then let me escort you to the outdoors. Because we wouldn't want to be destroying a fine family establishment, now would we?"

104

Shanty Bob didn't wait for an answer. He grabbed the guy by the arm and started to move.

Cherry on Top reacted, probably the same way he learned to get through the "tough times" in West Africa. He swung his arm up, breaking Shanty Bob's hold, and then, with his other hand, he delivered a quick blow to the throat, followed by a kick to the left knee. Shanty Bob fell to the floor, groaning and gasping for air at the same time.

That might have been the right move in West Africa, to show the biggest bully that he couldn't mess around with you, but here in Great Britain, in a pub no less, it just invited the rest of the blokes to step in and show their support.

Raymond calmly stepped back as everyone responded like ants to an attack on their hill. He would always give Cherry on Top credit for handling the first three lads. But the forth bloke delivered a punch that Cherry on Top could not shake off. He collapsed against the bar.

A few punches and kicks later, Cherry on Top's head lay on the bar's brass foot rail. Everyone took their turns kicking and punching.

In the middle of the ruckus, Raymond saw something squirt out of Cherry on Top's pants pocket. A syringe. Before he could get a better look, it was kicked away and out of sight.

Just a quick pint, he reminded himself, and started to back out of the pub. The last thing he saw of the fight was Shanty Bob stepping on the rooster claw around Cherry on Top's neck—and the rooster claw shattering beneath his boot.

Near the exit, Raymond ran into Mindy. They locked eyes. She wore the same look she'd had the night she asked him out for a date. Raymond shook his head, brushed past her, and slipped into the dark.

He only stopped running long enough to put in a call to Jenna.

CHAPTER 7

THE HELICOPTER TRIP LASTED twenty-five minutes, Jenna estimated. It was only an estimate, though. She had stopped wearing a watch awhile back because her smartphone had a clock, and she didn't care for things on her wrist anyway, especially considering the dirty, sweaty nature of her job.

But she couldn't necessarily whip out her phone in front of Carl. She counted herself lucky that his men hadn't confiscated her personal effects as it was. After all, he had gone to such great lengths to obscure their aerial view. Tel Aviv had been her last known landmark.

During the twenty-five-minute ride, the three passengers in the cabin spoke once, shortly after takeoff. Carl had given some heated towels and bottles of cold water to Jenna and George.

George used the warm, wet towel to wipe his face while Jenna uncapped his water for him.

As he drank, George's hand shook badly. Some of the water dribbled down his chin. Jenna had to hold the bottle steady for him so he could get a proper drink.

"You don't look well, George." When Carl didn't get a reaction, he turned to Jenna and said, "You see that he doesn't look well, right?"

She didn't say anything either.

"George, the place where we're going, I have a full-time doctor and nurse. If you would like, you can stay there and get well. And of course, you can leave at any time. That's better than any hospital."

"He's going to be fine," Jenna said before George could reply. "If he needs, we'll get medical attention back in Tel Aviv. You said three hours. You gave us your word."

"Yes, and I mean to keep it."

Carl probably hoped for, and even expected, a response. From both of them. Instead, he received blank stares for the rest of the flight.

———

THE HELICOPTER STARTED ITS DESCENT toward their unknown destination. Jenna had been in helicopters, airplanes, and even a biplane once, on a dare. The one thing that had always comforted her was that she could always see the ground, or at least the lights. Never once did she have to land in pure dark.

"Are you able to walk?" Carl asked George.

"Yes, I'm feeling much better. Thank you."

Jenna thought he couldn't possibly be getting better every time someone asked that. At such a rate, he would have a bit more life in his cheeks hour by hour.

"Okay," Carl said, "but let me know if you need any help. We're safe to leave the helicopter, no security precautions. However, do keep your head down. We wouldn't want to lose the contents of the Black Pages with an untimely accident."

Jenna and George looked at each other, but managed not to respond. They refused to give Carl the satisfaction.

Moments later, the helicopter touched down, and Carl jumped out of the cabin. He held the door for Jenna, and then George, who had no trouble at all getting down by himself.

As if conspiring with the blackened windows, the propeller whipped up sand and debris, so Jenna couldn't see much of their surroundings.

Carl shut the hatch, then tapped on the clear window of the cockpit. The helicopter's blades accelerated, and the dust whirls rose into a sandstorm, forcing everyone on the ground to shield their eyes. Thankfully, the helicopter began to lift off, and the storm dissolved, leaving a lighter veil of dust.

With a hand on each of their backs, Carl nudged Jenna and George forward. Vague impressions of the landscape began to surface through the haze. Jenna saw that the helipad sat on a flat mountaintop, and Carl was guiding them toward stone steps carved down into the cliff.

She tried to see what lay beyond the mountain, and, blinking back grit, she glimpsed a valley—a desert with no apparent signs of buildings or life.

She sensed movement on her left, and turned to look. A figure stepped in front of the dim sun and pulled a thick black cotton hood over her head. It all happened so quickly she didn't have time to react, or see anything.

"It's all right," Carl shouted over the fading sound of the chopper. "As soon as we get inside, we'll take off the hoods."

"George, talk to me!" Jenna called in the dark.

"I'm fine, Jenna. Let's just do as we're told."

A pair of meaty hands grabbed Jenna's arms and guided her in the direction of the stone steps. She doubted these paws belonged to Carl. From her observations at the airport and during the helicopter ride, he had smaller, manicured hands.

After walking a dozen yards, she heard an unfamiliar male voice whisper, "We're going to start stepping down now..."

Awkwardly Jenna descended the staircase. The meaty hands never let her go, not for a second.

Jenna wished she could see the ground, see where her feet were falling. All through her life she'd had a great sense of where she was going, but now she was blinded and had to navigate primarily by feel.

Here, even sound failed her. The chopper had faded, but the loud rotor must have temporarily impaired her ears, because her footsteps seemed muted.

So she counted. Nineteen steps. And then a landing. The meaty hands held her still.

She felt the door opening more than she heard it, even though it was loud and it definitely registered in her ears. But her senses seemed to have been disassociated.

A sudden rush of cool air rippled her jacket and hood. Jenna had been on digs all around the world. She had been in tombs and ancient undergrounds. And while the air here felt more conditioned, its pressure and quality and general smell suggested a cave.

The meaty hands nudged her forward, and then released their grip as Jenna walked into the cool.

The door behind her shut with a whoosh and a thud, and then the hood over her head was removed... by Carl. The only other person in attendance was George. No third man with meaty hands.

Jenna let her eyes adjust, glad to regain a sense she could believe in. Indeed, they stood in a hollowed-out limestone cave, in a vestibule of light cast by a dozen wall sconces. The poor illumination barely reached twenty feet above their heads to the ceiling.

Behind her, an iron door sealed the entrance, and in front of her, beyond the light, the darkness breathed cool air, as if they were standing on the threshold of something larger, and deeper.

Jenna looked to George. "Are you all right?"

"Yes," he said, "much better."

This time, she actually believed him. He looked surprisingly calm, and some color had returned to his face. His perspiration had cooled and dried.

"Although I could have done without the frat-house hazing."

"I do apologize," Carl said. "What you must think..." He tossed their hoods to the floor. "Ms. Grant, I know you've been in this region before on business. I didn't want to take a chance that you might recognize your surroundings. Again, for your own good as well as mine."

Despite his contriteness, Carl grinned with anticipation. Jenna wondered whether or not that was a good thing.

Carl raised a hand and waved at their surroundings. "So, this is what I call the Monastery. I guess I call it that because... I'm a bit pretentious. And because, thousands of years ago, that's exactly what it was... a monastery."

He flipped a switch on a wall panel built into the bedrock, and a series of lights flickered on down a long tunnel off of the cave—proving Jenna's suspicions about the depth of the place. How deep it went into the mountain was impossible to tell because of the angle of the descent, and the soft quality of light.

Carl said, "Now, George, you need to watch your step—the path is a bit steep. Although I bet you won't have any trouble breathing," he added with a smirk. "I pump in more pure oxygen down here than any of the casinos Jenna mentioned visiting in Las Vegas."

Motioning for them to follow, Carl began the long walk down the tunnel. Never once did he bother to look back and see whether Jenna and George were following. They stood in the cave until he faded out of sight.

"So how's Raymond?" George whispered.

Jenna had crossed her arms, not because of the cool, but because of the general atmosphere of the place. "I sent a text. I hope he'll be all right."

George nodded and started into the tunnel. Jenna stopped him after a few steps.

"Why are we doing this?"

He took in the surrounding bedrock, under their feet and far above their heads. "Look at all this. He's been dedicated in his effort for years... decades... perhaps longer. Carl has some answers, and we'll need them."

"But we can't trust him."

"Yes, I'm sure he'll never reveal the truth, only the facts. But you more than anyone should know how history can help us."

112

As he spoke, Jenna noticed something odd about him. His eyes had glossed over, and his voice seemed to echo from the light at the end of the tunnel, as if it were channeling from another source.

"And I caution you," George continued, "we shouldn't immediately dismiss his obvious lies without some thought. I have a feeling the truth may lie at the heart of his deceptions."

Before Jenna could respond, George started to cough.

"Hey..." She reached out to comfort him, but he stepped back, hunching over as he hacked and hacked and spewed violently at his feet. This time it wasn't just bloody spittle. It was mostly black mucus that stained the stone.

"Are you all right?" Carl shouted from somewhere deep in the tunnel.

George responded by not coughing. He motioned for Jenna to answer for him.

"Yes, we had a problem, but we're all right!" she said.

George wiped his mouth. With determined eyes, he took a few steps toward the tunnel. He abruptly stopped. Jenna followed his gaze and found words carved into the stone above the tunnel's entrance.

"Do you know the language?" he asked.

"Yes. The words are Sanskrit."

"Does it have any meaning?"

She said, "'The Devas around us are more influential than heaven.'"

———

JENNA AND GEORGE CAUGHT UP with Carl in the tunnel. He had clearly waited after hearing the coughing and was relieved to see they were now following him.

"George, are you—"

"I'm just fine. Thank you for your interest."

They both walked past Carl, who now fell behind them as they proceeded down the underground corridor.

They walked for a while in silence, but then George spoke up. "You said this was once a monastery..."

"Yes. As you've probably guessed, our surroundings are thousands of years old."

Jenna couldn't help but cringe at Carl's excitement. It was like watching someone show up at a party with a parrot on his shoulder to bask in all the attention.

"Before the monastery was built in 450, there was only a cluster of caves. According to tradition, an important Jewish leader wandered into the caves, thirsty and famished; ravens fed and watered him back to health.

"Two centuries later, after the monastery was built, an invading force massacred the monks and destroyed this place. Hundreds of years passed before Christian Crusaders attempted to fully restore it. But they ultimately failed in their effort. If we had more time, I would show you the shrine containing the skulls of martyred monks. One of my excavation teams discovered the remains after I assumed ownership."

Jenna thought Carl sounded like a giddy real estate agent listing all the selling points of a property. But she knew he was clever enough to either obscure the more identifying details of the location, or outright lie.

"Over the years, I've made some modifications. First, I subdivided the main cave into dozens of separate cells. And I made the facility entirely self-contained with airshafts that open above ground. I also installed a closed air-purification system in case the surface was some-how... contaminated. But the one thing I loved originally about this lo-cation still remains: there is only one way in and one way out."

They arrived at the end of the tunnel, which Jenna estimated to be at least four hundred yards long. They stood in an empty circular cavern with a high ceiling; a hub from which several narrow corridors stretched out like the arms of an octopus.

Carl brushed past them and led the way once again. "Please, follow me..."

He took them to one of the passageways, a sandstone hallway where they encountered steel doors every twenty feet. Halfway down the cor-ridor, they stopped in front of one of these portals. Jenna could make out air-tight rubber seals in the archway.

Carl slid a card across a security panel, and then stood perfectly still, eyes open, as the panel scanned his face with a red beam of light. A second later, Jenna heard a little hiss: the sound of the door's pres-surized seal opening. Carl grabbed the steel handle and pushed open the door.

"Please, make yourself at home..."

Jenna entered first, followed by George. Carl shut the door behind them. He hit some numbers on a wall pad, and the door began to seal itself with the hiss of escaping air.

In this chamber, the cherry wood conference table and leather chairs were the only part of their surroundings not made of either steel or glass. In stone enclosures, as Jenna knew, temperature control never worked well. So the glass had been installed to insulate the bedrock.

At the focal point of the room, steel-encased compartments lined an entire wall, much like at a city morgue. Although Jenna suspected the sophistication of these partitioned compartments far surpassed any coroner's meat locker.

The temperatures and humidity of each cubby could be customized to protect and preserve its specific contents, which she believed to be valuable ancient artifacts.

George walked over to the far end of the room to get a better look at the thirty-foot oil painting near the door. Initially, in passing, he had mistaken the image on the canvas for an abstract painting. Now, looking up at it, he saw the subject of the picture—a red amoeba-like mass with a mandala in the center. It was meant to be a depiction of something living.

"Please," Carl said, "both of you have a seat. George, do you need anything at all? How about a drink? At the very least, something to eat. You must be famished."

"A glass of water would be nice," George said.

A refrigerator was built into one of the cabinets lining the other wall. Carl grabbed a bottle of water from the fridge. He poured it into a glass with ice, then walked across the room and presented it to George.

Carl looked up at the oil painting. "Quite beautiful, isn't it? The artist was someone very close to Sandy Travis—"

"Sandy Travis?" Jenna asked. "You know that name?"

"Yes, of course," Carl said, looking back at her, but not bothering to fully turn from the painting. "The same people who were after her are after you."

Both he and George studied the canvas a moment longer, and then Carl finally returned to the miniature fridge. "Jenna, how about you? Can I get you something to—"

"Do me a favor. Don't offer me water, or some aged cheese to nibble on, or some wine you've bottled from one of your vineyards. Instead, what you can get me is the start of your presentation."

She stood absolutely straight as she spoke, with her hands on her hips and her eyes fixed firmly on Carl's. She had practiced this stance since she was a little girl, ever since her mother had told her about the research study of convicted rapists.

According to her mother, the predators had been shown videos of different women going about their daily routines—walking on the street, shopping, taking the bus. When asked which of these women they would rape, every single criminal had pointed out women who were, in fact, real-life rape victims. "These predators knew who to stay away from," Ruth told her daughter. "And who to attack."

Now, standing in front of Carl, the last thing Jenna wanted to look like was a potential victim.

"Fair enough," Carl said. "I promised you a show-and-tell item, and that's why I brought you to this room. But first... some background information."

"Bullshit!" Jenna grabbed the back of one of the leather chairs around the conference table. The legs of the chair bounced on the glass floor overlaying the bedrock.

"In the last few days," she said, "some really nasty people, along with my own brother, have attempted to kill me. Everything you've said or shown me up to this point only convinces me that you're the one standing at the podium waving the baton. So if you've got something to show us, I insist you get on with it... or get on with killing us. Which is, for the record, what I think you plan on doing anyway. I only tell you that now before you put a bullet in my head because I don't

117

want you getting the satisfaction of thinking that you fooled me for one minute."

Maybe it was all the oxygen pumping into the monastery, but Jenna was able to say everything without once catching her breath.

Carl looked over at George, then back to Jenna. "Well the truth is, I am, indeed, working with some dark forces. And I have been... for decades. But all this time I've also been a believer in Jesus Christ."

Jenna shoved the chair against the table, then turned to George. "Let's go. We're out of here." She started to walk toward the door.

Carl held up a hand. "Please, stop. Indulge me for just a few minutes."

"Open the door," Jenna calmly said. "Or put in a call to your execution squad. I'm sure you have one, because you look like the kind of guy who never gets his hands dirty."

"You've come this far," Carl said. "Will just a few minutes of... *preamble* really make that much of a difference?" It looked like this was the closest Carl ever came to begging in his life.

"Every second I stand here in your temperature-controlled *cell*," Jenna said, "I'm forced to suck down the same recycled air that's going through your nostrils, and that thought absolutely nauseates me."

"Yes, well... I'm not going to spend a lot of time explaining my motives, which would appear to elicit very little empathy on your part—"

"Zero," Jenna said.

"But you need to understand, I'm not some simple devil worshipper in a black robe killing squirrels in campfires at midnight. My philosophy is far more sophisticated than that and far more complicated—"

"I'm sure it is."

"In fact, what I believe in, what I've been working toward, is the reunion of God, his son, Jesus Christ, and the Angel of Light... Satan."

George, who had moved a few feet to look at the painting from a different angle, said, "For what purpose?"

Jenna glared at him. The last thing she wanted was to indulge Carl with a question. But George wasn't paying attention to her dirty looks. He had fixed his eyes on the red life form to see if it looked different from another perspective. It didn't.

Finally, George gave his attention back to Carl, who was obviously waiting.

"Reconciliation," Carl replied. "That's my purpose. Reconciliation between Satan and God. It's an absolute necessity if humanity is to be reunited with our father. It's the cornerstone of my beliefs and the foundation of what has motivated my actions for decades."

"So you admit you're behind everything?" Jenna asked, stepping away from the door.

"I confess... to playing my part."

Jenna positioned herself directly across from him. "So there are other people in your group calling the shots?"

Carl fell silent, which surprised Jenna. The loss of the Black Pages must have really forced this guy to throw away his compass.

"Like... Dr. Fincher?" George asked.

Carl didn't bother to hide his surprise at hearing the name. George stared at him, intense for the first time since Jenna could remember.

"Yes," Carl said, "he is part of the Red Veil." To Jenna, he added, "Dr. Fincher is the one who tried to have you killed. The one who... recruited your brother Neal."

Jenna noted Carl's phrase "Red Veil," but set it aside to learn more about Fincher and his relationship with her brother.

"Let's say you're telling the truth. Are you telling me that Dr. Fincher's in charge?"

"No. We all work for... him. The Angel of Light."

Jenna stared at Carl, trying to figure out what to accept at face value, and what to consider as counterfeit.

George plopped down into one of the leather seats at the table, exhausted yet relieved; finally he had confirmed his suspicions of Fincher. "All right," he said, "now it's time for you to prove it."

Carl nodded. He walked over to the wall of steel compartments and entered a code into a security panel, and then moved to one of the drawers in the middle. He opened it and removed a long steel container, which he set on the conference table.

"You already know the Codex Gigas was written sometime prior to 1229, because none of the pages reference anything beyond that year," Carl said. "However, the circumstances leading up to the conception and execution of the pages have been shrouded in mystery for hundreds of years."

Carl started pacing, like a college professor conducting a lecture in front of a class.

"Not long after the Codex Gigas was finished, the Benedictine monastery became financially troubled. The monks were forced to sell the manuscript to another abbey. A few years later, that abbey also went broke. And they sold the Gigas to the Holy Roman Emperor, Rudolf II.

"Now it's Rudolf who, I believe, first realized the supernatural value of the Black Pages. When the Swedish Army seized the Codex as the spoils of war, I theorize that Rudolf kept the Black Pages as he fled the country. Then, for thousands of years, Rudolf's treasure remained hidden."

As Carl continued to walk back and forth, spitting out dates and events, Jenna's eyes fixed on the steel container resting on the table. With every word coming out of his mouth, she became more and more tempted to leap on Carl, beat him unconscious, then, sans his verbal Cliff Notes, throw open the box and discover what lay inside.

"But then in the 1930s," he said, "the Nazi Party rose to power, and the Third Reich began a ruthless campaign to acquire every single ancient artifact that would help ensure their lasting supremacy. Their worldwide efforts paid off when they discovered, and then obtained, Rudolf's treasure. The Nazis were now in possession of the Black Pages."

Nazis, Jenna thought. *Great.*

"But whatever the content of the Black Pages—and I guess you're the only ones who know that now—the Nazis could not understand the significance of what they possessed. So the pages lay unexploited, along with all the other supernatural items underneath the Nuremberg Castle throughout the war.

"When the Third Reich collapsed, and Berlin was being overrun by the Allies, a high-ranking Nazi officer fled with the Black Pages, and whatever other artifacts he could carry. My theory is that this officer used the Black Pages to secure passage from Germany to Argentina. Whoever arranged for his escape ended up retaining his *payment* and doing nothing with it... for the next five decades.

"Then, about twelve years ago, the Black Pages hit the black market. By this time I had been tracking them for over a decade. At least twice during the next ten years, I came within minutes of acquiring them, first in South America, then in Canada. But I failed on both accounts. Not because of the ingenuity of the traders, but because of, I believe, fate."

"Fate," Jenna said, arms crossed.

"Yes, fate. Because only fate and I knew what I knew: that all these years, while the Nazis had been trying to figure out the key to the Black Pages, I had the key all along."

Tapping his fingers on the table next to the steel box, Carl said, "Fifteen years ago, I acquired the document you are about to examine. I was the only one who understood its connection to the Black Pages... and its true significance concerning the future of humanity."

Carl ended his briefing as if he were delivering the final line of a Shakespearean soliloquy.

Jenna clapped. She clapped like she was in the first row at the Globe Theatre watching a performance. "Bravo! Bravo! This is your 'victory lap,' right? Telling us this story is your way of finally sharing with someone—anyone—how brilliant you really are. Well consider my applause the validation of your cleverness and impressive determination—bravo!"

This time her words got a rise from Carl. He looked like a young boy who just found out his birthday party had been canceled.

"The point of telling you the background of this document is so you can appreciate the forces we are up against."

Jenna grimaced at his use of the word "we."

Carl opened the steel container and pulled out four weathered pages of parchment. They were half the size of the Black Pages, but on similar vellum. Next to them, he set another document, this one on acid-free paper with laser printed words.

"I call this 'Gabriel's Report.' It was written in 1201, and it details the circumstances that led to the writing of the Codex Gigas... and the Black Pages. I present the original to you, Ms. Grant, because I'm certain you would want to review the document itself, as well as read the content in its original Latin. I also provide a translation, perhaps for your review, George."

Jenna took a deep breath and moved toward the documents. Carl still stood in her way. He wasn't finished.

"Bernard Rose. Sandy Travis. Neal Grant..."

Jenna said, "If you have a point, then make it."

"They all died. Then they all had near-death experiences. After that, they were never the same. In fact, they were possessed. By demons. But only one, John Wolfenson, the Quartet's Envoy to the Middle East, is possessed by Satan himself."

He let his words soak in. And then Carl stepped aside and allowed Jenna and George to read what he had laid bare before them.

Brother Gabriel
July 11, 1201
Podlažice, Bohemia
Original Latin
English translation

Gabriel's Report:
Genesis of the Codex Gigas

To begin this gravest account, history has shown us that even angels fall, so what hope is there for men?

Brother Herman's fall came before Vernal Equinox, after Prime in the morning. He had chosen to climb to the library, where he would continue his penitent work with the quill.

A man of deepest faith, he challenged the steep stairs, heedless of recent rains, which bring flowers to Podlažice, and treacherous stone.

Though no one bore witness to the fall, we believe he lost his way at the height of his ascent. We found him in the dark of the stairs, with blood from his temple and crown.

We fetched blankets, water, and the barber-surgeon, who used the blankets as a stopper for blood, and who sprinkled the water on Brother Herman's head, as if to anoint him.

When Brother Herman opened his eyes, we felt supremely blessed. All here attest to his fellowship, and his devotion to Christ. He was our brother, as if of blood. However, as I write this, we fear that his resurrection is not a miracle, but only a trick of light.

For four days he lay in the infirmary, hands idle, flesh bare. We served him meals in bed, but he would neither touch his meat, nor breathe of it, else fall violently ill. Even after he rejoined us in labor and prayer, he would not eat of it.

We suspected a vital part of him had died in the fall, from which he would never fully revive, and at times we noticed his eyes were not his, but those of a stranger.

On the tenth day, he attacked one of the farmers who come to our monastery for alms of meat and bread. The farmer had accused Brother Herman of coveting his wife, and the men struck each other till blood made flesh of earth.

The almoner and the prior eventually restrained Brother Herman and confined him to his cell. When served dinner, he chewed it up and spit it out all over the door, even the meat of it, which made him vomit too, till dry heave and paroxysm.

Sometime after the twelfth hour, before Matins, he awoke screaming and tearing at his habit, as one might tear at foreign skin. His words still haunt our halls: "He has become me! He burns beneath the flesh!"

These statements, and his actions, led us to the unspeakable: that Brother Herman has been possessed.

A few days later, he broke from his cell and interrupted Sext. He defiled the altar and set candle to the sacristy before we bound him to his bed by common rope.

The infirmarian swears to this that Brother Herman's bed lifted as if by the hand of God, three inches from the stone, but no one else amongst us shares this claim.

Still others believe Brother Herman's presence here spoils the meat, and breeds mold in the bread; it has become increasingly common to fast, and our constitutions ail.

Twenty-one days after the fall, the Superior Elder, along with two other monks, performed an exorcism on Brother Herman. We held these brave men in our prayers, from Vespers to Prime, yet they emerged from spit and blood and a foulness best not described, having failed.

After twenty days of deliberation, the Elders of the monastery ruled that Brother Herman had succumbed to the evil within him, and for the sins of his flesh he was sentenced to death, to be sealed up in his cell.

It was at this darkest hour that Brother Herman awakened. His eyes seemed to be wholly his own, as if the stranger had passed, or was sleeping deeply.

In his enlightenment, Brother Herman requested breakfast, which was granted, for we were so relieved to see him eat. Even the lamb!

Afterward, he begged for an audience with the Elders. He behaved so well, he required neither rope nor chain, save for the watchful eyes and strong arms of our more sturdy brothers.

Brother Herman repented to the Elders, and confessed that since his fall and resurrection, the devil and our Lord had been embroiled to the death for his soul. The Lord, amen, was winning, and Brother Herman believed the demon might retreat under atonement.

So he beseeched the Superior Elder of the order to stay the execution but enforce his isolation: Brother Herman would be walled up in his cell, imprisoned but not entombed; he requested only a small slot above the floor for provisions, communications, and vellum and ink for scrolls.

Work with the quill often wore harder on his back than toil in the thorns of the field. So for his life, Brother Herman promised to deliver a codex of all knowledge, the bible of all bibles, and all under a single moon.

The Superior and the Elders granted Brother Herman's request, not for faith that he could complete such a tome, which would take decades. They agreed for the love of him; they did not wish to execute such a devout follower and friend if he could save himself.

And so it was: forty-five days after Brother Herman's accident, we laid brick in the doorway of his cell. He sat with his back to us, ruling his first page, one of 310 vellum leaves skinned from the calves.

As we laid the last brick, Brother Herman dipped his quill in the ink, which he specifically requested from the crushed nests of insects. Late into his incarceration, he sent a written order for eight extra leaves of vellum, for correcting his text.

Solely Brother Herman occupied the cell, and yet from the night of his prison, two voices echoed out: one from Brother Herman, of this we are certain; the other, no one knows.

When the abbot came to question him about this stranger, Brother Herman did not speak. Rather, he slipped a scrap of parchment beneath the door, written in insect ink and some twisted tongue: "We now speak as one."

Brother Gabriel, July 11, 1201
Podlažice, Bohemia

CHAPTER 8

WHEN JENNA FIRST FEASTED HER EYES on the medieval document, she was tempted to dive right in and read it. She resisted, though. She needed to authenticate it first, or why waste her time? Many experts made the mistake of reading an artifact before validating it. Oftentimes, compelling content swayed or blinded them to obvious forgeries.

Without any equipment, Jenna's authentication process had been cursory at best. She suspected Carl owned the tools she needed, but doubted he would loan them to her.

Brother Gabriel, if he, indeed, was the author, had written the report on vellum. To the naked eye, his ink seemed to radiate more than the insect ink used in the Black Pages. So, sans a black light to verify, Jenna assumed it was metal ink.

She scanned all four pages of text for a forger's tremor, but found no sign of hesitation or shakes in the lettering. Instead, she found evidence of authenticity: repeated signs of overlapping and layering, where ink lines crossed each other and pooled. This ruled out the possibility that the content had been drafted and then printed onto the vellum.

The pages themselves looked old enough. Again, without equipment, she couldn't conclusively say, but she could at least determine whether someone had tried to age or antique non-period vellum. Patterned, uniformed browning on the different pages of a document was a sure sign of forgery. Naturally, vellum aged in unique and unpredictable ways, just as these four pages had aged.

Jenna noticed, too, an overall similarity to the veneer of the vellum, which suggested one source. Acquiring four pages of the same thirteenth-century stock proved difficult nowadays, so forgers often settled for period vellum from two or more sources, contradicting the practices of thirteenth-century scribes.

Okay, Jenna thought, satisfied that she wasn't wasting her time. She stretched the kink out of her neck, cracked her knuckles, and began to read the original Latin document.

She was immediately stunned at how convincingly it contextualized the Black Pages.

Gabriel's medieval report indicated that Brother Herman had been possessed before writing the Codex Gigas. If that was true, what she and George had acquired, and then memorized, could be the written musings of Satan himself.

"I'll take that drink now," Jenna said after reading the document by Brother Gabriel. She caught the look of satisfaction on Carl's face, but didn't care.

"Water or something else?" he asked.

"Water *and* something else, if you've got it."

Carl turned to ask George the same question, but George was still reading the English translation.

Jenna's mind teemed with questions, contradictions, and paradoxes. She wished she could trust Carl to give her straight answers. Even if he told the truth, she suspected it would be self-serving.

"Here you go." Carl startled her. She had been so deep in thought, he seemed to have appeared right next to her without a sound.

He held a bottle of water in one hand, and a glass of brown liquid and ice in the other.

"Single malt Scotch whisky," he said. "I hope that's what you had in mind. And it's not from any distillery that I own, operate, or have ever been to."

Jenna took a gulp from the bottled water. Then she took a bigger gulp from the single malt Scotch whisky on the rocks. Her eyes watered as the alcohol burned her throat.

Even through the tears, she could see Carl standing next to her with that unmistakable look of anxious anticipation.

"Do you mind?" she asked before taking another sip from her Scotch whisky. "I need some space to process what I read."

"Well," Carl said, "I hope you're not concerned about authenticity. I've had Gabriel's report validated by two different experts in medieval documents. They used state-of-the-art equipment and techniques to verify the age of the document, the ink used, as well as their own expertise in judging the literary content. There is zero chance of forgery."

"Exactly the words I would expect from the owner of the artifact," Jenna said. "Believe me, I've heard it before."

"So does that mean you're challenging the authenticity?"

"No. Not at this time at least. But I admit to my concern about the health of the 'two different experts' after they authenticated your artifact."

The noticeable delay in Carl's response lent credence to Jenna's accusation.

"Both experts were handsomely compensated for their services. And they are alive and well."

"Fine. But I'm still going to ask you to give me some space."

Carl stomped away, unable to conceal his frustration.

She tried her best to turn her mind back to Gabriel's report. She had to reach a conclusion, and quickly, as to how the document impacted the content of the Black Pages. And since she couldn't trust Carl, she would have to sort out her questions and concerns by herself.

The first two lines of the first quatrain came to her as she mulled everything over: *"It was upon the fall when the light / From the morning star came upon me."*

Initially, she and Raymond had interpreted "fall" as a reference to Satan's fall from grace. But after reading Gabriel's report, Jenna believed the word "fall" was a double entendre—it also referred to Herman's fall down some monastery steps. A fall that somehow led to a change in his personality. Which begged the question, how many levels of meaning were hidden in the rest of the quatrains?

For all its obscurity, at least the report answered one question Raymond had asked all the way back in London: "What relevance do passages from the Bible, or anything that a monk wrote in the thirteenth century, have to anyone living in our century?" If the monk didn't simply suffer brain trauma from the accident and was somehow channeling Satan himself, the answer was—all the relevance in the world.

"I've finished," George said, stretching. "I believe this translation only confirms what we already knew. What Jenna and I have in our heads... it's perfectly consistent with Brother Gabriel's impressions hundreds of years ago."

Carl sighed with relief. "This is cause for celebration." He moved to the refrigerator, but Jenna interrupted.

"Can we take a time out on the celebration?"

She turned to George and hoped that her manner, and not just her words, conveyed her subtext. "George, I believe it's in our best interest to think carefully about everything we've read, don't you?"

Carl had already returned with two more Scotch whiskies on the rocks. He set one down in front of George and raised the other in a toast.

"To working together."

Carl held his glass out, but neither Jenna nor George made a move to clink glasses with him.

"I still have questions," Jenna said, staring at Carl's lonely glass.

"Of course you do." He withdrew the toast and took a sip. "Fire away."

Jenna hesitated, wanting to carefully craft her inquiries. She didn't want to inadvertently reveal any content from the Black Pages.

"I know what perplexes Jenna," George said. "It's the quatrains—"

"Shut up, George! Do you hear me? I don't want you to say another word!"

Jenna had never spoken to him like that. But she had seen the way Carl had lit up at George's reference to quatrains, and she needed to plug the leak as quickly as possible.

"I apologize for speaking out of turn," George said. He looked absolutely untroubled by her reprimand. "Please, you're the expert. Have your say."

Jenna noted that Carl had remained silent during this verbal exchange. The most effective kind of dissent within a partnership didn't need the direct involvement of a third party.

She took another sip from her drink. Now it was her turn to pace back and forth.

"If we're supposed to read into this document that Herman was possessed by... Satan... then my first question is, why would the great deceiver, the father of all lies, put down anything of value in writing? Unless, of course, it was one big lie, meant to send future generations running down blind alleys."

"If the Black Pages are all an elaborate lie," George said before Carl could get a word in, "then why would his... minions go through the deadly rampage to acquire them?"

"That's a good point, George. One you could have made after Carl dropped us off at the airport. At this moment, I think we should be more interested in hearing what he has to say, don't you agree?"

George nodded, still seemingly ignorant to Jenna's frustration, which she no longer bothered to conceal.

"Ms. Grant," Carl said, "I was convinced you would have some very good questions, and I'm glad you didn't disappoint. Please, let me try to answer your first one the best I can.

"Years ago, we received... signs that the Black Pages were a problem, so members of our group were tasked to acquire them. We knew nothing about the pages, only the facts behind their creation."

Carl set his drink on the conference table, and Jenna saw how little he had drunk. For all his enthusiastic calls for celebration, the last thing Carl intended to do was let alcohol guide his thoughts or decisions.

"Prior to our search for the Black Pages, we used Gabriel's report as a jumping-off point to answer the very question you now ask. I'm afraid we have no conclusive answers. But we had a few theories I'd like to share with you. The first theory comes from one of our members, an expert in the field of psychology."

Carl looked over at George, a clear sign that he was referring to Dr. Fincher.

"This expert theorized that Satan is the father, the founder, if you will, of all human psychopathology. Like genes from a parent, all of humanity's personality disorders or deviant behaviors can be traced back to his... fall from grace. Like any deranged serial killer, Satan couldn't resist throwing down the gauntlet and challenging God to stop him. The way it was explained to me, a person of superior intellect has trouble believing that anyone can keep up with them. So the Black Pages were the Angel of Light's way of putting it all out there, for all to see..."

Jenna watched Carl's delivery of Fincher's theory carefully. His summation seemed to bristle with subtle, non-verbal signs of derision and contempt. Carl probably had brought up Fincher's theory for the sole purpose of highlighting to George the doctor's involvement.

"Now my personal theory is quite different," Carl said. "And I would like to share it with you, not only to help answer your question, Ms. Grant, but also to bridge the gap of trust that's clearly still between us."

Normally Jenna didn't mind whenever someone repeated her name during a conversation—it was a standard memorization technique—but Carl's continual direct address was another transparent effort to achieve intimacy.

He said, "I've come to the conclusion that there is a protocol between the two competing parties. The envoy has hinted about a complex *understanding* in his relationship with God. A yin and yang to the way they conduct business. Whatever Satan intends to accomplish while he is here, there is a prerequisite: he is obligated to mitigate any direct efforts toward his goal."

Jenna and George exchanged a confused look. She wasn't sure whether Carl's abstract statement was symptomatic of the complex, almost esoteric topic, or just doublespeak from a smooth operator trying to "bridge the gap of trust."

"Yes, yes, I know it sounds vague," Carl said. "Let me try again." He took a deep breath before continuing.

"I believe the rules of engagement between the combatants required the Angel of Light to put down, in writing, information that would be damaging to him if he chose to directly influence events here. I suspect—and only either of you can confirm my suspicions—that he used the Black Pages to fulfill those obligations. Perhaps he even included information that details the exact method to end his presence here. That information might have been compulsory or... voluntary. I've spent time with him. I see an issue with his pride."

Jenna looked over at George and was ready to put her hand over his face if he tried to respond.

"And I can make the case that he probably didn't even think he was being reckless," Carl continued. "He figured hundreds of years would pass. How could these... mammals... God's higher-thinking creations... how could they possibly figure out what he was up to?"

"So it was sort of a fuck you to God," George blurted out.

Jenna cringed.

"Yes! Exactly!" Carl said. "Are you saying everything you know about the Black Pages confirms my theory?"

Jenna, after downing the rest of her drink, slammed her glass on the table. George, on the other hand, had not touched his drink, which surprised her; he sounded like he had downed a bottle of ninety-proof liquor laced with truth serum.

"Carl, if your plan is to get us drunk so we'll throw up the contents of the Black Pages, I urge you to give up that plan right now. And I also wouldn't be betting the rent money that this document, your lame attempt at intimacy, or your embarrassing effort at looking profound will end up being game changers."

Jenna's words sparked a twinkle in Carl's eyes, a bemused smile. He walked toward her, not in a straight line, but in meandering half circles; the kind of approach a four-legged beast uses as it zeros in on its prey.

"Ms. Grant, do you come from divorced parents? Because I can tell. Perhaps there's even a tragedy or emotional trauma in your past, before the age of maturation. My assessment is based on the fact that most people your age have the same amount of distrust and paranoia, but usually on the basement level of their mind, certainly no higher than the parking level. Yours, Ms. Grant, is even higher. I would say it's operating in the lobby. Because of some extreme hurt and profound disappointment, you have a dog in front of your building, barking constantly so no one ever gets inside."

Carl's words confirmed what Jenna had known for years. Success follows talent. Talent never follows success. But his talent for breaking down her personality, no matter how accurate, failed to breach the walls she had erected to protect herself from people exactly like Carl.

"Am I supposed to be impressed with the observations that a gypsy with a cracked crystal ball can spit out at any modern woman my age from a westernized country? That wasn't insightful. It was just playing the odds. I'd have given you more credit if you had guessed my astrological sign."

Her words stopped Carl's slow encroachment.

"Do you mind if I take a turn?" she said, and didn't wait for him to respond. "I see a control freak, not only because I saw you glance at the room's thermostat immediately when we walked into the room, but also because of the way all the bottles in your refrigerator were perfectly aligned. But the small beads of sweat that have gathered on the top of your forehead while standing in a temperature controlled room is just one sign that you're a control freak... who has lost control. The most telling clue is how you keep changing your approach to the way you're dealing with us.

"At the airport you started with intimidation, but when you realized that wasn't going to work, you quickly switched to the ingratiating host. Wine and dine us and somehow we'll all end up being comrades in arms, right? But when that didn't work, you switched again. This time you tried to portray yourself as a wise sage, the only man with enough insight that our only option would be to trust you for help. Problem with that plan is, it's not consistent. Somehow the wise sage screwed up. That's why we're now getting the floor show.

"So, what's your next plan, Carl? No, wait, don't answer. Let me guess. How about an appeal to our love for humanity? Or here's a good one—the sympathy card. Stop. Erase what I just said. I'm totally going with a variation of what you already tried at the airport. Shall I check my cell phone for a video of my cat being held at gunpoint?"

Carl turned away, and his head dropped until his chin rested on his chest.

"Yeah, you should look away. I didn't need to see your sweaty palms to know how desperate you are. It's in your eyes. Whatever yacht you've been skippering for years has obviously run aground, and you're terrified we'll see the driftwood washed up on the beach."

Carl opened his mouth to speak, but apparently Jenna wasn't finished.

"Oh, and you're a Gemini. Two-faced."

As Carl stared at his glass floor, George thought he looked humbled and embarrassed for the first time since they met. Or at least that's what he wanted to portray.

"I deserve that," Carl said. "All of it. For the way I've behaved with you both... but mostly because of my behavior the last twenty years. I was ignorant and... arrogant. Just like him. All these years it never once dawned on me that part of his plan would include my oldest son."

Carl's eyes pooled up with tears.

Jenna shook her head. She admired Carl's audacity. *Can you believe this guy? He's actually going to play the sympathy card.*

———

CARL LED THEM FROM his cabinet of curiosities back into the sandstone corridor, talking a mile a minute as they walked.

"For years we... received signs to focus on John Wolfenson. His wealth, his connections, his influence: they all made him the perfect possession. But, timing—timing was everything. Certain things had to be set in motion."

"The stars had to align," Jenna said.

Carl didn't respond to her sarcasm. He stopped at the end of the hallway, at the very last door. "When the timing was right, we made sure to try and kill him."

"Why?" George asked.

"So he would have a near-death experience."

Neal, Jenna thought. Neal had talked about dying and coming back, right before he drove his car into the train. Even in reflection, Jenna didn't interpret his description as an NDE. She had to wonder, though, is that how they got to him? Is that how he became someone other than her real brother?

Carl ran his card through the security scanner. After the red laser identified his face, the door unlocked.

Before opening it, he said, "Apparently, after all of our years of devotion and dedicated effort, the Angel of Light wasn't satisfied that he could trust us. So he created a test of loyalty."

They all entered the room. Not only was it smaller than Jenna imagined, it was not at all creepy. She had to admit the little schoolgirl inside her, who once enjoyed reading haunted house books, had hoped the last chamber in the hallway would be the biggest and scariest.

Instead, they stood in a space no bigger than a hospital's radiology room. A modular control panel, shaped like a horseshoe, featured rows of high-tech monitoring equipment. Spanning the back wall was a piece of opaque glass, which obscured whatever lay on the other side.

"One by one our loved ones died in tragic accidents. But then..."

"They came back," George said, when Carl could not utter the words. "Demonically possessed."

Carl pushed a leather office chair toward George, who took the seat.

"At first I tried to convince myself that the Angel of Light was using my son as a way to communicate with me through his demons. But when he himself finally took possession of John Wolfenson, and Ami wasn't released... I knew I had been deluding myself."

Jenna mentally flashed to the sixth quatrain. What was it? Loons? She had to think for a moment before it came to her.

Loons guide his descent
Preparing a nest for his landing
Never suspecting that the fish they gather
Will be snatched from the mouths of their own ranks

In Jenna's interpretation, the quatrain definitely corroborated that Satan, prior to his arrival, had sought leverage against the Red Veil.

She wondered if she could use Carl's revelation to latch the quatrains onto an accessible timeline.

In front of the room's opaque window, two hi-def televisions hung down from the ceiling. Carl hit a few buttons at the control panel, and one of the screens flashed to life.

Jenna totally expected it to show a live feed of whatever lurked behind the dark glass. It didn't. It showed a room inside a mansion, in Modern Moroccan style. Expensive, tasteful, with a mosaic inlay in the terracotta tile, the house could easily have been Carl's personal residence.

"My son Ami was hit by a car," Carl said, staring at the televised room, the intricate friezes above the doors. "In the few minutes that he was dead, he says that he saw an angel."

At the back of the room, an urn sat on a teak table. It memorialized the branches and husks of a Chinese lantern.

"And while my son never came back to life," Carl said, "his body got up and walked."

Footsteps echoed on the terracotta tile of the house as Carl made his grand entrance on the big screen.

Suddenly, something shrieked and leapt onto his back.

Jenna flinched.

At first, the screech and lethal pounce sounded and looked like a simian from the African jungle. But it turned out to be an Arab boy, apparently Carl's son.

"Eas incendit!" Ami screamed as he clung to Carl's back. *"Incendit omnes aves quae obscurant suam lucem!"*

Jenna quickly translated the Latin in her head: "He burns them! Burns all birds who eclipse his light!"

Father and son stumbled out of frame as the camera continued to hold on the shot of the empty room. The guttural noises, mixed with squeals and profanities, painted a very vivid picture of what was happening offscreen.

Just when Jenna couldn't stand it anymore, the image brightened to white, and the sound dimmed. Then it cut to black.

New footage came on the screen, this time from a hospital security camera. Several orderlies and nurses were trying to pin Ami to his bed, just long enough to subdue him.

The date stamp on this clip preceded the first home video. On Jenna's rough mental timeline, this record fell not long after Ami's accident, evidenced by his bandages.

Even here, bleeding through the gauze, Ami fought like a wild animal, with the lithe, frenetic, and unpredictable precision of a cat.

He bit and tore off an orderly's ear and shouted obscenities into it while his victim disentangled himself from the dog pile and stumbled back, holding the hole in the side of his head as if he didn't want to hear it anymore, these curses, this evil.

The clip, as the one before it, brightened to white, and then cut to black.

Then another video began. It had no date; three dashes substituted the month, day, and year. So Ami's bandages constituted the timeline. Pus either stained or suppurated through the gauze, saturating outward into reddish to brownish to blackish crusts. He must have made it difficult for anyone to change them.

The boy lay in a hospital bed, only this time in a house. Two middle-aged females, both Arabic, tried to pin him down while a priest stood by, reciting the exorcism rites. The priest attempted to lay a hand on the boy's forehead, but missed. Not only because the boy was writhing like a worm, but also, Jenna noticed, because the priest appeared to be blind. His milky eyes stood out in hi-def.

Then the video froze, and Jenna turned to see Carl lifting his finger from the pause button.

"Not exactly the home movies we want to share with relatives," Carl said.

"Was it you who shot the last video?" George asked.

"No," Carl said, "Zeinah, my wife—she took our boy to some close friends. The priest worked with Ami for two days. He failed."

"So you weren't actually there?" Jenna asked, with more than a hint of condemnation.

"I wish that had been possible, I truly do. But I believe Ami's possession serves as a viewfinder to my actions. Satan would have seen me if I were party to an exorcism."

"How do we know?" George asked. "How do we know what we're looking at isn't just... your version of a Hollywood production?"

"I would certainly sleep better if it were. But, no, George. My son Ami is the price I'm paying for my alliance with... him."

Carl fell back against the plastic veneer of the control panel, seemingly as exhausted as George. When he did finally speak again, he spoke in an intimate whisper, like someone who wanted to reveal the truth because they owed you that much.

"Ami is the reason I stopped you at the airport and flew you here. I hoped and prayed the Black Pages contained a way to... release my son."

"He's on the other side of this glass, isn't he?" Jenna asked.

Carl didn't bother to deny it. In fact, he seemed to have been waiting for someone to ask: he hit a couple of buttons on the control panel, and the opaque glass began to clear. Within seconds, the wall had changed into a window.

In the next room, Ami lay unconscious, strapped to a bed. Wires and tubes connected him to monitoring equipment.

"You asked why I changed my mind about helping Satan," Carl said, walking around the control panel. He approached a wall that looked like solid steel, and he rested his hand on it. Then he turned his head to look at them. "I wish one of you had children. Then maybe you would understand."

He stepped away from the wall and held out his palm in a gesture of urgent appeal. "Jenna, you're a daughter of a loving mother. I hope you understand my plea. Please, at the very least, did the Black Pages reveal a way to stop... him?"

"Perhaps," Jenna replied.

"*Perhaps*? *Perhaps*?! That's all you think I've earned with every-thing I've shown you?"

During the helicopter ride to this subterranean lair, Jenna had planned and rehearsed her answer. Now, seconds after hearing herself say it, she decided it was exactly the perfect response.

"I want to see him," George said. "I want to go in there and see your son. If you do that, I will give you more."

Jenna turned to George. "What the hell are you talking about?!"

"Shut up, Jenna. Stop trying to control me." George's eyes were fixed on Carl. "What do you say? I give you more information about the Black Pages in exchange for a visit with your comatose son? It sounds like a win-win to me."

———

CARL PUSHED ON A PART of the steel wall. It gave way to a hidden door and, behind that, a narrow passageway to Ami's room.

The entrance appeared to have no security scanners or guards. Jenna could hardly believe it.

After about a dozen yards, they ascended three steps. Then they passed through another solid steel door before entering the room.

All three took a few steps into the room and stopped. They stared at Ami, who lay comatose in his bed. Medical equipment beeped and whirred, and below those sounds, they could hear the boy breathing.

"Can he hear us?" Jenna asked.

"Believe me," Carl said, "if my son could hear our words, I would not have brought you here."

When he had first entered the room, George, feeling dizzy and weak, had leaned on the wall for support. But now, after staring at Ami for a bit, the strength began to return to his legs.

"Satisfied?" Carl asked him.

"In a moment."

"Please don't treat my son like he is a sideshow exhibit."

"Of course not. Just a bit closer and I'll be entirely satisfied." George took a step forward.

Years ago, his father had suffered a stroke while walking down some stairs. George had helped him recover. And whenever George Sr. tried to walk on his own, out of obstinacy and pride, each step was more diagonal than straight ahead. George Jr. now approached Ami's bed with the same awkward gait.

Carl leaned toward Jenna. "Look at him. You know he's going to die," he whispered, low enough that he probably believed the sound of medical equipment camouflaged his words. "And you will be all alone. Please, help me, and I swear to you I will not only reward you, but I'll see to it that he gets the comfort and support he needs in his final days. Trust me, if we do this together, we have a chance at putting an end to this... evil."

At Ami's bedside, George gripped the extended aluminum bar and balanced himself.

The child before him resembled a wax figure, or a corpse embalmed. And yet, for someone who looked so dead, the leather restraints suggested vicious life.

Slowly, sickly, a blue vein, shaped like a lightning bolt, began to emerge on Ami's forehead. George smiled.

"What did... the *envoy* tell you he was going to do?" Jenna asked. "What was his plan?"

Carl wasn't paying much attention to her. His attention was on his son. And George.

"His plan was to increase the brand name of John Wolfenson. This earthquake in Syria... he believes his personal response will put him dead-center in upcoming international events."

Ami's finger on his right hand twitched. Then the thumb on his left hand started shaking. George saw both movements and got a firmer grip on the rail of the bed. He had no way of anticipating how strong the boy would be when awakened.

"Carl, he's lying to you," George said without ever turning around. "We've seen the Black Pages. I can assure you his plan is not just some author book tour. This business in Syria... it's like the foreshock of something much bigger. Something worldwide."

Ami's eyes flashed open to the bloodshot whites. They stayed like that so long it seemed as if he had developed cataracts. But then the irises rolled down out of his head and fixed on George.

"Your dead wife is our whore," the boy said. And then he started to strain against his leather straps. Neck to torso, they began to snap.

"George..." Jenna warned, starting toward the bed.

But George stood perfectly still, even as Ami's right hand broke free and, quick as a striking snake, latched onto George's throat.

Ami sat up. The scars on his body and face, left by the car that had hit him, began to open up and fester with bloody pus. "She's our whore! And we fill her with our disease!"

George never retaliated, never moved, never even stopped smiling, despite the darkness eroding the edges of his vision.

"Stop it!" Jenna cried, prying at the hand clamped around George's throat. The boy's skin was slimy, slippery with infected secretions.

Behind her, the steel door flew open, and two men wearing black jeans and dark turtlenecks raced into the room. They helped Jenna release George, who crumpled to the floor, and then Ami leaned over the edge of his bed and spit in his face.

"You are nothing!" the boy screamed. "An empty glove!"

One of the turtleneck guys injected Ami in the thigh, and the boy's strength shut off slowly, like a faucet. They pinned him down, and, from gush to drip, to one last drop, the boy fell back into his quietus.

Carl's men moved about, trying to improvise new straps, while Jenna knelt beside George.

"Are you all right?"

He looked up at her, rubbing his neck. "Somehow I never get tired of hearing you ask me that..." He looked around and said, "Where's Carl?"

Jenna didn't know, and for the moment she didn't care.

"Come on," she said, and she helped George up.

Stumbling, rushing, they made their way down the dark hall from Ami's chamber.

"I'm so sorry," Carl said as they burst into the control room, both out of breath. He hovered around them like a pesky mosquito. He looked at George and said, "Do I need to call the medic?"

Jenna, catching her breath, said, "No, your three hours are officially up."

———

AS THE HELICOPTER LIFTED OFF from the flat mountaintop, Carl pulled the hoods off Jenna and George. He offered them warm towels and bottles of water, but they refused.

A few minutes into the flight, Carl tried again to engage them.

"So will you help me?"

"What if we said yes?" Jenna asked.

"I would applaud your decision. And I would start making plans for us to confront Wolfenson when he returns from Aleppo."

"Why wait?" Jenna said. "Why not right after we land in Tel Aviv?"

"Mmm, too risky. His bodyguards would be tough to break through. Believe me, I'm the one in charge of his security. But after he comes back from Syria, I can arrange for you to get close... if, indeed, the Black Pages have given you the means to stop him."

Jenna didn't respond. And once again, an awkward silence settled over the three of them for the rest of the trip.

———

APPROXIMATELY THREE HOURS after they first walked out of the Ben Gurion Airport in Tel Aviv, Carl's Humvee was taking them back to the curb near arrivals.

In the front passenger seat, Carl grabbed something from the glove compartment.

"I want you to take this," he said, turning to the passengers in the back seat. He held a mobile phone. Neither Jenna nor George moved to accept it.

"It's a satellite phone, completely charged and pre-programmed with a single number. You call that number and I will answer."

He extended his arm until the phone was practically in their faces. George finally accepted it.

The Hummer screeched to a halt at the curb. No one moved or said anything as the engine idled.

"You're not going to call me are you?" Carl finally said.

Jenna just stared at him.

"I swear on my son's soul I won't harm either of you, or your friend in London. I just need to know... what *you* know."

She unbuckled her seatbelt and leaned forward. "I think that's your problem, Carl. Always needing to know what other people know. Because you've never been able to figure out the answers for yourself. Why else would someone with all your resources make a choice that would end up causing so many people to suffer and die?"

150

Carl had nothing to say. He just stared at her with a blank look.

She moved to get out of the car, and Jenna had to admit she was surprised when Carl didn't stop her. She helped George out of the vehicle too. They stood just a few feet from where they had left hours ago, right in front of the main terminal—right in plain sight of anyone who might have been watching, or waiting to do them harm.

For some reason Carl was no longer concerned about their safety. Maybe they had never been in danger in the first place. Just one of Carl's strategies, Jenna thought, a scare tactic to get what he wanted.

Carl rolled down his window halfway and spoke to them over the glass. "I'm going to reveal something to you. And I'm only telling you this because I hope it will encourage you to use the phone I've given you."

"Go ahead, Carl, give it your best shot. I have to admit, after everything you've tried, I'm dying to hear what your fallback plan is."

Jenna's taunt didn't seem to register with Carl. He just stared at her, waiting until she was finished speaking. Then he said, "Helping the Angel of Light usher in the End Days... something of that magnitude requires contributions from many people. Dr. Fincher and I are just two members of a much larger organization. Another member of the Red Veil, in fact he's one of the founding members, is someone you know. Jenna... your father is one of us."

Carl didn't wait for her reaction. He motioned to his driver and the Humvee sped away.

CHAPTER 9

"**D**ID YOU HEAR WHAT I JUST SAID?" George asked, but Jenna ignored him and whipped out her cell phone.

"I said Carl is probably lying about your father."

They still stood on the curb outside the main terminal, watching the sun set on the earth. Jenna's phone only showed a few bars, and one unread text message. She opened it.

Spotted the fake, Raymond had written.

Oh, thank God! she thought. At the very least, that meant he had survived. She planned to make him regret it shortly.

Jenna punched his number into her phone and stamped her finger down on the talk button, as if she could somehow administer an electrical shock when he answered.

While the number rang, she looked over at George, raising her eyebrows to ask what it was he wanted.

"Why are you ignoring me?" he said.

"George, I'm not ignoring you. I'm ignoring what Carl said about my father."

Raymond picked up. "Before you say anything, let me just tell you I'm not currently drunk."

A bit of static crackled on the line, and she had to muffle her ear against the sounds of the airport. Other than that, she could hear his voice clearly enough. All she could do was close her eyes and wait until her heart rate settled.

Raymond, noticing the pregnant silence, said, "I am a little brassed off that I couldn't stay to the end of football, but... I'll be all right."

Jenna's eyes flashed open. "No, Raymond, don't you dare. Don't you dare try to pull the stiff upper lip thing with me."

"Oh, okay, I get it. You want me to say, 'Thank you so much, dear Jenna, for your text. It saved my bloody life.'"

"Yes," she said, "thank you."

"Oh, you're absolutely welcome. And I'll be sure to mention you in the next *Archeology Review*. But not without attaching a footnote."

"And what's that, Raymond?"

"That I'm thoroughly convinced I would've seen right through that *poncer* without any cell phone prompts."

"Poncer's inappropriate language for a footnote, don't you think?"

"Well let's just agree then, shall we? I owe you something for your valiant effort. Two pints ought to settle the account, don't you think? Because I surely won't be sitting around with you in public, perhaps with our friends, if you intend on dining out on this story that you saved my life."

"Fine. Raymond, I won't ever mention to anyone that I saved your life."

"Thank you."

"But I will tell anyone, and I mean everyone we know, what a complete moron you are."

"Thanks."

"Gerry's, Raymond? Honestly?" Jenna still couldn't believe it. "And on the *one night* I specifically told you to lay low. What could you have possibly been thinking?"

Over two thousand miles separated them, and yet she heard him sigh.

"I'm sure we both agree I *wasn't* thinking. I have no rational explanation for my behavior. So I'll have two rounds of drinks waiting for you when you get back, and we agree never to bring this subject up again. So now, with that agreed upon... let's move on."

"Gladly. Why don't we start with the man who was following you? Do you think he was the one I saw at the train station?"

"Oh, I'm sure of it. He had make-up on his face, for God's sake."

"Make-up?"

"Yeah, to cover up the wound George dealt him back in the States. No lone green eye, but... he could have been wearing a colored lens, I guess. Here's the real clincher: ask George if his guy was wearing a rooster claw around his neck?"

Jenna turned to George and asked him about the rooster claw. He nodded.

"George says yes."

"Well, then, we have our man. Serves him right too. I just checked the score on my cell phone, and Cameroon ended up winning the match."

"Raymond, what's that got to do with anything?"

"No, you're right—nothing. Sorry."

"So are you going to tell me what happened with this... poncer?"

"Not much to tell. I left the pub as they were giving him a real thrashing. So he could be dead, or still out there somewhere, probably feeling rather cheeky. How are you two?"

Jenna looked over at George. He was staring up at a plane flying in from some far corner of the earth.

"Let's just say we had an enlightening experience," she said. "But here we are, having landed over three hours ago, and we still haven't left Ben Gurion."

"Because of security?"

"No, long story. I'll fill you in once we get on the road. But I need to know something first."

He remained silent and waiting for her.

"Raymond, are you going to be all right?"

"Yes," he said. "Jenna, I'm fine, honestly. I'm having a pint with a mate at the King's College police station, and we're surrounded by at least a dozen campus bobbies." He lowered his voice. "Between you and me, I've seen tougher blokes at a boffin convention. But put them all together and I'm sure we can get in a few punches before any other poncer brings me down."

Jenna knew the term "boffin," in British slang, meant "nerd." She knew because Raymond often referred to himself as a boffin both on the radio show and at the pub. He was confident and comfortable enough with himself that cracking a self-deprecating joke was never a problem.

But hearing him rank his police officer friends below blokes at a "boffin convention"... whatever happened at Gerry's must have really shaken him up.

"Okay, Raymond, great to hear. But I need to say something, and I need you to listen, okay?"

"Okay."

"I'm sorry, Raymond. I'm really sorry for involving you in all this. The last thing in the world I want is for you to get hurt. But as it turns out, you were exactly the right man for the job. It makes me feel a tad better knowing you were on top of things."

"Well, then, let's say you make it up to me. I'm thinking another night on the balcony of the Hilton might just about cover it. What do you say?"

"It's a deal."

The plane George had been watching disappeared behind the massive airport. Jenna heard it touching down in the distant airfield. It reminded her of how tightly things were scheduled, and how sometimes you missed your flight.

"Look, Raymond, I need to run but... are you in a place with computer access?"

"Sure. As I said, I'm in my friend's office here at Campus PD."

"Good. Because I'm afraid my Internet will be even slower than usual here, and I need answers now."

"Okay, what's up?"

"When I looked up Sandy Travis a few days ago, I found some pictures from the day she was shot. There was a priest kneeling beside her as she died. I need one of the pictures where I see the priest's face. I'm trying to confirm something. When you get it, can you send it to me on my cell?"

There was silence. Then a rise of static... followed by more silence. She thought they had lost connection and somehow she hadn't heard it happen.

"Raymond, are you still there?"

"Yes, still here. But here's the thing, Jenna. I'm already calling in my marker."

"Raymond..."

"I want you to walk right past the rental car floor and go straight to a ticket counter."

"I can't do that."

"Yes, you can. You catch the next plane ride home, and take the train straight to the Hilton. Please, do it. You come and you meet me on the balcony of the junior suite."

Jenna started to tear up. *Oh my God*, she thought, wiping her eyes, *someone's taken over my body!*

The last time she had cried this much was when she found out her first boyfriend planned to go on a dig in Turkey without her. And it wasn't the boyfriend she had cried about.

"If you need to," Raymond said, "you pretend I was the one who saved your life. Pretend you owe me one."

Jenna cleared her throat. "Raymond, I wish I could. I've been living in England long enough, so try to imagine me saying this with a stiff upper lip. I've got to see this thing through to the end. You understand, don't you?"

The line went silent again. This time Jenna knew their connection was just fine.

"Raymond..."

"Have it your way. I'll get back to you with that information."

"Thanks, Raymond."

He ended the connection.

Jenna closed her phone and started marching toward the entrance to the airport.

"Where are we going?" George asked, trying to keep up.

"I'll tell you when one of us is behind the wheel." She suddenly stopped walking, and said, "And I'll take the phone Carl gave us, please."

George put a protective hand in his coat pocket, where he kept the sat phone. He was certain Jenna meant to throw it across the parking lot, or crush it under the heel of her shoe.

"Please," she said.

Finally, he relented and gave her the phone. She considered it for a moment, then put it in her coat and walked through the doors into the airport.

———

STEVE, THE GUY AT ELDAN CAR RENTAL who always helped Jenna, raised an eyebrow when she requested a compact car.

"No SUV?" he asked.

Because of the remote locations of her archeological digs, she had always requested something capable of transporting equipment over difficult terrain. For this trip, though, Jenna and George needed something reliable and inconspicuous. Something hopefully invisible to anyone who might be on the lookout for them.

Steve issued Jenna a light blue Ford Focus.

Soon, she was driving down Road 1 toward Tel Aviv. "What are you doing, George?"

"Trying to get this GPS to work."

"We don't need it to work. I know where I'm going."

He nodded and turned his attention to the car's radio. He fiddled with the knob long enough to drive Jenna insane, and then mercifully he settled on a classical music station. She recognized a piano concerto by Mozart, but couldn't identify which one.

George settled back and watched the passing scenery. Along the highway, lush plants threatened to overgrow the concrete barrier, and the silhouette of palm trees stood out against the dusk.

"So we're just not going to talk about it?" he asked as he stared out the window.

"About what, George?"

"About your father."

Jenna checked her speedometer and backed off the gas pedal. This part of the motorway had been raised to 110 kilometers per hour, and she was pushing it.

"I'm only concerned because it could distract you from what we need to do," George said.

"Do I look distracted, George?"

"No. But I'm still concerned the issue's on your mind."

"Based on what?"

He turned from the window and looked right at her. "You're gripping the wheel so tightly, the circulation to your fingers stopped two minutes ago. I'm afraid gangrene could set in."

Jenna, stubborn as ever, maintained her grip on the steering wheel. In fact, she tightened it.

"Okay, George, so let's talk. How can you be so sure Carl's lying about my father? You're the one who told me there may be some truth in his lies."

"That's not what I said. If you remember, I said—"

"I know exactly what you said! 'The truth may lie at the heart of his deceptions.' Right? Am I right?"

He didn't answer.

"Tell you what, George, ask me about anything you've said since we left London. Go ahead. Do it. You'll see. I can repeat it verbatim."

He didn't doubt her ability. And he wanted to reach over and touch her arm to calm her down. But he feared that she would throw his hand back with the fingers tied up in knots.

"That won't be necessary," he said. "I believe you."

"Are you sure? Because recalling everything you've said wouldn't be much of a challenge. You told a horse story. That was good. But you sort of peaked there. Since then, all I've gotten from you is a lot of ambiguous crap you could've cribbed from fortune cookies. Oh, except when you were spreading your legs for Carl, practically giving him the Black Pages. I thought you were going to request a stenographer. Brilliant. That's all I've got to say."

George stared at her for a few moments, then turned back to his window.

Back in Virginia, he had been convinced Jenna would dissolve into a puddle of despair. But he realized now that when people like Jenna have a meltdown, there are no waterworks, just clenched fists and a crimson face. Their blood turns to acid, and they stomp around looking for someone to bleed on.

"I'm sorry," he said. "Right now probably isn't the right time, but I've got to ask—you do still remember the exact words of the Codex Gigas pages, don't you?"

"Goddamn it, George, yes! I can't believe you don't trust me."

"I do trust you. But let's be real here..." He waited for Jenna to meet his eyes, and then he said, "It's you who doesn't trust me."

Her silence proved his point.

"Jenna, you said you would tell me where we're headed once you were behind the wheel."

"We're going to a Catholic church in Tel Aviv."

When she didn't say anything more, George said, "What are we—"

"We're getting a list of all the other Catholic churches in the city."

Again, she didn't continue. George gave her more than ample time before pursuing the issue. "Why do we need a list of—"

"Because, George, unless things have miraculously changed since I was last here, there are only three Catholic churches in all of Tel Aviv. But I'm betting it doesn't matter anyway. What we're looking for probably won't be in Tel Aviv. I'm thinking it will be in Jerusalem."

George frowned. He must have been tired. He certainly couldn't blame himself. The day had started out with a fainting spell at Paddington Station, and then a train ride to Heathrow Airport—a flight to Israel. And then a helicopter ride to some underground fortress where a deranged, demonically possessed teenager had tried to strangle him, followed by another helicopter ride. And now a car trip with a woman who looked like she was battling her own demons.

He must have been tired, because he had no clue why the plan was to visit Catholic churches.

"So you never answered my question," Jenna said. "Carl was talking about my father. You don't know my father. I don't even know him. So how can you be so sure?"

"Sure of what?"

"That Carl's lying."

"Of course Carl's lying. How can you trust anything from the man who sold out the world?"

Jenna only had a few seconds to ponder his point before her cell phone rang. She handed it to George and said, "It's probably Raymond."

"Yes, it is. Looks as if he's sent a text."

"Is there an attachment?"

"No. No attachment."

"Damn it, Raymond."

But then her phone rang again, and George opened the newest text. "Raymond says 'oops.'"

"Does that mean this time he sent the attachment?"

"Yes."

"Okay... can you open it please?"

George hit a few buttons on the phone, and the file took a minute to download. He opened it and saw a picture of a dead woman. Kneeling next to her was a priest.

"I think he sent you the picture you asked for."

"Can I see it?"

George showed it to her.

"Recognize the man?" she asked.

He took a closer look at the photo. "No, I'm afraid not."

"Remember the video Carl showed us? Do you remember the priest who was performing the exorcism on his son?"

George looked again. This time he saw it. The priest with Ami was the same man here with Sandy Travis.

"His name is Father Alan Olsen," Jenna said.

"So he was with Sandy Travis... on the day she tried to attack John Wolfenson?"

Jenna nodded. "Coincidence? Maybe. But that's why we're hitting up every Catholic church in the country."

"Jenna, think about this. Do you really want to involve another person?"

"Father Olsen's already involved," Jenna said. "And if the Codex Gigas pages are the key, we'll need someone who can perform an exorcism..."

CHAPTER 10

THE VIEW FROM THE TWO-STORY STONE HOUSE was lost on Father Olsen. He stood on the terrace anyway.

There outside his bedroom, anyone with the gift of sight could have seen the golden Dome of the Rock and the Temple Mount, and Mt. Zion, too, where Jesus and his apostles ate the Last Supper. Though he couldn't see it, just the idea of the view comforted the priest. It was one of the few things left in his life that didn't require a degree of faith.

Downstairs, his friend Jawad Bahar entered the apartment. Jawad owned the place, and every day on his lunch break, he brought haloumi cheese and fresh baked pita bread from the neighborhood market. He and Father Olsen would eat it for lunch over Arabic tea. But today, Father Olsen was surprised to hear Jawad running up the apartment stairs.

"Father, Father, can you smell the smoke?!"

Olsen moved too quickly from the terrace—his shoulder crashed into the doorframe.

"Jawad, I'm right here!" He stepped inside, rubbing his arm. "Where's the fire?"

His Arabic friend rushed into the room from the stairwell, breathing hard, but, as it turns out, not out of panic.

"I'm so sorry, Father.... there's no fire. What was I thinking? Please forgive me."

Father Olsen plopped down on the end of the bed, hoping to lower his heart rate. "Nothing to forgive, my friend."

He said it, not only because he was a forgiving person, but also because the mistake coincided with his desire: for his friends, and even his acquaintances, to forget he was blind. "You said smoke, what did you mean?"

"There are more clashes in the neighborhood," Jawad explained. "Let's go out on the balcony. You'll see..." He failed to choke off the final word. "Sorry, Father... I didn't mean it."

Father Olsen reached out, but touched only air. Jawad stepped forward and the priest patted his sleeve.

"My friend, we already talked about this. You've got to stop acting like you're walking on rice paper... as if rice paper were the cause of my blindness."

"Apologies."

"None necessary. I'm the one who should be wary of rice paper. I've overstayed my welcome here. It was only supposed to be a few days. Certainly not over a month."

"No, no, it's an honor to have you."

"Honor is too strong a word," the priest said. "Now please, lead me to the smoke..."

Jawad helped Father Olsen stand from the bed, and then guided him by the elbow to the terrace.

The house overlooked Abu Tor, a mixed neighborhood where Arabs, Palestinians and Jews lived side by side, just minutes outside downtown Jerusalem.

Jawad's father, who had immigrated here in the 1940s, had bought the house with earnings from his small restaurant. Five years ago he passed away, leaving the house to his son.

"It's complete chaos," Jawad said. "On the way to the marketplace, I almost got hit twice with some rocks the kids are throwing at the police."

"Who's involved today?" Father Olsen asked.

"Everyone: Palestinians going at it with the Elad; peaceniks caught in the middle. Then all three are battling the Israeli police, who want them all to go home."

Father Olsen, no stranger to Middle Eastern conflict, still found it difficult to keep track of the countless groups and sects and varying political beliefs. But he knew these particular players well. Elad, an activist group, defended the rights of Jewish settlement in Arab areas of Jerusalem. And "Peaceniks," a nickname for the grassroots Israeli organization Peace Now, promoted a settlement between the Israeli government, the Palestinians, and the rest of the Arab world.

"The police started with warning shots," Jawad said, "but then filled the entire area with tear gas. That's the smoke I was talking about." He stared at the white clouds billowing up from the distant streets. "Can you smell it, Father?"

167

"No, I can't. How close are the protests from the apartment?"

"Nothing to worry about. It's all happening near the marketplace."

"But, Jawad, that's... close to half a mile away."

"Yes, I guess that's right."

Father Olsen was genuinely confused. "Describe for me what you smell?"

"Father, I don't smell anything. Not even the flowers in the planter below us."

Now the priest understood. And for the second time that day, he forgave his friend. "Jawad, I'm not a superhero."

"Of course not, Father. I just thought... okay, now I'm embarrassed."

"Don't be."

When Father Olsen was younger, many magazines and newspapers had profiled him. And when the media needed a quote from the Catholic Church, they turned to him. He was articulate, provocative, and... blind.

Years later, in the middle of the church scandals, he remained the reliable source for background and opinion. His views on the church, though always progressive, never harbored an agenda, or even secrets. No illicit sex with female parishioners or underage altar boys in Father Olsen's confessional.

At the peak of the media attention, when the highest rated news magazine show, *24/7*, profiled Father Olsen, a cardinal in Rome referred to him as a "rock star." By that point, Father Olsen had become so disconnected with the rest of Rome, he took the remark as a compliment.

But so much had happened since then. Years had passed.

As he stood on the terrace of the "mixed neighborhood" in East Jerusalem, oblivious to the sectarian fighting, Father Olsen knew he was neither a rock star nor a superhero. He felt like a complete failure.

"Ready for lunch, Father?" asked Jawad.

"I thought you didn't make it to the marketplace because of the riots?"

"Please, Father. Only a nuclear bomb could stop me from my haloumi cheese on pita and tea!"

AFTER ALL THE EXCITEMENT THAT AFTERNOON, Jawad's lunch break had run long. He was late.

He worked as a security guard at the Four Quarters Hotel in Jerusalem, where he and Father Olsen had first met.

About three years ago, Olsen and his fellow priest Father Harris had visited the hotel during an inter-faith religious conference. Because of recent bomb and death threats against the venue, Jawad had been specifically assigned to escort the two priests during the conference. Probably because of Olsen's blindness, and his high profile. He and Jawad hit it off almost instantly. Not because they had a lot in common, but because they had so little. They chatted a lot between conference meetings and discovered they both shared a sincere and urgent desire to understand each other's beliefs. Besides, Jawad would be the first to admit, he was very excited to befriend someone who he constantly saw on TV.

Before leaving the apartment, Jawad performed his daily ritual; he walked over to his fireplace and touched a stone slab set into the wall nearby. His fingertips traced the engraving, "Al mulk lillah," Arabic for "Everything belongs to God."

Over the years, Father Olsen had learned that Jawad didn't believe in the sentiments of the slab. But he had promised his dying father that he would always, prior to leaving their home, touch the rock and think of his mother and Allah. A dutiful son, he had kept this pact for years, and had told Olsen that he intended to keep it until he, himself, died.

After the ritual, Jawad left the apartment. A few minutes later, Father Olsen did the same. He could not be late for his appointment.

Avoiding the main roads as Jawad had advised, he walked toward the bus station on Sultan Suleiman Street. If for some reason buses weren't running because of the protests, he would hail a taxi. Or, if no taxi, he would walk. He hoped that wouldn't be necessary. The church sat near the foot of the Mount of Olives, and he didn't think his tired body could handle the steep hills. The one thing that Father Olsen knew about himself was... he knew about himself.

He walked across the Gabriel Sherover Promenade, listening for any fallout from the protests, which, according to Jawad, were several blocks away. Father Olsen heard nothing—no sirens, no shouts or footfalls of protestors seeking refuge in the beautifully tended gardens.

He did not find comfort in this. For some time, the priest feared that he played a "blind witness" to tumultuous events, somehow either not in the right place at the right time to shape the outcome of those events, or worse: he was exactly in the right place at the right time, but his presence meant nothing.

Sandy Travis.

He could still hear her voice. Not the voice from when he first met her, when she was the producer in charge of his video profile on *24/7*.

That voice—energetic, personable, confident—he could no longer recall.

This voice, the one echoing in his head now, came from much later, after he had enlisted Sandy's help against a common enemy, foolishly assuming they could prevent others from being hurt or killed. He had offered her communion, for protection. She had refused.

"I appreciate your concern," she had said, "but I'll be okay." Despite her words, she had sounded scared, distant, lost. Yet for some reason, Father Olsen had let her go.

To her death.

He turned the corner onto Sultan Suleiman Street, which ran along the Old City wall. The high, imposing ramparts, erected by Sultan Suleiman in 1542, enclosed the heart of Jerusalem and its holiest sites. Seven gates granted entry to the Old City during the day, but the eighth gate, the Golden Gate, had been sealed for all time.

Father Olsen passed by the Souk Khan al-Zeit, an Arab bazaar and, in many ways, the lifeblood of Jerusalem. It spilled out from the Old City through the Damascus Gate. At this time of day, people bustled about, haggling over clothing and other wares. Someone who had never visited East Jerusalem would have found it difficult to believe violent riots were erupting blocks away.

But Olsen knew differently. He had been visiting Jerusalem for two decades, and he believed the fabric of coexistence in this holiest of cities was unraveling. Faster than ever before.

A few blocks from the bus station, he heard a very faint voice, which became louder as he drew near.

It was the voice of John Wolfenson.

"There are times when a disaster that befalls a nation becomes everyone's disaster," he was saying, "and it becomes everyone's obligation to help. We must remember we are all together, one family of humanity, no matter what the boundary lines of countries suggest."

The first time Father Olsen had heard the envoy speak, Wolfenson stood before thousands of people in the Western Wall Plaza. At the time, he sounded upbeat and triumphant. With good reason. He had just engineered the most far-reaching peace treaty the Middle East had ever seen.

The next time Olsen heard Wolfenson's voice, circumstances had changed. Sandy Travis was dead, and Wolfenson was just getting out of the hospital where she had put him. Jawad had found Wolfenson's discharge interview online, and he and Father Olsen had listened to it on his personal computer. The envoy had sounded... upbeat, triumphant.

Olsen believed it was possible that the man who had just survived a life-threatening injury could sound exactly the same as the man who had engineered a historic peace treaty. But he knew the story behind Wolfenson's miraculous recovery.

The beast seemed to have had a fatal wound, he'd thought at the time. *But the fatal wound had been healed.*

He knew the envoy sounded upbeat leaving the hospital because he felt like a new man, ready to begin a new mission.

"Father," someone said over the sound of John Wolfenson's press conference, "would you like a table?"

"I'm sorry," Olsen said. "Where am I?"

"Outside The Gates Café."

"Oh."

"Do you want to sit down for some coffee, or... ?"

"Excuse me, but will you be kind enough to tell me where that voice is coming from?" He braced himself for the worst. What if the answer was, "What voice?"

"It's the TV set at the bar," the waiter said.

"Is it... John Wolfenson?"

"Yes, it is. Good ear, Father."

"And what is he talking about?"

"Well, he's at a press conference in Tel Aviv. You know, he's here to help in Syria."

"You don't say..." Father Olsen turned his head toward the TV and listened for a moment. "Yes, I very much would like to sit down. Near the television, if that's possible."

The waiter led him to the bar just inside the main doors, and Olsen ordered a cup of house coffee, black.

"There is a crisis in humanity," Wolfenson was saying. "I am here to lend my humble aid in any way I possibly can. The victims of this great tragedy, a random act of violence, are in Aleppo. But it could happen anywhere to anyone. This is the time to unite under one common cause."

"Are you sure you don't want to hear our specials, Father?" the waiter asked.

"Thank you, but no. You see, I can't stay long. I have an appointment to make..."

CHAPTER 11

"THIS IS A BEAUTIFUL CHURCH," George said as they got out of the car. For one thesis paper and a book he was writing, George had travelled to different churches over the years. He estimated that he had visited at least two hundred in his lifetime, and had grown to appreciate the architecture. "What's the façade made from?"

Jenna slammed her car door. She didn't even look before answering the question. "It's black basalt."

St. Paul's Catholic Church, originally built in 1653, had been destroyed in the eighteenth century twice. The current structure had been erected between 1887 and 1893.

"It looks like they were trying to reach the sky," George said, pointing at the belfry tower.

"I think they would tell you they were aiming higher," Jenna replied. She clicked the lock button on the key fob and started toward the entrance of the chapel.

She obviously knew where she was going. The church complex consisted of several different entrances and buildings, and yet she had steered them directly to this one.

"You've been here before," George said, following her.

His observation surprised her. He had actually fallen asleep after Raymond's text, and had slept until she left the highway. For someone who seemed to walk with his brain in a cloud, George still managed an insight or two.

Jenna pushed open the main door to the chapel and said, "You're right, George. I'm practically family here."

———

FATHER ANDREW WALTON SAW JENNA walk into the chapel and he immediately excused himself from a group of people to greet her.

"Jenna, look at you! You've stopped giving yourself haircuts."

They embraced. With her chin resting on the priest's shoulder, Jenna said, "Only about fifteen years ago, Father."

He laughed. "Never gets old!"

The running joke had started when she was a teenager. On her first dig with her mother in the country, not long after her thirteenth birthday, Jenna met a local Jewish boy she liked. Somehow she got it into her brain that long hair wasn't cool. But her mother refused to get it cut, probably because she knew why Jenna wanted to cut it: to attract a boy.

So at that point, Jenna decided to cut her hair herself—but ended up doing a terrible job.

She lost the attention of the local Jewish boy, much to her dismay, but she did gain the friendship of an assistant priest, Andrew Walton. He had just started at St. Paul's, and would often visit her mother's excavation site. Growing up, Father Walton had worked in his father's barbershop in Wisconsin, so he volunteered to fix Jenna's botched haircut. It was something she would never live down.

"Well," the priest said, "whoever cuts your hair these days does a wonderful job. It looks beautiful, and so do you."

They had known each other for so many years, and had shared so many personal moments, Father Walton was one of the few people in the world who could compliment Jenna's physical beauty without causing her to look down at her feet.

She thought the priest had lost a few pounds and had gained a few wrinkles around the temples, but his warm smile remained.

"Why didn't you tell me you were coming?" he asked.

"It was a last-minute decision. Father Walton, this is George Wyatt. He's traveling with me this trip."

"George, so pleased to meet you."

They exchanged a handshake. The priest even threw in a second hand, to emphasize how happy he was to meet a friend of Jenna's. But as soon as their palms parted, Walton turned his attention back to Jenna.

"How's your mother?"

Jenna had prepared for the question. More than that, she had prepared to judge the priest's tone as he asked it. His inflection indicated that he had not, in fact, heard of what Neal had done in the States.

"Feisty as ever," she said.

"Hah! I imagine! Feisty enough to come back for a dig?"

"Oh, Father, I don't know if that's going to happen. A couple months ago, she called herself a fossil."

"Oh dear."

"Yeah, she said she was thinking about burying herself in the backyard to see if, after the excavation, I could figure things out just by examining the bones."

"Yes, that sounds like Ruth. I miss her. The both of you."

Over the years, Father Walton and her mother had spent many nights playing Scrabble. They also had taken two separate trips together to Syria, where she had guided him through the rock-cut architecture at Petra and the Citadel in Aleppo.

"I know my mother thinks of you all the time," Jenna said. "And of course I do as well." She squeezed Father Walton's arm to emphasize her point.

"I was just about to have a rather late dinner in the sanctuary," he said. "Please, you and George have to join me. Sister Anita makes an incredible fish stew."

Jenna wanted so badly to accept the invitation. Even more, she needed to tell him everything that had happened to her... and to Neal. But that would take time. And Jenna had a feeling time was the one thing they didn't have on their side.

"Thank you so much, Father, but we can't accept. Actually, we came here for a reason—"

"Oh, my," he said, "what am I thinking? You haven't seen the new display case!"

Before Jenna could stop him, he hurried to an adjoining hallway. George, grinning, pushed Jenna to follow him.

Father Walton led them to an eight-foot-tall wooden display case built into the wall. Behind lead glass, at least three dozen ancient artifacts lay arranged on the shelves, tastefully displayed under non-fluorescent lighting. Jenna saw wooden and stone crosses, papyrus scrolls, ancient tablets written in Hebrew, and other religious icons.

"One of our parishioners built this in his spare time. It was long overdue. Now we can properly display all of the objects you and your mother have graciously donated over the years."

Jenna scanned the shelves, recalling the discovery of each and every relic.

"What do you think?" Father Walton asked. "Wouldn't your mother be proud?"

She grinned. "Maybe not... proud."

"Yes, you're right," he said. "More like... chagrined."

They shared a laugh, and George smiled. He could clearly see a long, close connection between them. But then, he wondered, why couldn't Father Walton see, or intuit, Jenna's distress? George's smile began to fade.

"Seriously," Jenna said, "she always enjoyed sharing beautiful things from the past. I think she'd be very happy."

"And what about you? At least half of these objects are artifacts you donated. How does the display make you feel?"

For the first time since George had met her, Jenna looked uncomfortable.

"How does it make me *feel*?" she asked.

"Yes, mmm-hmm."

"Well..."

Father Walton, who had been smiling this whole time, grinned even broader. "Witness Jenna Grant," he said, letting George in on the joke, "speechless for the first time in her life."

This time, Jenna was the one who didn't join in on the fun.

"Humbled," she finally answered, interrupting them. "I guess it makes me feel... humbled." She nodded and then quickly changed the subject. "Listen, Father, we're looking for a man."

George watched as Father Walton's facial expression instantly changed from pride... to alarm.

"He's a priest and we're pretty sure he performed an exorcism recently. Right in this country."

"Jenna, are you all right?" Father Walton asked.

"Oh, totally," she said, brushing his arm to dispel such thoughts. Then she took a step closer and said, "But I do need your help."

She took out her cell phone and brought up the picture Raymond had sent. She showed it to Father Walton, who squinted.

"Father Alan Olsen," he said almost instantly.

"You know him?"

"Yes, of course."

"Because of what happened with Sandy Travis?"

"Well, yes. Afterwards, there was a lot of... gossip about how he was involved."

Jenna couldn't help but react to the words.

"Oh, forgive me," Father Walton said. "'Involved' was a poor choice of words. Did either of you know the Chinese symbol for the word 'gossip' is three women? I think it should be changed to three priests."

Both Jenna and George laughed.

"Look, the fact is I never met the man. But of course he's been quite the rebel with a cause in our church. So he was being talked about long before the assassination attempt at the Temple Mount."

"Actually..." Jenna said, "it was at the Western Wall."

"Oh, yes, you're right. If Father Olsen is who you're looking for, I suggest you try the Church of All Nations."

Jerusalem, George thought. Jenna had been right.

"From what I understand, Bishop Bynum has been dealing with Olsen the last three or four years."

"Thank you so much, Father," Jenna said. "I really appreciate the help."

"Are you sure you're all right?"

She didn't say anything. She just hugged him. With such ferocity and compassion, she hoped she conveyed everything she wanted to convey in words but couldn't.

In the middle of the embrace, Father Walton said, "Why don't you come with me into the chapel? I know there must be a wafer with your name on it."

Jenna giggled as she pulled away. "I'm sorry, Father, I'm not laughing at your offer. I just thought about what my mother said years ago when you asked her the same thing."

"Jenna, if we're going to repeat what your mother said, I insist we step outside the church."

She smiled and grabbed the priest's hand. "Father, thank you so much for your help."

———

"THERE ARE A COUPLE THINGS I don't understand," George said as he and Jenna walked to their car at twilight. "Your mother would apparently donate religious relics to this church, and yet she wasn't a believer?"

Jenna smiled. "The first time it happened, we were both working the entire summer on a dig in Jordan. I couldn't believe when she did it. Those three artifacts would have fetched a lot of money from a museum or private collector. I said to her, 'Mom, why are you doing this? You've told me time and again that religion is opium for the masses and all that. So, why?' You know what she told me? She said, 'I'm hedging my bets.'"

George laughed. Laughed so hard, it turned into a ten-second spell of coughing. When he managed to catch his breath, he looked to Jenna for the rest of the story.

"I told her, 'Mom, it doesn't work that way.' She just brushed it aside and said, 'How do you know it doesn't work that way?'"

"What'd you say to that?" George asked.

"Well, at the time, I didn't..." Jenna slowed down and then stopped, as if a sudden thought had taken so much brain power, she no longer could concentrate on walking as well. "I didn't have an answer. And maybe... maybe I still don't."

She mumbled the last part. Her vacant, tired stare indicated to George that she hadn't meant to share the thought.

She glanced at him, and then started walking again, looking embarrassed to have stopped in the first place.

"We need to get going if we want to make the Church of All Nations. I'm pretty sure we've already missed visiting hours."

"Not so fast," he said. "So your mother was hedging her bets. What about you? Why were you donating artifacts you'd found?"

Again, Jenna didn't answer. They arrived at the car and climbed in.

"If Father Walton is offering you communion," George said as he put on his seatbelt, "you must've been baptized."

She turned on the car and started to pull out of the parking lot. Just when George gave up on getting a response, she said, "I was baptized. But I'm a lapsed Catholic. I never attended church."

"Except to donate some relics."

She rolled her eyes, and George saw her do it. He looked away, out the window, and they moved on.

CHAPTER 12

"I'M SO SORRY FOR THE DELAY, ALAN," said Bishop Bynum as he walked out of his office into the waiting area. "I've kept you waiting too long."

Father Olsen knew his Excellency was hoping for forgiveness, but chose to say nothing.

"Alan, if you don't mind... visiting hours are over. And I've been in my office all day. Can we talk in the church?"

"Yes," Father Olsen said, "that would be lovely." He stood, feeling a twinge in his knees after sitting so long.

He had been in the waiting room for over two hours, well past his appointment with the bishop. And that wasn't counting the time he had spent at the café.

While sipping his coffee, Father Olsen had listened not only to Wolfenson's speech, but to the entire question-and-answer session afterward. By the time he arrived at the Church of All Nations, he was still early for his meeting.

The bishop's secretary had offered him a glass of water while he waited, and Father Olsen's answer revealed a dry throat. He couldn't decide whether it was from the ride over in the dry heat, or because he was anxious... and scared.

As he waited, he could hear the bishop's voice on the other side of his office door, talking on the phone, and, for a while, speaking with a few other people in the room.

Two long hours of muffled voices discussing things that had nothing to do with Father Olsen or the end of the world.

At some indeterminable point, his nervous energy wore him down to boredom, and then irritation, and finally frustration, which lingered even now as he and Bishop Bynum walked down the hallway to the chapel.

Father Olsen heard people approaching. Three of them, by the sound of their footsteps.

"How are you all doing tonight?" the bishop asked them.

No one responded, and Olsen wondered whether they all had simply nodded.

"Thank you for your hard work, gentleman. We'll see you tomorrow."

After the three sets of footsteps receded down the hallway, the bishop said, "That was the team who's replacing some mosaic tiles that fell off last year on part of the ceiling and wall."

"Oh," Father Olsen replied. "And how long will the work last?"

"They were supposed to finish last week." The bishop opened a door. "Here we are, Alan. Watch your step..."

He guided Father Olsen into the chapel, into the hallmark scent of stone, candles, and oiled wood.

Some called it The Basilica of the Agony, and between 1919 and 1924, twelve nations funded its construction in reparation for the First World War. Like many old things, the Italian architect had built it upon the ruins of something else: two bygone houses of God, one abandoned, the other conquered by a quake.

Father Olsen had first toured the church eleven years ago with his friend Father Harris. They both came absent their collars—as tourists, not as priests. Harris had done his best to describe the beauty for Father Olsen: first the triangular pediment outside, with its mosaic of Jesus Christ mediating between man and God; and, inside, the stunning night-sky domes of the cupolas over the aisles and nave; and the six Corinthian columns that held them up.

Judging by the reaction of their tour group, the true altar of worship resided in the presbytery, where a crown of thorns in wrought iron surrounded a large fragment of rock. There, Jesus had prayed in agony the night before the Passion.

When Olsen asked Father Harris for a more detailed description of the stone, his friend replied, "I wish I could say it's just a rock, Alan, but... I'm sorry, there really are no words for this."

Father Olsen, as many others had before, knelt to touch the rock, to pray upon it with the wrought iron thorns jabbing into his side. He had hoped to achieve something deeper and more meaningful than mere eyes could perceive, but he ended up feeling... just a rock. The *ooohs* and *ahhs* from the tourists made him acutely aware that, despite his efforts, his blindness prevented him from truly treasuring the physical beauty of the Agony, and from tapping into the very land that once played host to the Lord's son.

Beneath the twelve cupolas, six columns and two outer aisles flanked the nave; a central aisle divided it. Olsen remembered Father Harris describing the interior as "one large open hall." He also remembered letting his hand glide and bounce along the pews. He tried it this evening as he and Bishop Bynum walked the center aisle. But instead of pews, he found wooden chairs.

So much had changed.

"I know you've come to discuss your expulsion," Bishop Bynum said as they approached the altar and the rock. Father Olsen began to worry that their whole meeting would take place on the run, with an abrupt conclusion at the church's front gate.

"Well," the bishop continued, "I have some news. Why don't you take a seat?"

His Excellency guided Father Olsen to the foremost chair and helped him sit. The priest took a deep but inconspicuous breath.

"Alan, your expulsion has been lifted."

"Lifted?"

"Yes. Your letter of repentance has been accepted."

Olsen let the breath rush out of him, much less controlled and much more conspicuous. "By whom?"

"By Vicar-General Bartles and me. However, my understanding is that the official acceptance came from Rome."

"Ah..." Olsen said quietly. "Rome."

"Is this not what you wanted to hear?"

"No, of course. It's very good news." He stood up and reached out to Bishop Bynum, who cupped Olsen's hand in both of his. "I want to thank you, your Excellency. I'm grateful and pleased to be reunited with the faithful."

"Alan, please, sit down." He helped the priest to his chair and took the seat next to him. "I accept your appreciation, and I trust that you are sincere. But you still look troubled."

"I'm sorry, your Excellency. I suppose I expected to hear the same thing Rome has been saying for weeks—that my reinstatement was still under review. This all comes as a shock."

"But, Alan, you requested this meeting. What did you plan on talking about if not reinstatement?"

"I wanted to know, as an excommunicated priest... if I still had the power to perform an exorcism."

"Is it that local boy, Ami?"

"No," Father Olsen said. Initially he had planned to say more, but after his reinstatement, he feared that divulging his plans would put him right back in the doghouse.

"Well, to answer your question, Alan, you performing another exorcism would have been out of the question. Expulsion strips all ecclesiastical rights, privileges and powers. Now, whether that's true in the eyes of God, I won't comment on. But that's the church's official position."

The bishop stood up from the chair, but Father Olsen laid a hand on his arm.

"When does it become official?" he asked.

"It's official now. But why don't we go to the confessional and take communion?"

"Yes. Thank you, your Excellency."

"And then, Alan, I want to hear more about this exorcism." The bishop's tone made it quite clear. He wanted more details, not out of curiosity, but because he wanted to know if an exorcism was warranted.

"Of course," Olsen said.

He heard his superior step away, and he moved to follow, but after just a few steps Olsen crashed into his back. The bishop had stopped walking.

"Alan, I'm sorry..."

"Excuse me..."

"No, it's quite all right. The power just went out. All the lights are gone, and..."

"Your Excellency?"

"Very strange."

"What is it?"

"All the candles on the altar have blown out."

Father Olsen could smell the smoke from the snuffed wicks and wax. "Perhaps it has something to do with the restoration crew that was just here?"

"Yes, perhaps. Okay, so let's just wait here a moment. The emergency generator should switch on any second."

They waited in silence for almost half a minute before the bishop said, "Alan, do you mind staying here while I go to the administration offices? In this darkness, I don't want you to fall and get hurt."

Olsen couldn't help but laugh. The bishop eventually chuckled too.

"Okay, so falling in the dark isn't a new hazard for you. But do you mind staying here?"

"Yes, yes, of course. I'll stay right here."

Olsen took his seat.

After the bishop's footsteps had faded away, and Olsen was convinced he had left, someone cried out in pain.

"Ahhh!"

Olsen stood up, but before he could say anything, Bishop Bynum called out to him.

"I'm all right—sorry! I just stubbed my toe. Okay, moving again. I'll be right back."

A few seconds later the door to the chapel opened and closed, and the bishop was gone.

Father Olsen sat again and meditated in the peace and quiet.

While in seminary training in Eastern Europe, he had come across a Jesuit priest from an abbey in France where every day they observed many hours of silent prayer. He had expressed to Father Olsen that the sound of his own breathing often transformed into a separate "voice," with its own cadences and susurrations. And this voice, he said, guided his meditations and prayers.

Father Olsen listened to his breathing to see if he could detect a separate voice. But after great and lengthy focus, he heard only labored respiration.

The wheezing from his lungs reminded him of a forty-eight-year-old man he once visited in the intensive care unit of a hospital. This had been during his first year of God's work in a Brooklyn parish. The man, Henry Fisher, suffered from emphysema, yet he spoke optimistically about overcoming the disease. Unfortunately, his hacking cough and shortness of breath proved to be a more accurate prophet.

Father Olsen's breathing suddenly stopped—a hand had lit upon his shoulder.

"Are you going to be all right?" Sandy Travis asked. Months ago, after surviving a demonic attack, Sandy had helped Father Olsen escape his burning church. Afterward, while the firefighters worked to extinguish the blaze, Sandy had touched Father Olsen's shoulder and had said...

"Are you going to be all right?" the voice echoed again. Not aloud, but in his head. It sounded just like Sandy's voice. But the priest knew better.

Sandy was dead.

"I'll be all right," he said.

The hand lifted from his shoulder, but the weight seemed to still be there.

"Come with me, Father. Let me help you."

"Why not here?"

"No. In the garden. I'm worried about you. Worried about Tom. Please, Alan, hurry—he doesn't want me talking to you."

CHAPTER 13

"I NEED SOME MUSIC," Jenna said, and she turned on the radio to the classical music station. She recognized the song, something by Ravel. She couldn't identify the piece, even though she was sure she once knew the title. Maybe it wasn't Ravel. Now she wasn't sure.

She was tired. Actually, drained. Seeing Father Walton had exhausted her last bit of energy. She had been thinking about checking into a hotel near the Church of All Nations to catch a couple hours of sleep.

"Jenna, why are you ignoring me?" George said. He had been asking her all sorts of questions about her lapsed Catholicism.

She reached over and turned off the radio. Ravel, if it truly was his composition, was putting her to sleep.

"I'm not ignoring you, George. It's just that I don't understand why I'm answering questions that have nothing to do with anything."

"Okay, sorry. Now I understand."

They travelled in silence, and Jenna merged back on to Road 1 toward Jerusalem.

"I have a question for you," she said. "About something that does matter."

George sat up in his seat. His eyelids had already started to get heavy, but he was excited to be talking again.

"Carl's kid was in a coma, right?"

"Yes, that's right."

"To be honest, I thought he was dead when we walked in there. Believe it or not, I love being wrong. My life always ends up being more interesting that way. But I got more than *interesting* when Ami suddenly went batshit and attacked you. What I can't figure out is... why? What makes him wake up from a coma and attack you?"

"I don't know. I guess, sometimes, when you see the essence of what others really are, you don't need to open your eyes before you attack."

Jenna shot him a look.

"I'm sorry," he said, "you probably felt that was one of those fortune cookie responses."

"Yeah, kind of was. Next time, eliminate some syllables to your answer and you'll have a haiku."

George turned to look out the window. Her criticism had begun to sting. And the last thing he wanted to do was alienate Jenna. In fact, more than ever he needed to gain her trust.

———

GEORGE COUGHED HIMSELF AWAKE. He lurched forward so abruptly his seatbelt locked, and he spewed something all over the windshield: dots of bloody saliva, like small, bright-red balloons.

They had just passed a road sign with Hebrew, Arabic, and English translations: *Entering the city of Jerusalem.*

Jenna maneuvered their car to an outer lane and pulled to the side of the highway, despite the horns of objecting drivers.

George wanted to assure her that he was all right. But the words caught in his throat. It frustrated him, not only because he could not speak, but because he felt helpless to clean up the mess he had made.

Jenna parked and shut off the engine. The headlights, too. She feared that if someone, especially an Israeli police officer, saw them parked on the side of the road, she and George would have trouble ex-plaining the bright-red splat covering half the windscreen.

The interior of the Ford fell into darkness, except for the light of passing cars and the rising moon.

George continued to cough uncontrollably.

In the glove compartment, Jenna found a package of Kleenex. She used a wad of them to wipe up his sputum, only to discover that the tissues simply spread it around.

Against her better judgment, she turned on the dome light. She found one of their water bottles in back, and used it to dampen a new pad of Kleenex. This time when she tried, the bloody mix of saliva and mucus began to disappear from the glass. She shut off the dome light and continued to work in the dark.

"Please," George said as she soaked her fourth bunch of tissues. "Let me do this."

His coughing had blended so well into the background noise of traffic that Jenna hadn't realized he had stopped.

"No," she said, "I can do it."

"I know you can. But please, let me."

Jenna glanced out the windows and into the various mirrors. So far, no one had stopped to check out their vehicle.

Satisfied, she gave the wetted tissues to George and settled into her seat as he cleaned.

"Where are we?" he asked.

"I've never been to the church before, but I think we still have a ways to go. The traffic has been horrendous."

George looked at the clock in the car. He had been asleep for nearly an hour .

"Have you ever heard of the Shuar of Ecuador?" he asked, folding the dirty tissues to expose a clean side.

Even fatigued, Jenna perked up. The "Shuar of Ecuador" was the last thing she imagined he might say on Road 1, heading toward the Mount of Olives and the Church of All Nations.

"I'm ashamed to say the only thing that pops into my brain is the tribe's history of headhunting."

"Yes," George said, impressed she knew that much. "Exactly. They would cut off the enemy's head and then shrink it. I did my dissertation on the tribe and spent nearly a year in their country doing research. I didn't plow any new ground, but I did confirm that they weren't interested in the heads themselves. I mean, they didn't value them as trophies. Instead, by shrinking the heads, they believed they could control the victim's soul."

In any other situation, Jenna would have been riveted by his story. But given the circumstances, she wasn't so interested.

"George, if you're done cleaning, maybe we should get going."

"I understand." He looked at the windshield. The tissues had left streaks, but otherwise he had cleared the glass of any obvious signs of blood. "Just give me another minute here."

He looked down, trying to gather his thoughts. He wanted to phrase what he had to say precisely.

"The instant I woke up from the train collision I could think of only two things: saving your life and... rescuing Carri's soul. That's why, after saving you, I went to see Dr. Fincher. Because he had Carri's heart."

He enunciated the last sentence with naked disgust.

"We had a drink, and I couldn't stop staring at him. Because he looked just like one of the Shuar men that shrink their enemies' heads. All I wanted to do was kill him because... I couldn't let him control my Carri."

"Why didn't you?"

"I don't know, I just couldn't. I still don't understand why. There are a lot of things I don't understand. At times, there's been clarity, better than any time in my entire life. But most of the time I just feel like a puppet."

"A puppet?"

George's eyes lit up. He threw the wad of Kleenex onto the floor and leaned toward Jenna. "Yes, that's what I wanted to tell you. A puppet. I look for them, but I can't find them. I feel them, but I can't see them. I try to cut them, but there's nothing to cut. But I know they are there."

"What, George? What's *there*?"

"The strings."

A pair of high beams appeared behind them.

They completely lit the interior of their car.

"Crap," Jenna said, fumbling for the keys in the ignition. She fired up the engine, put the car in gear, and then slammed her foot on the accelerator so hard they lurched forward and George fell into the dash.

The Ford kicked up dust and then its tires screeched on the pavement. Someone honked as Jenna cut off a couple of cars and established her own space in the long parade.

She looked into her rearview and saw the set of high beams still parked beside the highway. She hoped that, whoever it was, they were simply good Samaritans and nothing else.

CHAPTER 14

"**M**Y FATHER, IF IT IS POSSIBLE, may this cup be taken from me. Yet not as I will, but as you will."

Matthew had written these words, 26:36-39, because Jesus had spoken them, on the rock that the basilica now enshrined. Christ had come to the Garden of Gethsemane, as he had many times before, usually to meditate about his future, but this time in agony, and sweating as if hemorrhaging blood. He had prayed upon the rock, "May this cup be taken from me."

"In the garden..." Sandy's imposter had said back in the chapel. "Please, Father, hurry."

Traveling in the deepest of darks, Father Olsen had certainly tried. All the way, he had bumped into walls and other objects that any sighted person could have seen, even without a light. He tried very hard not to lose his surefootedness—and then lost it anyway.

After navigating almost the entire route down unfamiliar passages, pain had stabbed him in the leg—he had collided with something, he didn't know what. His knees buckled, and he dropped to the ground.

He applied his hand to his shin and felt something that could have only been his own blood. He tasted it. Indeed, he had been scratched. Nothing deeper than that.

"My Father, if it is possible," he said, "may this cup be taken from me. Yet not as I will, but as you will." He climbed to his feet and persevered.

Almost forty minutes since the candles had first blown out in the basilica, Father Olsen came to a familiar stone entryway.

He knew of the engraving over the garden gate: "Hortus Gethsemani." But he could neither see it, nor reach high enough to feel it, so he couldn't be sure whether he was at the right place.

On his way here, he had hoped to run into someone, *anyone* from the church. Somehow he never did. And a part of him felt relieved. The blood of Sandy Travis already stained his cassock. He didn't think he could live with any more death on his hands. And yet, he was terrified to enter the Garden of Gethsemane alone.

"My soul is overwhelmed with sorrow to the point of death," he said, putting his hand in his pocket and clutching the object he found there. "Stay here and keep watch with me."

The priest pushed open the gate.

After hours, it should have been locked.

Earlier that evening, when he arrived at the church, his throat had been parched by the heat. But here at the threshold, he felt as if he were entering a gateway to the Arctic.

Cold air stung his eyes and swatted at his cheeks. His nose instantly started to drip.

At that moment, he knew what he had known since performing Sandy's last rites: that it was inevitable, this meeting with... him.

The priest stepped through the gate.

Much of the Garden of Gethsemane remained as it had for two thousand years, as stones unturned. Olive trees grew there, gnarled and twisted, with a bush of green leaves. Eight of the oldest olive trees in Jerusalem still clung to that holy earth. They produced fruit with essential oils.

Olsen knew olive trees aged like people: the older they got, instead of getting taller, they just got wider. And he had learned that they didn't grow tree rings. So no one knew the true age of these trees.

Since his initial tour with Father Harris, Olsen had come to Gethsemane dozens of times. He eventually formed the opinion that the garden no longer provided sanctuary for serious thought, especially during visiting hours. Too many tourists, too many activities.

This evening, all those conditions had changed. The channels for meditation, contemplation and prayer had been left wide open, clear and silent and as receptive as the night. Father Olsen could hear only a gentle wind in the trees. And, from somewhere in the cold, he could feel a warm presence.

Someone else waited in the garden.

As Olsen ventured forth, he feared he might stray from the path and trip on the gnarled roots of the olive trees, or maybe run into the stone pillars supporting the old, arthritic limbs. "Walking canes," the pillars were called; Father Olsen could not ignore the phrase as he weaved his

RICHARD FINNEY AND D.L. SNELL

way slowly, carefully through the garden like an elderly man in need of his own support.

Finally, he arrived in the heart of the garden. Irritation, anger, shock, and exhaustion had long left him. He stood fully erect, like a lightning rod in a storm, waiting for the first shock of contact.

"For we walk by faith," someone said. "Not by sight."

It was not Sandy's voice. And it was spoken aloud, but barely above a whisper. Father Olsen recognized it, had listened to the same voice over coffee that day.

It was the voice of the Angel of Light.

"I admire your tenacity, Alan. It's something we have in common."

The priest knew better than to engage Satan in conversation. No man alive was invulnerable to his temptations, his lies. But Olsen also had no choice—engaging him in a dialogue would draw him in closer.

"I fight for the ones I love," Father Olsen said. "*You* want to kill them and everyone else. What exactly do you think we have in common?"

"Alan, you think you know who I am. But I suggest that you have no idea why I'm really here."

The next time Wolfenson spoke, his voice came from an entirely different direction, causing Father Olsen to whirl around.

"I leave in a few hours for Aleppo. I thought it was important that I meet with you."

"For what?"

"To discuss working together."

"Working together? How is that possible? Why would you even want that?"

"Alan," Wolfenson said, from yet another corner of the garden. "Have you ever read Voltaire? His account of the Lisbon earthquake in 1755, in particular."

Father Olsen said nothing. He wanted, he *needed* to listen. Not only to the voice, but to where it was coming from.

"The quake struck the country at 9:40 in the morning on an important holiday. Practically every church in the country crumbled, killing thousands of worshippers inside.

"The *Aleppo* earthquake hit at 3:25 in the afternoon," he said, and from his voice, it sounded like he was circling closer, like a predator in the high grass. "Most children were in school. Their mothers were at the marketplace, buying that night's bread and wine. And, coincidentally enough, the most prominent Catholic church in the city was right in the middle of mass."

Father Olsen could not get a fix on his adversary. The object in his pocket grew slippery with the sweat of his hand.

"Trust me, Alan. Like in Lisbon, once the numbers are tabulated... the death and destruction in Aleppo will be shocking."

The angel drew ever closer, and Father Olsen began to feel waves of heat cutting through the cold chill, like the warm caress of the morning sun.

"In all your years as a priest, I'm sure you've been asked this many times: 'Why does he do this if he loves us? Why does he shake down our homes? Destroy our cities? Let our children starve?' They ask these questions, not because they are confused... but because they suspect the truth. And you share their suspicions."

Out of his coat pocket, Father Olsen pulled the silver cross. He knew the Angel of Light had probably seen him do it, but it was far too late to stop now.

"If you were to come with me to Aleppo, Alan, you will see how he allows it all to happen. The destruction. The suffering. The evil. He doesn't care because... he's turned his back on you, a father so disgusted by his own children that he no longer feels anything at all for his creation."

The angel's heat completely enveloped the priest. Strangely, this close to the man, Father Olsen could not smell him. He had assumed the Beast always smelled of shit, decay and death.

"Oh, I apologize, Padre. I said 'you will see.' I forgot that you can't, in fact, see. So I apologize, but only for the slip of the tongue. Because you and I both know your infliction is something for which the Landlord alone is responsible."

Father Olsen held up his silver cross and reached out with his other hand. He was startled for a moment when his fingers found the top of the envoy's head, but then he jumped into the exorcism rite.

"In the name of Jesus Christ, our God and Lord, strengthened by the intercession of the Immaculate Virgin Mary, Mother of God, of Blessed Michael the Archangel, of the Blessed Apostles Peter and all the Saints. I command you, unclean spirit, and unclean legion, by the mysteries of the incarnation, passion, resurrection, and ascension of our Lord Jesus Christ, by the descent of the Holy Ghost, by the coming of our Lord for judgment—I command you to obey me, I, who am a minister of God; nor shall you be emboldened to harm in any way this creature of God, or the bystanders, or any of their possessions. And powerful in the holy authority of our ministry, we confidently undertake to repulse the attacks and deceits of the devil."

Father Olsen paused for a moment, sweating and out of breath, and anxious to know whether God's words were having any effect. He noticed the head beneath his hand felt completely dry. Not even the slightest hint of moisture.

"We drive you from us, unclean spirit, with all of your satanic powers, all infernal invaders, all wicked legions, assemblies and sects; in the Name and by the power of Our Lord Jesus Christ, may you be snatched away and driven from the Church of God and from the souls made to the image and likeness of God, and redeemed by the Precious Blood of the Divine Lamb!"

Father Olsen stopped again to catch his breath.

"Alan," Sandy's voice interrupted, "let him help you! He can help us all. Let him help!"

The priest shook his head, having lost his spot in the exorcism.

"Don't you want to see me, Alan? See what I look like? Don't you want to touch me with your eyes?"

A warm, supple hand took Olsen's, and guided it to the lips of a soft, moist kiss. Then the smooth, strong fingers glided over the priest's face, spreading warmth to his cheeks, his chin, and his forehead, and finally his eyes.

Father Olsen shut them, but the warmth penetrated his eyelids, and got hotter and hotter until he feared his eyeballs would shrivel up or burst into flames. And yet somehow, he did not recoil—could not.

"Together," Wolfenson said, "we will make the Landlord pay attention. He will see us for the first time in a very long time."

The envoy's fingers fell away from the priest's face, and Father Olsen no longer burned. He noticed, too, that the chill had vanished, along with the waves of morning warmth. He heard only his own breath and, beneath it, the wind.

He remembered Henry Fisher, the emphysema patient, the day of his last rites.

"I know my wife and kids are angry with me," Fisher had said, "angry that I continued to smoke all these years. Please tell them not to be, Father. I'm certainly not."

He had seized the priest's hand then, and had pulled himself up a few inches off the bed, his voice a raspy but urgent whisper. "I have seen the beautiful faces of my children, and a grandchild. I have enjoyed a hundred sunrises and a hundred sunsets. I have gotten drunk while staring up at the full moon. I look at you now, Father, and you have seen none of this. Tell me, how can I not feel blessed?"

Remembering Fisher's dying words as he stood in the Garden of Gethsemane, Father Alan Olsen, for the first time in his life, stared up at the beauty of a full moon.

CHAPTER 15

THE CHURCH OF ALL NATIONS, and the entire Mount of Olives, had ceased to exist in all that darkness.

"I don't see anything," George said.

They had parked on an embankment along Jericho Road, close to where the church should have been. They didn't see any lights.

Jenna looked back the way they had come. There, too, she found darkness, which both comforted and distressed. She kept expecting to see two lonely high beams coming their way.

"What do we do now?" George asked.

Jenna had expected a different question. She had expected him to press a response to his confession that he was some sort of puppet. But how could she even respond? Was George delusional, insightful, or was he trying to tell her something? Jenna didn't know what to believe.

"So what do we do?" he repeated.

"I don't know why we don't see the church," Jenna said. "Maybe my sense of direction is off, but I don't think so."

George reached for the dashboard and the GPS. He never got the chance to use it. Up the road, a whole hillside of lights suddenly switched on like a commercial for the local power company.

"Look at that," Jenna said. She didn't know what the Church of All Nations looked like during the day, but at night, lights illuminated the domed cupolas and tympanum as if the basilica had been built on constellations.

Jenna took off her seatbelt and checked her cell phone. No messages. She turned to George. "Why don't you stay here?"

"I knew it," he said.

"Knew what?"

"You're already fitting me for that black hood."

"George... why do you say that?"

"Because. You don't trust me. I was honest with you about what I had been feeling, and now you want to leave me behind."

Jenna sighed and looked at the time.

For some reason, she didn't doubt that Father Olsen was here at the church this evening. He seemed to be in all the right places at all the right times. And just like his attendance at Sandy Travis's death, this power outage could not be a coincidence. Someone had beaten them to the punch.

"Come with me if you want," Jenna said. "I'm just looking at that steep hill to the church and I'm thinking, maybe you ought to sit this one out."

George looked at the hill. He grinned and turned to Jenna. "So you trust me?"

"Sure I do, George. Which is why I'm letting you watch my back. You've got my back, don't you?"

"Yes, of course I do."

"Then be on the lookout for two high beams behind us. I won't be long."

———

HE DEFINITELY COULDN'T HAVE MADE IT, Jenna thought, sweating and breathing hard. George would have died.

Jenna should have fared better up the incline, though. She thought she kept herself in greater shape than this. The hill wasn't *that* steep. And it was a cool night, no more than seventy degrees. Yet she had perspired so much, she had to wipe the sting of it out of her eyes.

A tall wrought-iron fence ran the breadth of the church's façade— closing off its stairway. Jenna almost expected it to be locked this late after hours. Someone had left it unlatched.

She watched through the bars before letting herself in. She peered up the church's stone steps and scanned its portico, the shadows behind the pillars.

Three archways, formed by four clusters of Corinthian columns, supported the entablature and pediment of the roof. Men and women knelt and prayed there in the triangular tympanum of the façade, all part of a gold-leaf mosaic. In agony, they fell to either side of Jesus, who knelt in the center, wearing red robes and a halo, beseeching God with the angels above.

As Jenna let herself through the wrought-iron gate, her eye caught a snippet of Latin text in the frieze below the mosaic: *Preces supplicationesque cum clamore...*

She translated as she read and realized it was from Hebrews 5:7, "Who in the days of his flesh, when he had offered up prayers and supplications with strong crying and tears unto him that was able to save him from death, and was heard in that he feared."

Jenna started up the church steps and tried her best to straighten the wrinkles in her blouse. She wanted to come off as someone looking for answers, not a handout.

Behind her, hurried footsteps approached.

She whirled around.

"Please!" a woman shouted as she came up the stairs. "Visiting hours are over—you can't come in!" She brushed past Jenna and hurried through one of the tall heavy doors of the church, which she slammed shut behind her.

Jenna almost laughed, it was so absurd. But she didn't. The woman had been genuinely panicked: she hadn't even locked the door to the church.

So Jenna let herself inside.

————

"EXCUSE ME," A CLERGYMAN SAID, "can I help you?" He looked almost as alarmed as the woman Jenna had encountered a few minutes ago. His thick glasses created part of the effect, magnifying his eyes so that they seemed to bug out of his head. His mussed white hair topped it all off.

"I'm looking for someone," Jenna said. She had made her way through the chapel and down some long corridors to the administrative offices. She had run into the clergyman in an outer office area. "I, uh... I know it's not visiting hours but... I'm wondering if you can help."

"Well, we just had a power failure," the man said. "We're just now trying to get things back in order."

Jenna hadn't noticed at first—the clergyman had startled and distracted her—but now she noticed that the place was a wreck: overturned chairs and desks, shattered glass everywhere, and a large wooden cross lying in the middle of the floor.

"My name is Jenna Grant," she said. "I'm a friend of Father Walton."

The clergyman extended his hand, and Jenna shook it. She saw the dazed look in his eyes and thought the blackout must have really upset him.

"I'm Bishop Bynum," he said. "Welcome."

He tried to move away from Jenna, but stumbled, regained his balance, and then walked over to the fallen cross.

"Sorry to bother you, Bishop, but I'm looking for Father Alan Olsen. Do you know him?"

The clergyman paused for a moment. Then he leaned down and picked up the cross. "Are you a friend of Father Olsen's?"

Jenna looked away, pretending to survey the wreckage. She didn't have a hard time lying if necessary, but not to a priest in a house of worship.

"Father Olsen and I are actually really good friends," she said, "yes."

"Then you will be overjoyed to hear that something extraordinary occurred to him this evening." The bishop set the cross down on the only desk left standing. "Father Olsen has regained his eyesight."

Jenna's mind raced with dozens of thoughts, and they all wanted to spill out of her mouth at once. She stammered as she tried to form a coherent question.

"Speechless," Bishop Bynum said, "I understand. But I assure you, I witnessed it myself. Father Olsen is no longer blind."

She moved toward him, but stopped when her shoe crunched in a pile of glass. A framed photograph of the clergyman and the Pope lay nearby, shattered.

"Bishop Bynum, I'm sorry but I'm confused. What happened here? Who did this?"

He looked around at the mess in the office, then smiled. "It was your friend, Father Olsen. He did all this. Right after I said what had happened to him was a miracle."

CHAPTER 16

ON THEIR CHARTERED PLANE TO ALEPPO, Patricia Wolfenson looked over her husband's shoulder as Carl Saracen showed them satellite imagery before and after the quake. Dr. Fincher sat across from them, observing.

Nearly two dozen other passengers, including Reitz, occupied the plane. Some of them were part of the security team; others were part of the rescue mission, sent from the U.N. and the White House.

In Carl's satellite photos, Aleppo radiated outward from its citadel like a pile of boulders and rocks. The Al-Hamadaniah Stadium had fallen in segments and looked more like a Stonehenge around a green patch of grass. No siege before it, nor the medieval religious crusades, had conquered the ancient city so thoroughly as the earthquake.

"It's not unprecedented for the area," Carl was saying. "Built on a nest of fault lines as it is."

Patricia nodded. Before she and John had gone to Aleppo to broker the peace treaty, she had researched the city. "Didn't a pretty horrible earthquake hit in... I forget the year, but... wasn't it a big one?"

"Yes," said Dr. Fincher, "August 9, 1138. It killed over two hundred thousand people. Of course, this is according to ancient records."

"Flawed as those ancient records may be," Carl said, "this recent quake may have already exceeded that toll."

Patricia closed her eyes and shook her head. She still remembered the Arab mother on TV, grieving over her children. That memory, more than the god's eye view of the rubble, made Carl's estimate all the more immeasurable.

Wolfenson spent the rest of their trip poring over the latest reports from the region. When their plane began its final approach toward Aleppo, he visited the cockpit, only to return minutes later with an announcement.

"Bad news, everyone. I just overheard our pilot communicate with the control tower the coordinates for our landing. The controller on the ground admitted that they were communicating with a portable radio because all of the main power at the airport is still out.

"Fortunately," Wolfenson continued, "we have received reports from an advance contingent of Mr. Saracen's security team, already on the ground in Aleppo. They have assured me that the airport has experienced no difficulties with incoming flights, or any close calls since the earthquake. I have every confidence we will arrive unharmed. That's all."

Carl nodded, and watched Wolfenson return to his seat beside Patricia. If the envoy was nervous, he didn't show it. Carl wasn't nervous either. Not about the landing. He was more concerned about the security situation on the ground.

"Mr. Envoy," he said, leaning closer to his employer for privacy. "I think now would be a good time to put on a flak jacket."

"Absolutely not."

"Are you sure?" Patricia said.

"Yes, dear, I am very sure."

Carl had suspected this answer, but went through the motions anyway. "Sir, do you see my head of security?" He nodded subtly toward Reitz, who sat opposite them in a bulletproof vest; Reitz had holstered a pistol in plain sight on his shoulder. "I have been in disaster zones all over the world. People get desperate. And when they get desperate, they *act* it. Sometimes, it's only the threat of force that insulates us from their desperation."

Wolfenson shook his head. "I appreciate what you're saying, but we want the victims of the quake to fear the aftershocks, not the people who have come to save them. We don't want to send the wrong message."

"I understand," Carl said. He knew the original plan was for the angel to have a presence in Aleppo at a time when the rest of the world would be watching. It would increase Wolfenson's visibility and credibility as a future leader. But after hearing George's claim that it was all a lie, Carl now questioned whether that was still the plan.

Patricia turned to look out of the plane. She had landed in countless airports around the world, so many that she had lost count, and while each one was unique, they all shared one commonality: their airfields looked more like star fields. This evening, as they prepared to land at

Aleppo International Airport, Patricia worried that there was nothing beneath them but the dark.

———

JOHN WOLFENSON'S CHARTERED AIRPLANE came down without incident. It parked on one of the tarmacs adjacent to the runway, and the rescue team began to debark with their gear.

Carl, the first one down the exit ramp, noticed large quantities of food, water, and medical supplies piled up on a patch of grass near the landing strip. According to reports from his advance team, delivery into the city had been obstructed by fallen buildings and other debris in the streets. It was one reason Wolfenson's mission was so critical.

Not only was the envoy bringing helicopters packed with more food and medical supplies, but also cargo planes full of transport vehicles, flatbed trucks, excavators, and other earthmoving machines on loan from the Israeli government. Wolfenson's first goal was to clear a roadway into the city.

Downed phone lines and cellular towers made it impossible to communicate in Aleppo. Which was why Carl's team never depended upon what was on the ground, but in the sky. He pulled out his sat phone and pressed the speed dial for his tactical-operations center, set up in the heart of the city. Then he handed the phone to Wolfenson as the envoy exited the plane.

"This is Envoy Wolfenson," he said, plugging one ear against the noise of air traffic. "Yes, we just landed. Can you give me a status report of the present conditions in the city?"

As Patricia stepped off the plane's ramp, Carl offered her a hand. He was concerned she would be overwhelmed not only by the situation, but by the chaos, and the sound.

"There's going to be a delay before we can make our trip into the city," he told her. "We need to offload the earthmoving equipment coming in from the other planes, so we'll try to create as comfortable a situation for you as possible."

"No," she said, but the rest of her reply was lost under the roar of a departing jet.

"I'm sorry, what did you say?" Carl asked.

"I said I don't want to be babied! I came to help, not to be some movie star who needs to be pampered. Just point me in the right direction. I want to help!"

He held up his thumb. "Yes! Got it! Sorry!"

From the window of a building near the tarmac, one of Carl's security guards signaled to him: the building was secure.

Reitz escorted the envoy inside, intent on being the flak jacket that Wolfenson refused to wear. Carl ushered Patricia, intent on being hers. It was exactly where he wanted to be.

———

THE DOOR OPENED FOR CARL and Patricia and then quickly shut behind them. All the noise from the airfield immediately cut off, as if someone had pulled the plug on a stereo.

In the dim light provided by emergency generators, Carl met the head of his advance team, an American of Korean descent, Mark

Tanaka. Since Carl had personally recruited the guard years ago, Tanaka had quickly become one of his best field operatives.

Like Reitz, he launched directly into his status report. "Power and telecommunications are still out in ninety percent of the city. We have some vehicles ready to go, but, Mr. Saracen, I strongly recommend that you only go with a solid contingent of body guards. A city-wide curfew doesn't kick in for another three hours, and looting and other crimes are a serious issue. The local authorities are shooting and asking questions later."

"Understood, Mark. Thank you."

The door behind them opened, and Reitz, along with a pair of body-guards, ushered in John Wolfenson. Behind them, Dr. Fincher led the other passengers from the U.N. and the White House. Tagging along were two reporters and their photographers, who would be covering the team's rescue effort for the rest of the media, both print and network TV.

As soon as the door shut, Wolfenson disconnected his phone call and turned to his wife. "Pat, how are you doing?"

"Everybody, stop worrying about me. I'm fine."

"Okay, good." Wolfenson turned to the gathering. He started to speak, but fell silent.

Patricia worried about his state of mind. He had barely slept the night before the trip, making arrangements for the Israeli rescue team and their equipment. He had also written his own speech for the press conference. Then, after delivering the speech, he had stayed at his podium for two hours, answering questions from a group of international journalists. To make matters worse, he hadn't slept on the flight from Tel Aviv, not a wink.

"The city's main hospital was destroyed in the earthquake," he finally said, regaining his composure, and his confidence. "Some patients are being transported to hospitals outside the city, but the victims trapped in and around the epicenter are being treated in tents at the public park, and at other key locations.

"In a minute, I'm going to call the main Emergency Response Unit at the Red Cross to let them know our supplies and equipment are here. In the meantime, I need to make an advance trip into the city. Carl, can you get one of the off-road vehicles ready for that trip? And a few loaves of bread?"

Wolfenson returned the sat phone to Carl, but didn't wait for his reply. Instead, he put his hand on Patricia's waist and gently steered her away from the others, to address her privately.

"Honey, I'm going to meet you in a couple of hours at the main Red Cross tent in downtown Aleppo. Right now, I need to deal with a situation."

"Why can't you wait for the rest of the caravan?" Patricia asked.

"Because I just got off the phone with one of Carl's contacts here. Apparently there is a special-interest group using the disaster to put pressure on the locals. They've paid off the police, and even some government officials. So I need to intervene. They know who I am, and I might be able to change their minds."

"Then let me go with you."

"Pat..." he said, taking her hand. His was dry, hers was not. "I need you to stay and help Carl at the Red Cross. That's where you'll be the most help. Please, will you do that for me?"

Patricia studied him, his eyes. She knew he was lying. The true reason he didn't want her to go was because his mission was too dangerous; she knew that. But she couldn't see any hint of the lie in his eyes. She saw only excitement. Her husband, if this man truly was, hadn't been so excited since the signing of the peace treaty.

"Okay, John. I'll stay."

"Thank you." He opened his arms to embrace her, and out of pure instinct she almost stepped away. But she didn't. She let him envelop her and hold her in his warmth, and she hugged him back, wondering if it would be the last time she ever saw him.

Carl, holding the sat phone, approached Dr. Fincher.

"Nothing to worry about," Fincher said, noticing the concern on Carl's face.

"A few loaves of bread?" Carl asked. "Where's he going?"

"There's been a slight change of plan."

"Are you going with him?"

"Yes. And we'll need Reitz as well."

"You should also take Blatchard and Tanaka, don't you think?"

"Trust me," Fincher said, "where we're going, that won't be possible. We'll meet up at the Red Cross."

Carl glanced at the envoy and traced the power button on the sat phone.

"Don't worry about it," Fincher said, laying a hand on Carl's shoulder. "Just stay with Patricia. Proceed as planned."

Carl nodded.

Proceed as planned.

CHAPTER 17

"THIS IS ONE OF THE MOST extraordinary events in my life," said Bishop Bynum, his tears brimming, glistening, but never spilling over. "Extraordinary!"

Jenna didn't want to leave the church office. She and the bishop had never met, and yet here he was, feeding her a blow-by-blow of his meeting with Father Olsen that night. As if she were his wife, or part of the Catholic hierarchy—neither of which was a possibility.

Unfortunately, Jenna also had her eye on her phone. Specifically the clock. George had been alone in the car for close to thirty minutes. Keyword, alone.

And with him, the question was, how long was thirty minutes, exactly? You just could never tell.

But as Jenna listened to the intimate details of Father Olsen regaining his sight, she felt as if the floor had turned to wet concrete, drying around her feet.

"Oh, my dear Lord," said Bishop Bynum, "what will the media think? Father Olsen's already a rock star, but this? They'll give him his own TV show at the very least. My God, we'll all be working for him."

Jenna's eyes skimmed the room, pausing on the toppled furniture, shattered picture frames, and broken flower pots. She wanted to say it was, indeed, the destruction a rock star would make out of his hotel room, but she managed to squash the attempt at a joke.

"I'm still not sure what happened," the bishop said, needing no encouragement to continue. "One minute he was standing right there, and the next... he flew into a..."

She thought he was going to say *a rage*.

He said, "A temper tantrum. As if... as if someone had *taken* his sight, not given it to him."

"And this happened after you used the word *miracle*?"

"Yes. What word would you have used?"

Jenna held up her hands. "Sorry, your Excellency, I'm not questioning your word choice. I'm still just trying to understand what happened."

"Well, I repeated the word *miracle*, because I thought maybe he didn't hear me, and at this point my eyes were all clouded over with tears, so I thought he was walking away to get me some Kleenex. But then I realized he was lifting a chair over his head."

"Oh my God," Jenna replied, just to let him know she was listening. "Really?"

"Yes, and then he threw it through my office window. I was absolutely stunned. I was even doubting that I saw what I plainly saw. But then he continued with his rampage. He pushed over that desk..." He pointed to a desk. "Then he took his right arm and... wait..." He lifted his left arm. "It was his left... Yes. He took his left arm, and he swept it across the wall there, knocking down all these pictures. And then..." The bishop stopped and surveyed the scene, as if recreating it in his head. "He picked up each picture and he *threw* them, one by one... like Frisbees." He flung pretend picture frames toward the real ones lying shattered at the base of the far wall. "Finally, I managed to say, 'Alan, what are you doing?' and he just... stopped."

Jenna glanced at her cell phone again while the bishop caught his breath. She did it so quickly, and was so deep in thought, she didn't really register the time.

"So," she said, "what did he do next?"

The bishop wiped his eye and stared into space. "He had his back to me but... I could hear him crying."

All through his reenactment, his Excellency had been very sure of exactly where everything in the room had taken place. Now, he was looking beyond the room to something he couldn't quite see. "I should have consoled him but... I was still scared." For almost the first time during his retelling, he looked Jenna in the eye. "Do you know what I mean?"

She nodded sympathetically. "So what did you do?"

"I said, 'Alan, are you all right?'"

"And what'd he—"

"He didn't say. He just left the office without another word." Exhausted, finished, the bishop eased himself into the only chair that stood upright.

Jenna looked at her cell phone. She really looked at it this time—and blanched.

"Your Excellency, my friend in the car... I need to go see him. Do you mind if I come back with him?"

"Yes, yes, you're friends of Alan... and Father Walton. I want you to feel at home."

"Thank you, sir. You're very kind."

As Jenna turned to leave, she realized she had failed to ask the obvious question. Fatigue had clearly taken its toll on her mind.

"Sir, one more thing: did Alan tell you what really happened? I mean, specifically, did he tell you how he regained his sight?"

The bishop had been leaning forward in his chair, reaching for a broken picture frame on the floor in front of him. He stopped and leaned back.

"No, I don't think he did. He just said *where* it happened."

"Where—"

"He said in the garden. The Garden of Gethsemane."

———

JENNA MOVED QUICKLY DOWN THE HILL toward the rental car. Finally, she thought, they were in the right place at the right time. And she wanted to exploit their good fortune. She only had to get George out of the car and up to the church while the bishop was in a chatty mood.

Only one problem: George wasn't in the car.

Jenna glanced around—no sign of him. She rushed up to the Ford. He wasn't inside. The car was locked, empty, and the windows were unbroken. And the keys, which Jenna had left in the ignition, were gone.

"George," she said, afraid to yell.

If anyone heard her, they didn't answer back.

She pulled out her cell phone and dialed the emergency number in Israel: 1-0-0. If George was in trouble, there was no time to waste.

Jenna started to press talk.

The rustle of leaves stopped her.

About two hundred yards from the street where they had parked, the foliage grew thick, blighted with night and something else.

Jenna looked at her phone, at the three digits she had entered. Her finger gently rested on the talk button. Indecisiveness—yet another sign of fatigue.

She folded up her phone. Put it back in her coat. And then she started walking toward the bushes.

About fifty yards from the shrubbery, she heard the sound again. The sound of someone or something moving around in the leaves. She fought the urge to run forward like a madwoman, screaming, just to shock the prowler into thinking she was enraged. But she knew that would probably just end up getting her shot or worse.

So she pulled her phone out of her pocket again, ready to call the police, but accidentally dropped it, watched the back come off and clatter on the dirt.

As quickly as possible, Jenna swooped down to snatch it up. And as she bent over, the bushes rustled and she knew she had made a mistake, had left herself wide open to attack.

And then she heard sharp coughing.

"George?" she asked, running forward. She helped him out of the brush. "Are you all right?"

He was gagging, and trying to catch his breath. "Yes. I'm fine."

"George," she said, "what were you doing?"

"Hiding."

"From what?"

He took a second to recover. "While I was waiting for you, I saw the same car drive by twice. I didn't want to be in our car when it drove by a third time."

Jenna looked up and down the road that lined the hillside. From where they were standing, she could see through the darkness for at least a quarter of a mile. She didn't see any headlights. At least no lights that were moving.

"So you think we're being followed?" she asked.

"Yes, I guess it's a possibility."

"Did you get a good look at the driver?"

"Just for a few seconds."

"What'd he look like, George, come on."

"Um, an older man, fifties or sixties. Caucasian—" he coughed. "He had black hair. Or brown. Hard to tell in the dark. That's all I saw."

"What about a license plate?"

"Two and seven."

"What?"

"Those are the numbers I remember."

"Were they in red?"

"Why does that matter?"

"The Israeli police have red number license plates, George."

"It wasn't a police car."

"They'll often use unmarked cars. You can tell because the license plates are always the same."

"Oh. Well, I don't know what color the letters were, but they were definitely not red."

Jenna looked around again, but was practically blind out here. "Let's go up to the church. We'll be safe there, okay?"

She held out her hand for him, and after a long considerable silence, he took it. Then together they started back toward the road.

CHAPTER 18

ON THE ROAD OUT OF THE AIRPORT, Wolfenson's team was delayed at a checkpoint. The Syrian military had formed an armed perimeter with roadblocks and hundreds of men.

Luckily one of the guards recognized the envoy from his talk show appearances. "You were funny, sir," the guard said in plain English.

"Shukran," Wolfenson replied. He had rolled down his window so he could talk.

The guard gestured into the other back seat next to Wolfenson. "What is that?"

"It is bread."

The guard nodded again, as if in perfect understanding. He pointed to the far fields, where hundreds of lights flickered and flagged. "Be careful out there. Some of them are dangerous."

"Are they refugees?" Reitz asked.

Before the guard could answer, Wolfenson said, "If you don't mind me asking, soldier, do you have a wife and children?"

"Yes, sir."

"Excellent. Do you have a picture?"

The soldier paused, surprised by the question. He dug a photograph out of his wallet and handed it to Wolfenson, who studied the image thoughtfully.

"Your little one," he said. "What's her name?"

"Aisha."

Wolfenson nodded. "And is she safe?"

"Her name means 'alive and well,' sir," the guard said with proud relief. Wolfenson laughed, and the soldier smiled at having entertained a great man. "My wife says her name's a sign from Allah."

Wolfenson nodded and handed back the picture. "Your wife is right. Mashallah, soldier. She's beautiful."

"Mashallah," the guard said. "Fe Aman Allah." He let them pass, let them out toward the flickers in the field.

Reitz's vehicle, a Humvee, handled well over the roadway, which was as full of faults as the ancient earth.

"So, Reitz," Fincher said as they travelled. "I haven't had a chance to talk to Carl—how is he doing?"

"He appears to be fine, sir."

"And his family?"

"I'm afraid I can't say." Ahead, road barrels reflected in Reitz's headlights.

"Yes, I understand. Your relationship is strictly professional."

"Not exactly," Reitz replied. "Mr. Saracen is a private man, so I don't know much about his family. But we've been through a lot together and he's more than earned my undying loyalty. So things are more than professional between us." He squinted at the road barrels ahead. "Overpass is out."

Guided by GPS, Reitz took an off-ramp, and then an on-ramp, by-passing the whole mess. In a minute they were back on the main road. "Eyes sharp," he said, pointing at the flickers in the field, which were fires.

Immediately, a loose squad of men spilled out of the night, waving. Some could have been mistaken for Westerners by dress, while others, Muslims, wore red-and-white checkered headdresses.

Reitz slowed and swerved around them, but Fincher told him to speed up.

"Don't give them a chance to get in front of us."

Reitz complied.

The men in the road had come from makeshift camps where chil-dren and women, veiled to the eyes, huddled around burning trashcans. Thousands of Syrians inhabited the dark farmland, naturally segregated by Muslims and minorities, like Christians, but also naturally brought together by the quake. They had migrated from the city knowing that aid would come by air.

"So where are we headed, sir?" Reitz asked.

"To the trade market in Khan al-Shouneh."

Reitz glanced at him in the rearview mirror. "Sir, surely you've seen the satellite pictures of that area. It's devastated."

"Sadly, that is the case. But it's the survivors we need to speak to, not the dead."

"And I must warn you," Dr. Fincher said to Reitz. "These people we're going to see, they'll be spooked by a U.S. soldier carrying a weapon."

"I haven't been a soldier since my tour in Baghdad, sir. I'm a private employee now, have been for years."

"Just the same, we'll need you to hold your position outside. Can we count on you to make that happen?"

Reitz addressed Wolfenson in the rearview, as if the envoy had asked the question and not Dr. Fincher. "Sir, that request makes me very uncomfortable. I've never lost a client. I refuse to start with you."

Wolfenson unbuckled his seatbelt and leaned forward to squeeze Reitz's shoulder. "That's very commendable, soldier. I can see why Carl holds you in such high esteem. But trust me, behaving rashly is the one thing that could get us killed."

Out of the darkness, a roadblock materialized, a building collapsed into the road. And in the desert directly before it, several eyes shined.

"What in the hell?" Reitz slowed down and looked through a pair of night vision binoculars. "Canines of some sort. Three of them, just standing there by the side of the road." He zoomed in and then lowered his binoculars as the beasts resolved in the headlights. "I think they might be coyotes."

Wolfenson leaned forward again to stare out the windshield.

"Impossible," Fincher said, squinting. "There are no coyotes in Syria."

"They could have escaped from the zoo," Reitz suggested.

"Aleppo doesn't have a zoo."

"And yet," Wolfenson interjected, "Reitz is correct. They are coyotes."

The animals weren't moving, even as the Humvee roared near and spewed its exhaust. They stood as monuments unshaken, even by the faults of the land.

Since he was a boy, the hairs at the nape of Fincher's neck had been sensitive. He had always thought of the hairs as an extrasensory organ, feelers that bristled cold against a very specific stimulus. Out here, at the edge of catastrophe, his hairs should have been on end—he knew that. But they weren't.

"Pull over," the envoy said to Reitz.

"Sir—"

"Please."

"Yes, sir." Reitz parked on the shoulder of the road, but kept the engine running. Wolfenson threw open his door and got out. With the confidence of an accomplished man, he strode toward the feral trinity.

"Sir!" Reitz shouted, scrambling for his submachine gun, an HK MP 5. He turned to Dr. Fincher and said, "What's he doing?!"

Fincher, ignoring him, got out too.

"Damn it!" Reitz jumped out of the driver's side and chased after them, breathing in the smoke and the night.

About two dozen yards from the canines, Wolfenson halted. Fincher and Reitz stopped with him. The coyotes' six eyes shined like moons in the headlights, fixed solely on the envoy.

This close to the threat, Fincher still didn't feel the chill down his neck, the one that told him which instinct to follow.

Slowly, calmly, Wolfenson took another step forward. The coyotes crouched in unison, moving as one beast with three heads. It growled, six eyes flashing.

Reitz stepped between Wolfenson and the predators, aiming his weapon. The eyes looked right past him to the envoy.

"Sir, if you would, please back up toward the Hummer. Slowly..."

"Yes," Fincher said, and started to back up himself. "Excellent idea."

A second later, Wolfenson backed up too, and the coyotes began to bark.

When they could talk privately near the rumble of the Humvee, Wolfenson leaned toward the doctor. "Where are we at with acquiring those pages?"

Fincher hesitated, embarrassed. "We're working on it."

The envoy didn't react to the news. He was too fixated on the coyotes, which Reitz seemed to be holding back with his weapon. "*Canis latrans*," Wolfenson finally remarked.

Fincher furrowed his brow. "Latin for... *barking dog*?"

"Yes, the coyote. They have a gift of making the howls of a few sound like the howls of the many." He looked toward the roadblock of brick and mortar. "I believe that's why the Landlord chose them as his messengers."

Fincher glanced at him and noticed that, for the first time, The Angel of Light's look of fixed confidence had disappeared.

The doctor opened his mouth to say something—but then Reitz fired his submachine gun into the air. The coyotes no longer barked at Wolfenson. They growled.

"Should I shoot them?" Reitz asked.

"No, let them be!" the envoy shouted over the sound of the Hummer. "Time to move out! We need to find a way around!" He and Dr.

Fincher got into the vehicle, and Reitz started to retreat slowly from the beasts.

Taking advantage of the brief privacy, Fincher turned to the envoy, who sat beside the bread. "Messengers. For what?"

Wolfenson stared out at the roadblock, resting his elbow on the door rest, resting his hand over his mouth. "To issue a warning," he said. "A final caveat about my plan."

With that, Reitz opened his door and climbed in. Behind him, the coyotes howled, and the hairs on the back of Dr. Fincher's neck finally shivered on end.

CHAPTER 19

APPROXIMATELY TWO HOURS after Wolfenson departed on his trip, the convoy of relief vehicles left the airport for the city. Five SUVs led a parade of half-ton trucks, which carried the Israeli disaster equipment and supplies.

After easily circumnavigating a devastated overpass, they came to a field of refugees. Patricia wanted to stop—how could she not? Men groveled at their caravan for water and food. Babies cried in the field. But another charity was already gearing up to assist these people, and Patricia's team was focused on clearing the road and getting supplies to the Red Cross.

Not long after the refugee encampment, her convoy came across the first impasse. A building had collapsed. Its massive blocks had spilled into the roadway. Nothing but a motorcycle could have passed without a detour off-road.

A team of rescue workers immediately set upon the rocks with jack-hammers. They stood aside periodically while bulldozers scraped debris into the desert. Forty-five minutes later, it was clean.

They drove five minutes to the next blockade, and an hour later they drove to the next. Patricia stood outside her SUV, staring at the latest fallen concrete goliath. Carl stood nearby, watching the men work.

Patricia kept dreading that they might find someone under all that stone. She could only hope any victims would survive, and not just die in some tent, or worse, die at the very moment of being saved.

"At this rate," she said, "we'll never get into the city."

She had said it to herself, but loud enough for Carl to overhear. He looked at his watch and fretted over the hold this would put on Wolfenson's plan. Their ropes and pulleys would definitely work better on Patricia in the smoke and mirrors of night.

That was a small concern, however, when compared to the Black Pages. Or more accurately, the two new keepers of their ancient knowledge. Dr. Fincher's mission was to erase the document, and all memory of its contents. He claimed to need Carl's help, but with Fincher, Carl had learned over the years that the doctor preferred to work alone. So there had to be a compelling reason for his request.

Since their conference in the freezer, Carl had come up with two theories. One, Fincher really needed his help because he was afraid to disappoint the envoy. Perhaps *very* afraid. That's why he was willing to change his *modus operandi*. Or two, Fincher already realized he was going to fail in his task, so his new plan was to make sure the blame fell on Carl. The envoy's target list of Red Veil names didn't include Dr. Colin Fincher. No doubt the doctor wanted to maintain the special relationship he enjoyed with the angel. A bond that apparently included the envoy's full confidence in sharing with the doctor the real reason they were in Aleppo.

Patricia, deafened by the jackhammers and earthmovers grumbling into position, winced and covered her ears. She had barely tolerated the first few excavations, but this latest one shook her to the bone.

Then Carl saw Patricia's face freeze.

The rescuers had just uncovered part of a body, a hand poking out of the rubble. It shook and dangled limply as the team continued to dis-inter the corpse.

Patricia raced back to the SUV and climbed into the passenger side, slamming the door behind her.

Carl waited a beat, then got in behind the wheel.

"Patricia, are you all right?"

"Yes, I'm sorry. I'm fine."

"Don't apologize," Carl said. "Those kinds of sights are shocking. I don't care who you are."

"It's not just that. It's everything. It's John being gone. It's me feeling like a fly on the wall in a... busy beehive. It's a million and one things you couldn't possibly understand."

She noticed Carl react to her voice. Patricia closed her eyes and took a deep breath. "I apologize. I'm completely all right now."

Carl smiled—and then laughed. "Are you sure you're *completely all right?*"

Patricia blushed at having her words playfully thrown back at her. She certainly felt better, having released all those pent-up emotions. "Well, maybe not... *completely all right.* Look, I'm really sorry. Despite what I just said, I'm sure you're more than capable of understanding."

"Is there anything you want to talk about?" Carl asked, choosing his words for the effect he knew they would have on her.

Patricia chuckled. "It's funny, you have no idea how hearing that makes me immediately feel better. Maybe I should turn that into my mantra."

Carl pretended to be confused, so Patricia touched his arm to explain.

"A lot of things have happened in my life, Carl. Unfortunately I've said more to therapists than to anyone else."

He nodded and fell silent for a few moments, demonstrating that he truly was listening. "So I guess the phrase 'Anything you want to talk about' is like... comfort food for you."

Patricia laughed and reached over again to touch him, lingering longer this time before withdrawing her hand. "That, and a cigarette on the side," she said, "yes."

Nothing about their effortless interaction surprised her. When they had first met at Balshem Medical Center, after John's attack, Carl and Patricia had talked for hours in the waiting area and cafeteria. In her experience, most of John's security operatives acted as cold and multi-dimensional as the guns beneath their coats. But Carl, just minutes after they had become acquainted, was proudly showing off pictures of his wife and two sons. Patricia had wanted to show him a photograph of her son, Scotty, but with the added turmoil of John's attack, she hadn't risked the tears.

The drama of that moment paled in comparison to the anguish she now felt. Just the thought of what lay on the other end of the hand they had found disturbed her. Patricia feared she would lose it if the victim turned out to be a child.

240

"Well, then fine," Carl said, "talk to me. Tell me about those other problems you mentioned. I'm already on your husband's payroll, so I won't be charging you by the hour."

"No," Patricia said, "I don't think so. It all feels so... petty and trivial complaining about my personal problems in the middle of all this. People have lost their families out here. People have lost their lives."

Despite her noble words, Carl could see that she wanted, and even needed, to talk. He didn't want to push her too hard, but he also wanted to get her to open up.

"I understand," he said. "But I hope you don't mind me asking... what in God's name are you doing here, Patricia?"

She had devised a whole repertoire of answers to this type of question, on the plane ride over. Her answers ranged from excuses to outright lies, but one version came very close to the truth. Patricia wanted to give Carl that version, if she could. But every time she opened her mouth, she couldn't figure out what to say, or how to say it.

She almost came right out and said that John wasn't John, he wasn't her husband, but that had started to sound crazy even to herself.

"I'm sorry," Carl said, "I shouldn't have said anything..."

"No," Patricia said, "I don't mind you asking. It's just... I'm not sure I can answer you. I *can* tell you I'm not here for some adventure to tell my girlfriends about. And I'm not here to..." She looked over at the rescue team as they continued to dig up the body. "Not here to find myself in the reflection of some poor earthquake victim's eyes. But I guess I'm still not answering your question." She turned away, frustrated and confused.

"Patricia, I only ask because..." Carl pretended to shift uncomfortably in his seat. "Everything we're about to see and experience... it's probably the worst this planet has to offer." He let the words resonate with her a second.

In no way did Patricia believe Carl was exaggerating. She had often heard John criticizing the media's running theme that tragedies brought out the best in people. They ran stories of heroic rescues or selfless conduct. But, as John had informed her countless times, the news also shelved stories about how tragedies brought out the worst in people.

"Are you prepared to handle that?" Carl asked her.

"What about you?" Patricia asked. "Why are *you* here? And don't tell me because you're getting paid. Your security team could keep us safe without you here, endangering yourself too. If this is the worst the planet has to offer, why come? Why not be with your wife and children?"

Carl didn't have to pretend to think about the question, because he hadn't expected it. "Well, Patricia, I'll be honest with you. I'm not a religious man, but my answer will sound religious..."

Outside, the jackhammers suddenly stopped. Indeed, it was a child at the end of the hand.

"I believe that on any trip to heaven, there are always detours through hell."

CHAPTER 20

REITZ DROVE JOHN WOLFENSON'S Humvee into the Old City, where the Citadel of Aleppo on the hill once shined. He parked near a tourist bus crushed under white bricks.

In this part of the city, those bricks were thousands of years old. Fincher wondered if the envoy had planned them too.

Candles, oil lamps, and fires burned here, outside the stone wall of Khan al-Shouneh. Their light erected a golden dome upon the ruins of archways and towers. In this glowing sanctuary, people had gathered, as they had for centuries.

Aleppo had long served as a nexus for the great trading routes, including the Silk Road. Once an inn for traders, Khan al-Shouneh had become an extension of over nine miles of covered marketplace: stone archways sheltering a narrow cobbled maze, where all manner of God's people haggled. Imports such as Damascene coffee, Indian spices, and raw Iranian silk; domestics, such as wool and soap.

Tonight, three guards stood at the khan's intricately carved door. They looked as if they would haggle for nothing. But Dr. Fincher knew every man had his price, even if just the one on his head.

"This is exactly the type of situation I was trained to avoid," Reitz announced.

Fincher laid a hand on the guard's MP 5 to steady it. "Don't let your emotions control you," he said, hoping his psychoanalysis would help.

"And lead with your ears," Wolfenson added. "A calm reaction is key to a satisfactory outcome."

Fincher was amazed each time when the envoy's grip on Reitz's shoulder put the man at ease. As if the envoy knew some age-old pressure point.

"In fact, let us lead," Wolfenson said. "Our hosts will want to see our faces."

Before either of his men, the envoy got out and took the loaves of bread. Several sacks in each hand. Fincher followed after him, and obediently, but not blindly, Reitz trailed behind.

A congregation of women wore black veils, revealing only their mourning eyes. As Wolfenson entered their temple of rubble and light, they all gathered around for alms of bread. Each woman accepted her loaf with a respectful bow and blessings and thanks: *Shukran, Mashallah*, and *Allah Ma'akom*. Wolfenson, too, repeated *Mashallah, Mashallah*: God bless you all. Reitz watched all of this, clearly confused, and uncertain what to do with his gun.

At the entrance to the khan, the armed guards caught sight of Wolfenson and his entourage. Two of them tossed their cigarettes aside and raised their guns. The third, to the right of the door, stopped petting a dog to grab a pistol from his belt.

Fincher checked on Reitz, who was itching at his trigger guard. The doctor opened his mouth to whisper more consolations, but then Wolfenson chuckled and surprised them both.

"Gentlemen, gentlemen," the envoy said to the guards. "I expected a warmer welcome." He lifted his arms, as if inviting a congregation to stand. Under his breath, so that only those closest to him could hear, the envoy said, "While the trumpets are silent, my voice will lift the veil. I will raise the dear departed to rebuild on shattered stone."

Dr. Fincher listened carefully to this incantation, taking comfort in the cadence and tone. He didn't know how, but this prayer played a necessary part of what they were about to do.

The door to Khan al-Shouneh suddenly opened, and a man stood in the shadows. He said something to the three guards in Arabic, and for several seconds no one moved.

"No Jews and crusaders can see the Imam in this state," the man in the shadows said.

Wolfenson nodded. "We are neither." In Arabic, he added, "We are from the Red Veil."

The shadowy figure stepped quickly into the light. Long white robes draped his skeletal frame, and a headdress and beard lent a fullness to his hollow face. "We are from the Red Veil," repeated Ilyas Saeed in Arabic. "Nahno min jama'et Alkoofeyah Alhamra."

At Saeed's command, the three guards lowered their weapons. Two of them lit new cigarettes, and the third went back to petting his dog.

To Reitz, the envoy said, "We won't be long." And then he and Dr. Fincher disappeared into the shadows, leaving their bodyguard behind.

Hopefully, Fincher thought, Reitz's nerves wouldn't get the best of him.

Once the khan's heavy door had shut, the women in veils picked up their bread, but did not eat of it, not yet.

Aleppo's marketplace had several khans, each named after its location and function: such as the Khan al-Gumruk, caravansary of customs and excise, including the consulates of French, English, and Dutch commerce.

Khan al-Shouneh specialized in the trades and traditional handicrafts of Aleppine art, none of which was on display tonight. The khan resembled a colossal dark shell: a corridor of tall archways, arcaded with wooden shop fronts and their fanlights. The brick walls had cracked, as had some of the huge tiles on the floor. Otherwise the building remained intact.

Ilyas Saeed led Wolfenson and Fincher down the arcade. He spoke quietly, and yet his voice traveled far. "I am sure you have heard. The infidels sent their fireflies to burn down the Imam's home in Beirut."

"Yes," Wolfenson said.

Fincher had heard this too. For ten years the United States had been trying to kill the man named Omar Sheikh Kashmiri—or OSK, as the intelligence community referred to him. Kashmiri and his terrorist group had bombed American military outposts in Afghanistan and Iraq, killing soldiers, U.N. aides, and civilians alike.

Recently, the CIA had launched drones to the Shuf Mountains to fire missiles into the Imam's castle.

"I trust the Red Veil gave him fair warning?" Wolfenson asked.

"Yes, and he escaped. The Americans believe the Imam is hiding in Jordan. They are fairly confident in stating it."

"Perfect," Wolfenson said.

Saeed's eyes became even sadder. "I am afraid *not* perfect, my envoy. I am afraid not." He grew gravely quiet as they came to an intersection and turned left, over a decorative grid of tile work in the center.

Down this covered street, there was lamplight, and a group encircling a crudely constructed bed. Half a dozen of them knelt in prayer. The other half simply stared at the body laid out on the thin, lumpy mattress. A white cotton kafan shrouded the man's corpse all the way to the neck, and an open copy of the Koran rested beside his head.

Years ago, when Carl Saracen had first given the Imam's dossier to Dr. Fincher, the psychologist had been struck by the terrorist's profile, which seemed to run the table on the psychopathy checklist, the PCL-R.

In Egypt, during the 1980s, the Imam had founded the terrorist organization Zulfiqar, a reaction to the Soviet Union's invasion of Afghanistan. Since then, the group had become more anti-Semitic, anti-Western, and anti-modern, and OSK had personally masterminded the deaths of hundreds of people. He alone had become one of the most wanted terrorists in the Middle East.

Though members of Zulfiqar preached Islamic fundamentalism while proselytizing at mosques, Fincher knew from the files that OSK cared very little for religious texts. Almost as little as he knew about them. Which ruled out the initial diagnosis from another member of the Red Veil—borderline personality disorder with extreme disassociation.

No, OSK was a man who loved to make video threats, spouting more than just a black-and-white ideology. He was a killer, indiscriminately. Not just of Westerners, but of Sunnis and Shiites alike. And if those targets included women and children, all the better.

Each of these traits and tendencies led Fincher to label OSK with an amoral, narcissistic personality. More than that, the doctor felt certain he was looking at the profile of one of the modern world's most prolific mass murderers. A perfect recruit for the Red Veil.

Now, as Fincher loomed over OSK in the dim lamplight of the khan, he was underwhelmed by the corpse's stature. Surely this body, this sunken-in meat, was not the legendary OSK. Too garden variety. The dead man certainly wasn't recognizable: his face, although cleansed of blood, had been pulped and bruised in death.

But indeed, this was the man they had come to see. The man who had long ago told his followers that he wanted to brand himself, not only as the spokesperson of their group, but as the face of destruction itself. And here, the Imam's face had certainly been destroyed.

"There is the brick that took him," Saeed said, pointing to a bloody chunk of rock, around which more people were praying for some ungodly reason. It looked older than the masonry in the khan, and had a different color too, as if it had come from a different building altogether.

Again, Wolfenson and Fincher had already heard this news, but the doctor admired the envoy's show of sadness and surprise.

Fincher himself found it difficult not to comment on the irony of OSK's death: after the U.S. military and intelligence had spent millions of dollars and thousands of man hours trying to eliminate him, it had been a simple brick that had taken the Imam's life.

"Who knows of this?" Wolfenson asked. "This tragedy?"

"Only those amongst us," Saeed replied.

The envoy nodded. Fincher, as well. Like the envoy had said before: perfect. All according to plan.

"Could we have a few minutes alone with the Imam, please?" Wolfenson asked Saeed.

"Yes, but I must stay."

The envoy smiled. "I understand."

Saeed nodded and then executed a flourish to everyone surrounding the bed. The people instantly scattered into the darkness, their robes dusting old floors.

Wolfenson stood by OSK's bedside and stared down at him, as if trying to read the Imam's mind. Saeed shifted uncomfortably and took a step toward Wolfenson, who acknowledged him.

"It was not his time," the envoy said. "There are things he still needs to do."

Fincher noticed Saeed trying to hide his confusion, but a slight crease in the man's weathered brow betrayed him.

"We believe that Jesus Christ is not dead," Saeed replied obliquely. "We believe he was taken to heaven by Allah, peace be with him. And I personally believe Imam Kashmiri will soon return to the army of Allah."

Wolfenson did not respond, vastly more skilled than Saeed at hiding his reactions. He knelt and laid a hand on the cotton kafan over OSK's chest. Once again, he stared at the terrorist before closing his eyes.

Fincher waited eagerly for something to happen. After a full minute, he glanced at Saeed, who now looked openly confused, but also intrigued. He did nothing to stop the envoy.

Eyes still closed, Wolfenson turned to Saeed. "I need your help. Our friend Kashmiri has fallen asleep, but I am going to wake him."

"Suras..." Saeed stammered, "holy warrior... Allah..."

After a few long, anxious moments, the envoy spoke again, this time loudly. "Take away the stone!"

It was not clear who Wolfenson was speaking to, and Saeed looked to Fincher with concern. The doctor kept his eyes on the envoy.

"Saeed," Wolfenson said, his eyes still closed. "Your brother will rise again. He who believes in me will live, even though he dies. Do you believe this?"

"Yes!" Saeed said. "Yes, I believe!"

With that, the envoy removed his hands from the Imam's chest. Then he opened his eyes.

Omar Sheikh Kashmiri opened his eyes as well.

CHAPTER 21

AS SHE AND GEORGE WALKED up the narrow path to the church, Jenna summarized the "miracle" of Father Alan Olsen's eyesight, and the priest's rampage after the fact.

She had plenty of time to flesh out her summary because George was struggling to make it up the hill. They even stopped a few times so he could rest.

When they finally did make it to the front of the church, he insisted on stopping again. He stared up at the mosaic of God, Christ, and man, and caught his breath.

"What do you say we approach things differently this time?" Jenna said. "Not like what happened with Carl. I've already bonded with the bishop, so... why don't you let me handle the situation."

"In other words, you want me to shut up."

"Hey, I tried to say it in a nice way."

"Well, it came off like you were talking to a first grader about his potty accidents."

Jenna rolled her eyes. "Are we ready to go?"

With great effort, they made their way up the stairs and into the church, then to the outer offices. Over a dozen people were now cleaning up the mess Father Olsen had left behind, and when Jenna approached Bishop Bynum to resume her interrogation, she found he had transformed into a completely different man.

Rather than the callow, confused bishop from earlier, his Excellency was now stoic and decisive. His verbal diarrhea had given way to constipation. She didn't sense anything sinister about the change. He was surrounded by church employees and parishioners, and was back to being their leader.

"Excuse me, your Excellency," one of the employees interrupted. "You need to see this. Apparently Father Olsen ran into some tables and statues on his way to the garden."

"Yes, of course, Jessie." The bishop turned to Jenna. "I'm sorry, I need to..."

She nodded, deciding she wouldn't get anything else from him anyway.

The bishop followed Jessie toward the hall, but stopped when he caught sight of George, who had been hanging back as per Jenna's instructions.

"My son, you look terrible..."

"Thank you, your Excellency, for noticing."

"Is there anything we can do?"

Before George could answer, Jenna said, "Your Excellency, this is George, the man I needed to check on. The one waiting for me in the car, remember?"

"Oh, yes, that's right. Your friend does not look well."

George coughed a couple times. "I'm very sick," he said. "And tired."

"Yes, you do look tired. You should rest."

Jenna noticed how the bishop stared at George as he spoke, as if entranced, either by his frail appearance or the cadence of his words, or something else.

"Perhaps you're right," George said. "But it's late, and we have no place to stay."

"Jessie," the bishop said, still looking at George. "These are friends of Father Walton's... and of Alan's. Can you see to it that they have a couple spare rooms in the rectory?"

"How kind of you, your Excellency, but—" George coughed again and cleared his throat. "Excuse me. I appreciate the offer. But Jenna tells me Father Olsen is no longer here. I've come all the way to Israel especially to see him."

"I understand. I'll just have Jessie here check with Lisa to get you Alan's address in East Jerusalem."

"Thank you, your Excellency." George held out his hand, which visibly shook. "For your hospitality, and your kindness."

The bishop wrapped both hands around George's, as if creating a protective shell. "Yes, of course. I hope you feel better."

———

JENNA OPENED HER DOOR CAREFULLY and looked up and down the hallway. Jessie had just finished showing them their guestrooms, and now Jenna confirmed that he had in fact left the rectory.

Quietly, she moved across the hallway and knocked on George's door. When no one answered, she checked if it was locked. It wasn't. She let herself in.

George lay in bed, on top of the sheets, wide awake.

"Are you all right, George?"

"I'm sorry, I just couldn't go on."

The way he looked, all sunken in, she started to worry about what he meant.

"I just need some sleep," he said.

"What about Father Olsen? It can't be a coincidence that on the night we're looking for him, he somehow regains his sight. We need to find him."

"Yes, I agree. But I also think it would be unwise to go wandering around at night when I'm sure we're being followed."

Jenna pulled out her cell phone and looked at the time. "Okay, we sleep until 5 a.m. Not a minute more. Deal?"

He didn't answer. He just closed his eyes and rested his hands on his chest, which showed through his shirt because of the sweat. The green bruises had deepened in color, and the skin on his face had become almost translucent, as if she were reading a street map and all the veins represented highways and toll roads, and his chest was the sea. She was afraid of what she might discover if she held a mirror beneath his nose.

Jenna set an alarm on her phone and then opened the door to leave. But when she looked out across the hallway to her own room, to the cold floor between it and her, she stopped. The last thing she wanted to do was sleep alone. If this was the night George was going to die, Jenna wanted to be there for him.

She closed the door and went back to his bed.

"Scoot over."

He opened his eyes. "You're going to sleep with me?"

"Mmm-hmm." She took off her coat. "We just have to make sure we're both out of here before the house deacon does a bed check in the morning. Otherwise we'll have hell to pay."

George rolled to the other side of the queen-size mattress, and Jenna lay down next to him. She looked over, but George had already closed his eyes.

So she rested her head on the pillow and looked around the guest quarters. A college dorm room had more furniture. And there was practically no décor. Just a tiny wooden desk and a cross hanging above it on the wall. A small oil painting near the door, depicting Jesus Christ. And a bookshelf, almost completely empty except for five books: a Catholic version of the Bible, a Bible concourse, a Catholic liturgy manual, and the *Oxford History of the Christian Church*. The fifth book had lost its cover.

Jenna wondered if the other rooms where the full-time church officials lived were equally as Spartan. She figured if the church still operated on the principles of the Jesuit order that founded it, every room would have the same POW feel. Simplicity reminded the priest that their sole focus should be God, not their own personal desires, choices, or ambitions. The priests would have no reason to complain about the rules either. Each one became part of the church because they had heard the calling. They hadn't been drafted. Every priest fighting in God's army actually volunteered.

Jenna stared at the little desk, and thought about her own workspace at the radio station. She had covered the tabletop with souvenirs from her trips, and with dozens of framed photographs of friends or other significant people, like her high school science teacher who had recently passed away. The photograph that probably meant the most to her sat next to the phone. In it, she posed in a great big family hug with Neal and her mother the day of her college graduation. They were all smiling.

Carri had hung pictures up around her workspace too, Jenna remembered. All those photographs of George pinned to her bulletin board.

Everywhere, people decorated their office or workspace in similar fashion. Jenna had never really thought about why, though. She thought one reason was to give any visitors a taste of their personal life outside the job. But she felt the other reason was more important. Pictures that your kids painted in school; a baseball you caught at a game; the pair of men's socks you won playing strip poker—all mental sticky notes, reminders that you were a real person. Not some cog in the machinery, or a faceless voice at the other end of a customer service call—and certainly not just a set of numbers on a middle manager's department budget. A real person.

All of her life Jenna had always felt in control, making her own choices, and living with the results. Sure, random events occurred in the world all the time that no one could control. All you were left with was your reaction.

But the last few days felt different. She wasn't sure how much of it had been random. Jenna wanted to believe she was involved in a large puzzle, and her goal was to put it all together. She could embrace that scenario. What she didn't want to hear was George talking about strings.

Jenna had her own personal reasons for continuing the fight and was convinced her decision was a conscious one, of her own free will. She bristled at the thought that she might be someone's puppet. Even the notion that she might be a pawn made her want to scream. Jenna knew enough about chess to realize sacrificing your own pieces was part of a winning strategy. And pawns were almost always never left standing in the end.

"Amazing Grace," George whispered, so quietly Jenna wasn't sure he was awake.

"George, did you... ?"

"The song, 'Amazing Grace.'"

"What about it?"

"It just popped into my head. Probably because of Father Olsen. 'I was once lost, but now I am found, was blind, but now I see.' I didn't even know I knew the words."

Jenna rolled over the other way, so that her back was to him.

"Don't you think it's significant?" he asked.

"I don't know. Maybe. Look, George, if we're going to stay here, then let's get some rest."

He didn't say another word. He rolled over too, and less than a minute later, his breathing deepened.

He was asleep.

Jenna didn't think what George had said was significant. She was pretty sure "Amazing Grace" was the soundtrack in the brain of a lot of people when they died.

CHAPTER 22

THE RUINS LOOKED BUILT OUT OF BODIES. Pillars of them. Archways. Buttresses for shattered stone. The relief convoy drove past Aleppo's new monuments.

Patricia, Carl, and two U.N. workers all shared the same SUV. Tanaka drove. Carl rode shotgun. It had been Patricia's idea to roll down all the windows, to listen for signs of life.

"Oh God," she said, overwhelmed by the smell. "It's worse than the year of the garbage men strike." Trash all across Washington, D.C. had rotted for weeks. At the time, some of Patricia's social circle had characterized the conditions as scenes from a third world country.

Across the back seat from her, one of the U.N. workers, a Polish Jew in his thirties, was thinking of the Third Reich. "My grandparents..." he finally said, staring at the bodies. "They died in the Holocaust. I've always only had photographs to understand what that must have been like for them."

Patricia stared at the young philanthropist as he gazed out at the deaths. Though it wasn't intentional, his musing made hers seem trivial, a reminder of how she and her friends all lived on a hill.

"I'm sorry, people," Carl said, "I can no longer handle the smell." He rolled up the windows via the controls in the center console, and then switched the SUV's filtering system to recycled air. For him, it wasn't the stench of the bodies, but the nauseating, all-encompassing stink of piss and shit.

"Better?" Carl asked Patricia, who was gripping the armrest of her back passenger door.

She took a deep, cleansing breath and nodded, but didn't let go of the armrest. Her fingers dug into the veneer. "Yes."

But it wasn't. The immediate comfort just gave her more time to think. The most horrific thing now, she thought, was how disasters desecrated even the sanctity of death by making each body indistinct. It blurred them until they weren't even human, just unceremonious meat.

One of Aleppo's biggest hospitals had once stood nearby. Now it was one of its biggest gravel pits. At every intersection, Syrian soldiers stood with their backs to each other, assault rifles cradled. Their sights were on the earthquake survivors, who scurried around the streets.

In all the disaster zones Carl had ever visited, the survivors all moved the same, like a hive of insects that had just been sprayed: the asphyxiated shambled like zombies, while the not-yet-dying ran away. He knew that the quick ones scurried to save their families, or to loot for food and gain. At some point, Carl had realized the difference.

"Almost there," he said as they approached the park. Around the fountains and in the lawns is where the Red Cross tents had been set up. The loud hum of portable generators had attracted people to the park from all four quarters.

Tanaka steered their SUV toward the storage area designated for food and medical supplies.

"I've been here before," Patricia suddenly announced, recognizing one of the fountains. "Every day, I bought us lunch in the open market right around here. For John and me."

After a few seconds with no response, a U.N. volunteer from Ecuador said, "Yes, but I think now you were here in another life."

The relief caravan came to a stop, and the screeching of brakes cut through the din of the portable generators. Immediately, hundreds of earthquake survivors descended upon the SUVs. They slapped the windows and clamored for handouts.

Some of them looked angry, shaking fists, beating at the metal and glass. Others had tears cutting down their dirty cheeks. Patricia couldn't understand what they were saying, but she heard an underlying chant: "*Raja'an, raja'an.*" In other words, "please." Even the angry ones were saying it.

From out of the military trucks nearby, Syrian soldiers emerged to push people away from the SUVs. The armed men formed a human shield around the caravan, and a few soldiers fired their AK-47s into the air.

Patricia watched the civilians scatter. "Is that really necessary?" she said. No one in the SUV answered her. Everyone was getting out.

Carl came around and opened Patricia's door for her. "It's okay," he told her.

"I know it is." She took his hand and let him help her out, knowing it was acceptable to show the occasional weakness, but hating it anyway.

The convoy began to unload the supplies into the storage area. "I don't understand it," Patricia said, as she and Carl ran into each other at the back of one of the trucks.

"What's that?" he asked.

"Why are we bringing supplies to some roped-off guarded area? Why aren't we just handing them out?"

Carl said, "You have to believe me, there's a reason this sort of thing evolves a certain way."

"The worst this planet has to offer?" she said, and her tone confused Carl. He couldn't tell whether she was reminding herself of what he said, or accusing him of living down to his own words. He decided to give her the benefit of the doubt.

"Trust me," he said, and he left it at that.

She learned what he meant quickly enough. Several refugees tried to sneak past the armed guards to steal food and medical supplies. Some of them pushed whoever got in their way. One of them pushed Patricia. She dropped the box of bottled water as she fell, and the man swooped down upon it. The guards struck him with their batons and forced everyone back.

"Are you all right?" Carl asked, helping Patricia up.

"Yes," she said, dusting herself off and glancing sideways at the man who'd pushed her. She had never felt so afraid in her life of someone she was trying to help.

Carl picked up her spilled water and gave it back to her.

"Thanks."

He nodded, and then went to get his own box.

Patricia carried hers toward the storage area. She glanced again at the man who'd pushed her, and saw him sitting on a park bench, holding his bleeding head. A young Syrian girl, no older than eight or nine, stood by him, folding her headdress for his wound. No one scolded her for taking it off. His blood was already on it anyway. And on her face.

The little girl looked over and saw Patricia staring, saw the box of bottled water in her hands, none in her own. The girl coughed.

"I assure you," Carl said, startling Patricia from behind, "helping her will only get her trampled to death."

"Then why did we come here?"

Again, her tone confused him. He had already proven that point to her. "There's a right way to hand out these supplies, Patricia. The other way will kill more than it saves."

She didn't like being taught the same thing twice, but she carried the water to the storage area anyway and went back for another load. She hated that he was right.

Unloading the supplies took hours, and took even longer after a group of U.N. workers split off to set up a water treatment system. Patricia offered to help, so one of the workers handed her two steel-reinforced suitcases containing some of the hardware for the system.

"We're setting up the first one near the refugee camp," the U.N. worker said. Patricia told him she hadn't been there yet, and he said, "Just go through the main medical tent, and then out the back. I'll be right behind you."

Before Patricia even reached the tent, which served as the emergency triage center for the Red Cross, she could hear the dull, monotonous moans and piercing screams.

The sights inside were worse. Row upon row of cots. People practically mummified in bandages. Crushed body parts. Missing limbs. Some of them amputated, for the lack of better medical equipment. Amputation was the only viable option at that point.

Patricia realized she was looking at the living dead. The idea hit her so hard and so fast. These people weren't here to be saved, they were here to die.

One girl was screaming down at her missing feet while her father and a nurse tried to console her.

Patricia stumbled through the tent, saw a young boy lying on a stretcher, motionless yet crying. His mother, in broken English, was trying to explain to a nurse that a wall had collapsed on the boy while he lay in bed; the nurse, on the other hand, was trying to use the few Arabic words she knew to explain that the boy's back might be broken. Neither of them fully understood the other.

Almost all of the emergency medical personnel were not locals, Patricia noticed. She had heard that many of Aleppo's medical experts had been killed themselves, or had ended up here on a stretcher.

Near the back of the tent, she heard an old man speaking to the nurse who was changing bandages on his amputated arm and leg.

"Ma ne'dar n'aared 'el 'arwah. 'Eqabna men 'el 'arwah."

Patricia couldn't fully understand the Arabic, but she heard several word repetitions, as if he were reciting some kind of prayer to comfort him.

As Patricia moved past his cot, trying not to stare, not wanting to, the old man's eyes locked onto her as intensely as he gripped the sheets. "We cannot go against the Deva!" he said in English, but with a heavy Arabic accent. "Our punishment is from the Deva!"

Again, he repeated the verse like a prayer. But his piercing eyes and indignant tone added an edge to his words, turned it into a fervent chant that echoed in Patricia's head, joining the cacophony of pain and despair and other prayers so that it seemed louder than the jackhammers and bulldozers before it, louder than anything, and all one song. Something mounted beneath it, a thrum of generators and something else, almost like machinegun fire, only more uniform and more powerful, and quickly on the approach.

Patricia dropped the suitcases and rushed out of the back of the tent, but found no relief. She found acres and acres of the wounded and dying. Some of them lay on bed sheets, cardboard mats, or mattresses. Others just squatted on the streets that usually accommodated hundreds of market stalls. Smoke from campfires and burning trash loomed higher and higher over the camp.

At a distance, the things with loud wings looked like a plague of locusts to Patricia, black through the smoke. Until she realized they were helicopters. It hadn't been machinegun fire she had heard, but propellers, loud enough that she could see the people screaming, but not hear them.

Apparently the Syrian military had begun their curfew sweep, herding everyone off the streets. The helicopters provided guidance from above, while scattered dogs howled and barked.

In the last few seconds, Patricia had lost feeling in her legs. She had almost collapsed, until something caught her eye: Carl Saracen, overlooking the wounded too, and weeping.

"Carl?"

He heard her and quickly turned away, as if she hadn't seen, and Patricia realized the opposite truth to what her husband once said: that tragedies brought out the best in some people.

After drying his face on the sleeve of his coat, Carl turned to Patricia with a look of determination. She admired his attempt and tried to match it. She was no longer quite as faint. And she could feel her legs again. She stepped toward Carl.

"You tried to prepare me..." she said.

"I probably didn't prepare myself," Carl admitted. He pretended that he was just clearing his voice on the last word.

"Tell me that you're all right," Patricia said. "Tell me that you're..." she forced a smile, "completely all right."

Carl broke into a smile too, and then into a genuine chuckle. "Yes, I'm completely all right."

The U.N. worker appeared, carrying more parts of the water treatment system. He saw Patricia standing with Carl, but didn't see her suitcases of equipment.

"I'm sorry," she said, "I left them in the tent." She touched Carl on the arm, and he immediately moved closer to her. "Want to help us construct a water treatment system?"

"I would love to," he said. "I'll go get the stuff you left in the tent."

"No, it's okay. I'll get it."

"Then we'll go together," Carl said, and he followed Patricia toward the tent. She was glad for his company.

———

IN THE TWO HOURS AFTER they had assembled the water treatment system, Patricia estimated that they had given out one hundred two-gallon buckets to as many refugees. She felt proud, as if she had purified the water by running it through her own fingers.

"Can you help me, beautiful woman?" a little girl asked, the same girl with the father who'd tried to steal the bottled water.

Patricia shook her head. "I wish I was half as beautiful as you."

The girl's sweatshirt, several sizes too large, sported a Celtics basketball logo from the U.S. She had rolled up the sleeves so that she could use her hands, and the hems of a dress, pink and cotton, peeked out from beneath the sweater. Under other circumstances, she would have warranted squeals of adoration, which only made the situation more heartbreaking.

"What is your name?"

"Tira." The young girl spoke almost perfect English, with very little trace of an accent.

"Where are your parents?" Patricia asked.

"My mother is back there making dinner. My father has gone to get us more food."

"How's he doing?" Patricia asked.

"He's okay. He says this *whole thing* hurts his head."

One of the spigots from the filtration system continued to pour out clean water into a bucket for the young girl. It burbled half full.

"Well, I'm glad he's okay," Patricia said. "What else can I help you with?"

"Please," she said, "can you help my brother?"

"Your brother? Where is he?" Patricia looked around, wondering if Tira had brought her sibling with her, or if he was somewhere in the refugee camp, one of those who had yet to receive medical help.

"He was in school at the time of the earthquake," Tira said. "He still hasn't come to join us."

Patricia, upset by the news, didn't realize the bucket was full until it overflowed with water. She knelt and twisted the faucet shut, then, still taking a knee, turned back to Tira. They were at eye level now.

"Please, beautiful woman," Tira said, "help me. I miss my brother!"

"Hey, hey, hey," Patricia said, taking out a Kleenex from her pocket. She dampened it a little and cleaned the girl's face. "Sweetie, how do you know your brother is still... ?" She stopped, wondering why she had even started the sentence.

"No, I know he's alive," Tira said. "I saw him and his classmates in a building nearby after the shake-shake. Please, you must go to him and bring him back!"

Tira jumped into Patricia's arms and started planting kisses all over her face, as if to sweeten her request.

Carl came over to empty a bit of water from the bucket, so that it wouldn't spill when the little Syrian girl carried it.

"Did you hear this?" Patricia asked him as Tira continued to shower her with kisses.

"Yes, I heard."

"What do you think?"

"I think the curfew is in effect and there's very little we can do."

Patricia managed to pull Tira away from her face, but the girl wiggled free and resumed her obsessive show of affection.

"Oh my God, look at her. Please, Carl, we need to help."

He shook his head.

"Oh, Carl, how can we not?! Tell me you will help."

He paused, wanting Patricia to think he was torn by the decision. Finally, he nodded. "Fine."

Patricia smiled at him. "Tira," she said, "we're going to find your brother."

The young girl stopped kissing and threw her arms around Patricia. As they embraced, Tira looked up at Carl. He saw she had the same vacant look in her eyes that his own son Ami possessed.

CHAPTER 23

MEN IN THOBES, ANKLE-LENGTH AND LOOSE, carried the brick that had killed their leader, Omar Sheikh Kashmiri. Behind them, even more men carried a stretcher and the body of OSK himself, the body of the face of destruction.

Ilyas Saeed held open the heavy door of Khan al-Shouneh. Wolfenson, who was leaning on Fincher for support, exited first.

"Sir," Reitz said, "are you all right?"

"Prepare our transport," Fincher said when Wolfenson could not. "We'll also need you to pop the hatchback."

Reitz glanced at all the people gathered outside the khan, then at the body and the brick. He finally nodded to Fincher and moved to carry out the requests.

Candles, oil lamps, and fires guttered, and the flickers and shadows congregated around OSK's living corpse as his men carried him toward the Humvee. Some of his followers trailed behind the procession, whispering and eager to catch a glimpse of their fallen leader.

The women came forward, chanting *Mashallah, Mashallah* beneath their shrouds, blessing Wolfenson for the bread. They kissed the brick, or touched it, and they laid pieces and loaves of the bread on OSK's stomach and chest, so much that the pieces tumbled off and were trampled to crumbs beneath their feet. They laid jewelry, too, pendants and rings and bangles of sterling silver and gold. Much of it clinked and clattered to the stone, but some caught on OSK's hands and feet. Medallions dangled by precious chains and caught the twinkling lights.

Reitz started the Humvee and then hopped out. He walked around and opened the hatchback. The guard had laid down one of the seats to accommodate their patient.

Into the plumes of exhaust, the men carried OSK, and carefully, reverently, while everyone looked on, they placed the brick into the vehicle's cargo area and slid the terrorist's stretcher in beside.

Reitz stared at the body. Fincher stepped in front of him and slammed the hatch.

Ilyas Saeed, who had been following in the procession, turned to everyone gathered there. He raised his arms, draped in voluminous robes, and in Arabic he said, "The Imam, our lord, has come back to us from the dead!"

Saeed turned then and kissed the envoy, and everyone knelt in prayer at the diplomat's feet. Wolfenson, given all this attention, blushed. But Fincher realized modesty had nothing to do with the increased blood flow to his face. The Angel of Light was in distress.

"Shukran," said the envoy, barely louder than a breath. "Thank you." He offered a humble bow, but started to fall forward. Fincher grabbed him before he tumbled headfirst into the cobblestone. He helped the envoy into the backseat of the Humvee, and as the doctor was strapping him in, Wolfenson, somewhere between consciousness and somewhere else, said, "I need a... I need a drink..."

Fincher paused—shivered despite the sweat dripping down his side, the perspiration beading on his nose and brow. He clicked the envoy's safety belt and took a seat next to him, shifted once and then settled in.

Reitz shut the back door, then got behind the wheel. As he put the SUV in gear, he checked the rearview, checked on his passengers.

"Where are we going?" he asked.

Fincher said, "Just drive," and then he continued to focus on the envoy.

———

THEY HAD BEEN TRAVELING for a few minutes, back the way they had come, when Reitz spoke up.

"Sir, what's going on?"

Fincher didn't have a satisfactory answer. He had no idea what was happening with the envoy. And he had his doubts about whether they should proceed with the next step in the plan.

"Sir?"

"Reitz, I heard you. I just need another minute."

Fincher had never seen Wolfenson in this condition, even after the attack in Jerusalem when the Angel of Light had first inhabited his host. Slumped, head rolling, the envoy would have slid straight to the floor if he weren't belted in. And his skin tone had changed again, chalk white and covered in sweat.

273

"Sir," Reitz said, "I'm trying to be patient here, but—"

Fincher spoke right over him. "Mr. Envoy, please..." He steadied Wolfenson's head, hoping to rouse him.

"You're not giving me anything to go on. Now I demand to know where we're going—"

"Speak to me."

"Who is this man in back?"

"Can you hear me?"

"And what's wrong with Envoy Wolfenson?"

"John!" Fincher said.

At the sound of his name, Wolfenson twisted his head to look at the doctor, but his eyes never focused. He just stared right through Fincher, as if he were part of the window.

At that moment, the doctor decided to move forward with their plan. Even if the envoy's condition worsened, Fincher would still need a quiet, deserted place to clean up.

"Reitz, take a look at what the envoy programmed into the GPS. That's where we're headed."

Reitz took the device and held it up near the steering wheel, glancing at the touchscreen as he continued to drive. "I'll double-check the latest intel report, but... I don't recall any Red Cross or medical stations anywhere near this location."

"Just drive to those coordinates," Fincher said. "Give me a heads up when we're getting close."

Reitz tossed the GPS onto the passenger seat, then steered the Hummer to the side of the road and engaged the parking brake.

"What the hell are you doing, soldier?"

"Dr. Fincher, I've already told you: I'm no longer part of the military. And even if I was, I don't take orders from you. The man next to you is my client. Now, he either tells me himself where we're headed, or I immediately contact my superior and get the location of the nearest medical station. Because that's what's best for both my client and the critically injured man loaded in back."

To reinforce his threat, Reitz reached into his coat and withdrew a satellite phone, which he showed to the doctor.

Fincher believed the bodyguard was waving the device near his face to taunt him, but before responding rashly, he scanned the neighborhood to assess his options. He discovered they were limited.

This area had not escaped the same wholesale devastation that had affected the rest of city—buildings had been reduced to piles of brick on either side of the street, water erupted here and there, and downed power lines stretched like tentacles down the street. But the real problem was parked on the concrete median.

Two tanks from the Syrian military.

Fincher didn't see any soldiers, but that meant they were either patrolling nearby, or performing their own recon, getting ready to check out the Humvee.

"Listen, Reitz. We have reason to believe all communications around this location are being monitored. With the man we have in the back of our vehicle, a simple phone call might lead to all of us being dead men. Do you understand?"

Reitz unbuckled his seatbelt and turned around in his seat. "No, sir, I do not understand. I demand that you tell me immediately what is happening so I can take the appropriate action."

Fincher pretended to hesitate. "The man in the back... his name is Omar Sheikh Kashmiri."

"OSK? The terrorist?"

"Yes. The U.S. government has been searching for him for years. His group, Zulfiqar, masterminded the bomb plot that—"

"Sir, I know who OSK is. What I don't understand is why we're transporting him in the same vehicle with Envoy John Wolfenson—the very man I'm supposed to protect."

"Because what you don't know is that the U.S. government has asked the envoy to accomplish what no army, spy network or drone has been able to achieve."

"Are you telling me we're bringing OSK in?"

"Correct, soldier. Now if you'll take us to the coordinates programmed in the GPS, we will be rendezvousing with a helicopter sent by army intelligence who will then take custody of OSK."

A steely quality came over the guard's eyes, and Fincher knew he had finally engaged the former soldier's sense of duty.

"And what about the envoy, sir?"

"Let me worry about him. But I know he was proud to be working with the President to locate and secure a very dangerous terrorist." Fincher looked at his watch and shook his head. "Listen, soldier, there's a two-minute window before our contact aborts the extraction. If we don't leave immediately—"

"Understood," Reitz said.

He released the parking brake, put the Hummer in gear, and steered back onto the road. Once again they were driving down the streets of Aleppo, which at one time bustled with honking cabs and cars and dusty buses, and pedestrians trying not to get hit, but now there was nothing except the Humvee.

———

HAVING TALKED HIS WAY INTO MORE TIME, Fincher turned his attention back to the envoy. He noticed that Wolfenson's breathing, which had been labored since loading him into the vehicle, now sounded shallow.

He reached for the envoy's carotid artery, but stopped. Checking Wolfenson's pulse meant touching the scar on his neck, soiling it. The idea made him uneasy. But his emotions only paralyzed him for a few moments. He took a deep breath, then applied his index and middle fingers to the envoy's throat—to the smooth, raised flesh of the healed wound. He quickly added a third finger, and still felt nothing.

Fincher remembered something Carl had said in the hotel freezer—that there were restrictions to the envoy's abilities. Restrictions that made him vulnerable. "The envoy's wearing a human suit," Carl had said. At the time, Fincher had dismissed the idea, choosing to believe the Angel of Light was capable of withstanding anything that would kill a normal human being.

Now he faced the real possibility that the envoy had lapsed into cardiogenic shock, or, more likely, cardiac arrest.

He lifted the envoy's head, intending to check his eyes, but recoiled when Wolfenson began to twitch. Just minor contractions at first, muscles rippling beneath the skin. It stopped briefly, and the doctor almost believed it was over, until it started again, worse than before—violent spasms wracked Wolfenson's entire body. His legs flew out, and his feet thumped the seat in front of him, while his head slammed again and again into the headrest.

Fincher reached out to comfort the envoy, even though he knew his attempt would be ineffectual. Wolfenson lurched forward and knocked the doctor back. If not for his safety harness, the envoy would have wound up in the front seat, as if their vehicle had just been in a head-on collision.

"Doctor," Reitz said, watching the rearview mirror more than the road. "What's going on back there?!"

Fincher didn't respond. He didn't know how to.

When someone was seizing, you could only clear any nearby objects and cushion the head. There was practically nothing else you could do. So the doctor had to just sit there and watch while everything he had built toward for the last two decades came to an end, not with an epoch-changing bang, but with an artery-blocked whimper.

"Doctor, answer me!"

"Reitz, I'm trying my best back here! Just get us to the rendezvous point!"

"Okay!" He checked the GPS and said, "We're about two minutes from the coordinates. Is it possible they'll have a medical team standing by?"

Under other circumstances, the bodyguard's words would have amused Fincher. He had always marveled at how people he was manipulating would, themselves, offer up the means to their exploitation. This time, however, it came as a small relief.

"Yes, Reitz, they've been alerted to the critical condition of OSK. No doubt they can handle the envoy's medical needs too. Just get us there!"

Reitz stomped on the gas, and the sudden acceleration pushed Fincher back against his seat. At the same time, the envoy's spasms came to an end.

The doctor checked again for a pulse.

Nothing.

And then, something.

Very faint.

Fincher timed it on his watch. Only three beats in thirty seconds. But at least the envoy had not gone into cardiac arrest.

He looked up from his watch, only to be greeted by a horrific sight: black foam bubbling out of the envoy's mouth. And his face—the skin had degenerated into a transparent veneer, clear as glass, revealing all of the veins, nerves, and muscles contorting.

Slowly, deliberately, Wolfenson lifted his head from the headrest. He fixed Fincher with completely black eyes and said, "Losing... control..."

Black foam bubbled from his mouth as he tried to say more, and his words faded away, as if he were being pulled from a microphone.

The envoy's skin tone returned to normal and then his eyes also changed, became softer somehow.

Fincher knew immediately it wasn't the Angel of Light who had been revived. It was the *real John Wolfenson*.

John's hand shot out and latched onto the doctor's biceps with almost inhuman force. Fincher struggled to get away, but couldn't.

"Help me," John said, gurgling as if drowning in his own black vomit.

Fincher glanced into the rearview and met eyes with Reitz. Only for a second. And then they both focused on the envoy.

The real John Wolfenson continued to stammer and choke, but finally managed to speak. "A demon is... possessing me... controlling me... *Please... help...*"

"What the hell did he just say?" Reitz shouted.

Fincher winced as he tried again to break the hold on his arm. "The envoy is having a seizure. He's delirious. Just ignore everything he's saying."

John tried to utter more, but mumbled something incoherent. He kept trying, though, as if his life depended on it, and soon enough his words became clear.

"Someone help me... my soul... he won't... release it."

Fincher wanted to cover John's mouth, wanted to silence him, shut him up. But he could do nothing except pry at the bear-trap grip on his biceps. The nails had already punctured his skin.

Then the real Wolfenson pulled Fincher close, close enough that he could feel John's breath on his face, breath that smelled... almost human.

"Please, help me... get rid of him! Doctor, I made a mistake. I've changed my mind and... don't want this anymore. Get him to release me!"

Fincher finally managed to free his arm, but John's other hand snatched him by the throat, clamped down with equal ferocity.

"You have reached your destination."

It was the artificial female voice on the GPS.

Cold, clinical, British.

Gurgling, fainting, clawing at the hand around his neck, Fincher stared into John's wild eyes as the voice reverberated in his head. The eyes, they were still pleading with him, even as the hand was crushing his windpipe.

Either because of the announcement on the GPS, or because he could see Fincher being choked to death, Reitz stopped the Humvee. He jumped out, threw open the back door, and dove headfirst into the fray.

It took all of his strength, but Reitz broke the envoy's hand from around the doctor's neck. Fincher, gasping and hacking, tumbled out of the vehicle and landed on all fours.

He tried his best to regroup. There was no telling what the envoy would do in this frenzied state. Fincher wiped the water from his eyes and checked his surroundings. Beyond the vehicle's headlights, darkness cloaked everything. He had no way of telling whether they had arrived at the place the envoy had pinpointed prior to falling ill.

Fincher climbed to his feet and scrambled to join Reitz, who stood at the back passenger door, frozen in horror as he stared in at the envoy.

"What the hell is happening to him?"

Fincher looked in too. He had no idea whether he was staring at the real John Wolfenson or the possessed one. The envoy's body had lapsed into cyanosis—his skin blue, the tissues near the surface oxygen-starved; and his jugular veins bulged, as if the air was piling up in the circulatory system, piling up against a clot.

Fincher put a hand on the bodyguard's shoulder, but Reitz barely noticed. The doctor knew the guard's inattention would make the next part easy.

"There's nothing more I can do," Fincher said. "We need to just wait for the helicopter. It should be here any—"

John let out a gasp and crumpled into the seat. His head fell back as he slipped into unconsciousness. Fincher was relieved to see his skin tone warm up from blue to red, glad when all his veins retreated beneath the flesh.

"Is he going to be all right?" Reitz asked.

"Yes, soldier, thanks to you. I think I hear the helicopter..."

Reitz turned to look, but ended up staring down the barrel of his own gun.

Fincher had stolen it from his holster.

The single shot rang out in the night, and the bodyguard stumbled backward, clutching at his throat, kicking up dust into the headlights. He staggered silently for a dozen feet and then fell onto his back in the road, right in the high beams of the Humvee.

Reitz's hand, still at his throat, began to tremble, no longer able to apply pressure. Blood bubbled up between his fingers and flowed from the wound, draping his neck in a red scarf.

Fincher waited to see whether Reitz had any fight left in him. He was pleased that his shot had hit above the guard's bulletproof vest, but disappointed at his own marksmanship—Fincher had been aiming for the head.

After a few muscle contractions in his legs, Reitz finally lay still.

The doctor looked around to see if anyone was watching, but he had to admit, in this darkness, his effort was rote. He wasn't too worried. They were operating in a disaster zone, and like a war zone, the normal rules didn't apply.

Holding the gun at arm's length, Fincher crept closer to Reitz. As he came within a few feet, he leveled the weapon at the bodyguard's head.

"Doctor, please," Wolfenson said, laying a hand on Fincher's shoulder. "There's a better way."

He was pale and sweating, and his voice was barely above a whisper, but the Angel of Light stood beside him, once again in control of John Wolfenson's body.

"Envoy, sir, are you all right?

"Yes, I believe I've squashed the rebellion. I'm feeling much better now."

The envoy turned to Reitz's corpse. After a heavy sigh, he took a step toward it.

"Sir, what are you doing?"

"This dying man is too valuable, doctor. He is one of Carl's own, and that connection should serve us well..." The envoy trailed off as he caught sight of Fincher's arm and the bloody nail indentions in his skin.

"Did I... ?"

Fincher covered the marks, ashamed. "Don't worry about it, sir. I'm fine. Absolutely fine."

Despite the doctor's words, the envoy lowered his head in embarrassment.

But his contriteness only lasted a matter of seconds, and then Wolfenson was raising his head and moving toward Reitz all in the same motion. Fincher felt sure there was an internal clock ticking away inside the Angel of Light's head, and he only wished he could tap into it, somehow download the settings into his own brain so that he could better anticipate and service the envoy's next move. The best he could do was simply follow with all of his senses on full alert.

He was just a few steps behind as Wolfenson moved with determination toward the bloody corpse in the glow of the headlights. But then, as they both stood above the bodyguard, Fincher saw the same look on Wolfenson's face just before he resurrected OSK, and all he wanted to do was pull the envoy away before he tried to reverse the doctor's own thoughtless, impulsive act.

"Mr. Envoy, please take a second. After what we just experienced, another... *miracle* might prove to be even more debilitating."

The Angel of Light stepped away from Fincher and repositioned himself in the center of the Hummer's high beams, so that he cast a shadow over Reitz. "I don't blame you for your doubts, doctor. Indeed, you always prove to have our best interests at heart. But please understand, some of the actions you have witnessed... I was undertaking them for the very first time. I wish I had a guide, but like all of your kind, I have been thrown into this world without one. So now I ask you to keep the faith, not only as I handle the problem that lies before us, but also as I overcome all the obstacles on the road ahead."

The envoy dropped to his knees at Reitz's body, and, shutting his own eyes, extended his hand toward the bodyguard's throat. But just as he was about to apply his fingers to Reitz's neck, he looked back.

"Doctor, can you do me the favor of shutting off the headlights? The very last thing I want to do is perform on a stage..."

———

THEY HAD JUST ONE FLASHLIGHT, but the envoy assured Fincher it would be enough. Indeed, as they walked toward their destination, Wolfenson maintained a slow but steady gait, and, for the first time since they had seen the coyotes, his eyes beamed with confidence and determination. The doctor became convinced that wherever the Angel of Light was headed, he could find it in the dark.

"Do not be concerned, doctor. Our new congregation is not much farther." He pointed to the area ahead, and as his hand passed through the doctor's flashlight, Reitz's blood glimmered along the envoy's knuckles.

"Sir, I am not at all concerned," Fincher replied. "I will go wherever you lead."

"Where I lead us is in response to the Landlord. Believe me, doctor, there is no other choice. I had always known my time to execute the plan would be short, but the Landlord continues to enact measures that make it shorter."

The doctor stopped walking. His flashlight illuminated a sunken road, where major sections had collapsed into massive sinkholes. Beyond lay the vague outlines of a once prosperous community.

"Shall we find another way?" Fincher asked.

"No. You need to just walk with me. And with your trust in me, I, in turn, will trust and share with you what I have seen..."

The envoy led the way down the sloping street and around the edge of the first sinkhole. The doctor followed, but had trouble not only with his patience as he waited to hear what the envoy had to share, but also with his own fear. Fincher followed directly behind Wolfenson, but each step he took felt like he was traversing a bed of wet clay.

"Before flying to Aleppo," the envoy said as he pulled Fincher around the other side of a sinkhole, "I saw a man who breathes. But without the lungs of the living."

Perhaps it was Fincher's previous brush with death, or the distraction he felt staring down into the face of death at that very moment—whatever the reason, nothing the envoy said made sense.

"Sir, I'm afraid I don't understand."

"Sorry, it's not my intention to speak in riddles. Let me be clear—there is a man who pursues us both, but he is not truly a man."

"You say he pursues us both?"

"Yes. But as I said, he is not a man. He's one of the Landlord's agents; therefore, I believe he can do me no harm. But he guides and watches over a woman... someone who could be more than an obstacle."

"Who?" Fincher asked, worried that the envoy would consider any human being to be an obstacle. "Do we know her? Have we—"

"Yes. Her brother was possessed by one of my minions."

Fincher paused. "The woman who escaped the train accident, then."

"Yes, I believe that's correct."

The doctor tried to mitigate his reaction to the news. But there was only so much he could do. Not only had he failed to retrieve the Black Pages, he had also failed to eliminate the one woman who now posed a very real threat to their plan.

"When I saw her, she still had cuts on her face," Wolfenson said.

"Envoy, sir, how did you come to know all of this?"

"My eyes are everywhere, doctor. You already know that one of my own possesses Carl's son, Ami. I saw the Landlord's messenger and this woman. They were there to see the boy and to discover answers about our plan."

"Sir, that's evidence Carl has betrayed you."

"Very possible, maybe even probable. But I still allow, indeed hope for the possibility that the Landlord, not Carl, has given these two special guidance."

Wolfenson stopped walking.

"We have arrived at our destination."

Here, the street widened into a courtyard, where a public water fountain stood dry. Next to it, a shrine to display statuary had crumbled into a heap of broken plaster.

"Beyond this fountain, we will find our followers."

"Sir, if I may first ask a question..."

"Of course."

"What shall we do about Carl?"

Even in the dim glow of his flashlight, Fincher could see the envoy's face tear with indecision.

"You know, doctor, I trusted him."

"But it appears he betrayed that trust."

The envoy didn't respond.

"Sir?"

"I'm reluctant to take any action at this time."

"Because of Patricia?"

"Yes. But even when Carl is finished with that role, his services might still be necessary."

"Envoy, sir, we should not allow anyone to get away with such a betrayal. Especially someone so close to you."

Wolfenson stepped away from Fincher, out of his beam of light. As if he no longer wanted his face to be seen. They stood in silence until the envoy's voice eventually emerged from the darkness.

"I am rewarding your loyalty, doctor, with the task of dealing with Carl's betrayal."

Fincher suppressed a grin. "Thank you, sir. I applaud your wise decision."

————

AS THEY WALKED BEYOND the water fountain and shrine, Fincher's flashlight shined on a series of rectangular ventilation shafts at street level.

They approached an oblong building with a massive archway at the front portico. The envoy nudged Fincher to the right of the archway, toward some stone steps descending along a limestone wall.

The stairs appeared to lead to a doorway, but because the opening was located in the middle of the stairwell, Fincher theorized that it originally had been designed as a window, as if the building had been constructed over something else, something older. The window had only recently been widened with hammers and picks.

"This is the passage where the followers of OSK retrieved his body, so they could honor it aboveground."

Dr. Fincher shined his light into the hole. "Is this one of the ancient tunnels to the citadel?"

"Yes," Wolfenson said.

In medieval times, homes in the Old City came with underground escape routes to the fortress on the hill, in case of invaders. The tunnels had been sealed off for ages.

"OSK had a section of them opened as a refuge for Zulfiqar and members of his family," the envoy added.

He squeezed through the opening in the stone wall and disappeared.

Fincher knew better than to hesitate. He stepped into the hole right behind the envoy.

Near the bottom of the stairs, he had to climb over a mound of rubble to the passageway on the other side. The walls were rough in sections, finished with brick in others. Water lapped at the stone, hip deep. Fincher could hear it gushing out from somewhere ahead.

The envoy had already waded into the pool and was proceeding down the tunnel. Fincher, too, lowered himself into the water, which chilled him, enveloped him, but he couldn't falter or tarry long. He had already lost sight of the envoy around the bend.

The tunnel sloped downward as it went, and the water got deeper and deeper until it was chest deep, and the doctor felt as if his heart were palpitating, it was so cold. He came to a large chamber, supported with groin vaults, a nexus for several other passageways, most of them collapsed. Part of the chamber ceiling had also crumbled, exposing plumbing, a busted pipe, which surged and flooded and spurted everywhere, with errant jets of it darting here and there, hissing, and beads of water running along the vault and dripping like rain.

The envoy stood there beneath the falls, arms spread out as the water poured down on him, matting his hair and clothes.

Fincher stepped into the chamber, blinking rapidly as droplets bombarded his eyelashes.

Something bumped into him. Something floating.

A body.

The doctor long ago had mastered his fight or flight response. He grabbed for Reitz's pistol, hands trembling. He brandished it along with his flashlight and turned in a circle, inspecting the chamber, detecting all sorts of floating debris: clothing and bedding and scraps of food.

The envoy stepped in front of him.

"You are safe here, doctor. We are amongst the dead."

Fincher lowered his gun out of respect for the envoy, and wiped the water from his face. Finally, he realized it wasn't just debris floating all around him, but more bodies—dozens of bloated bodies, with long hair and black veils drifting about their heads.

He turned to the envoy for help, only to discover that Wolfenson now stood a dozen feet away, with his body twisted and contorted in a very unnatural pose. John's eyes were shut, and his palms were pointed downwards, with his upper torso rotated in a completely different direction than the lower half of his body. The envoy almost looked as deformed as one of the corpses drifting in the water.

The envoy began to mouth words Fincher could not hear, as if Wolfenson needed his invocation to be part of the hiss and spray of water. But then his words became louder and louder until they overpowered the natural sounds.

"Now hear me, for I am your Deva, your Angel of Light, and I call to those who wish to rise to the top and stand with me!"

All around, Fincher could see waves in the water emanating from the envoy, a vibration that conducted through the floor and the air itself, and small chunks began to fall from the extant parts of the vault.

"I will fill you with the air of life and lift the weight of death that has filled your lungs. Hear me now—come forth! Rise into the vessels I have laid before you! Come!"

Fincher had seen and smelled his share of corpses in all stages from flesh to bone, but never like this. And some of the offal and sewage in the water had collected around him, like filth against a dam. He almost retched.

Only the shock of a more foul sight stifled his compulsion to vomit—a hundred more corpses bobbed to the surface, all in response to the envoy's call.

"I am the Angel of Light, and I will shine the way out of this sad domain! Let us ascend! Let us all storm the gate! Now rise, stand before your lord! Rise!"

The scar on Wolfenson's neck parted like two lips whispering, and vomited blood. Red splats and drops diffused in the water, but, as if it were oil, did not dilute, swimming in ribbons toward the bodies like hundreds and thousands of tiny eels.

One of the floating bodies spit up water. Another sprang upright, its hair whipping and splashing. A third one tried to stand, but its leg must have given out because the corpse fell back into the water and disappeared. Seconds later, it surfaced and started limping forward.

Fincher watched as the crushed, bloated, and misshapen dead emerged from the water all around and, one by one, staggered toward the envoy, who moved toward them as well, touching them, kissing them, and embracing them all, even the ones who couldn't lift their broken arms to envelop him. He let them kiss him, the wound on his neck, as if to feed them, his children, his newborn kin.

Soon, he had disappeared amongst the hundreds.

Fincher stood outside their huddle, barely aware of the water pouring down on him. He tossed the flashlight aside, and it was swallowed up in the flood, the very flood that had taken the lives of the lost and the broken who now gathered around the envoy as if he were God.

CHAPTER 24

"IT LOOKS LIKE THE MOON," Carl said as he maneuvered the SUV over the rocky remains of the Christian Quarter, al-Jdeideh.

They had traveled less than two miles from camp. At least a dozen military patrols had stopped them, though no Syrian soldier kept them long; Patricia and Carl each wore a jacket designating them as volunteers from the Red Cross.

On the dash, the GPS directed them to the school where the girl, Tira, had last seen her brother. The screen showed evidence of streets and city planning. The windshield showed something else.

"Blocked," Carl said, pulling to a stop. "I'm afraid we'll have to go on foot."

Patricia leaned forward and studied the map.

One Sunday morning, over a year ago, she and John had toured the citadel walls. The whole world had stood silently below them. The amphitheater had stood quietly behind. And then all of a sudden, all the church bells in the Christian quarter had begun to sing: Armenian Catholic, Greek Catholic, Maronites, Armenian Orthodox; Greek. John had remarked that it sounded as if the air itself were made of bells.

Patricia had been writing poetry at the time, and she discovered that he liked to feed her lines, like some subliminal muse. He had, as everyone said, a way with words. Some of that was honestly earned. But other times it was because he practiced too much. John liked to hear himself speak.

"You know," he said, "they used to recast the metal of cannons back into bells."

She held up her hand to silence him. Patricia just wanted to listen to the beautiful sounds.

John waited until the last bell had rung, then he added, "It was in medieval times. Sometimes the bells would be named after saints."

"Interesting," she said, because Patricia didn't want to fight. But she was always disappointed when her husband would not allow a special moment to speak to him simply because he was so busy getting ready to speak himself.

According to Carl's GPS, one of the churches with bells stood just in front of them. The windshield showed a roadblock capped in a dome and a leaning cross, as if cannons had blown it all down. It was the first real sign of al-Jdeideh.

"We don't have to do this," Carl said, engine idling. "We could always go back."

Patricia ignored him and started getting out. "Where are the flashlights?"

Carl nodded. "I guess we really are doing this then."

They gathered their backpacks and trekked toward the school through a sprawling, narrow brick maze, obstructed with new mountain ranges. All through her life Patricia had loved hiking. Usually tame trails. But every now and again she challenged varying terrain. She remembered Table Rock, and how, on top, where you could see everything, for 360 degrees, the basalt made interesting cubic architectures of steps and climbs. She could imagine the moon had similar courses, as Carl had implied. But not just the moon.

She opened her mouth to tell him Aleppo was more like the rockier Mars, but he spoke first.

"Did you know al-Jdeideh, in Arabic, means 'the new'?"

"No," she lied. "I wasn't aware."

"Yeah. The Christians were able to build so many mansions and palaces because they built outside the Old City walls, in their own little cell. So they became kind of like the brokers between foreign merchants and the locals."

"Interesting."

Patricia knew the history lesson was meant to calm her down, which was why Carl had omitted the part he obviously didn't think she knew: that the Christian quarter had been built after a Mongol siege—after the Mongol leader had ordered the construction of a tower outside the city; a tower of twenty thousand skulls.

But Patricia didn't need a tour guide or anyone to comfort her. For the first time in Aleppo, she felt she had a chance to make a real difference.

She didn't stop Carl from prattling though. His lecture seemed partially for his own benefit, something to keep his mind off the endless

295

mineral mounds and mountainous dead ends to which his GPS always seemed to lead them.

Sometimes the destruction had been retained by the fragment of a westerly wall, which probably had some great historical significance, as most walls in the area. As if every single unit of masonry had been individually blessed, or bled upon, or consecrated by someone's tomb.

"Oh, this isn't good," Carl said, shining his light on one of the very few shops left extant. People had shattered the storefront glass, and had stripped the shelves completely bare. Judging by the glimmering chandeliers and Persian rugs, with their geometrical pattern and sub-patterns, and their number of floral and fractal motifs, the shop had dealt in antiques.

"If the quake didn't destroy your business," Carl said, "the survivors finished the job."

Patricia put a hand on his arm. "I know. The worst this world has to offer. That's why we need to find this school."

He shook his head. "With all due respect, this GPS is the only thing that's kept us from moving in circles. We've been walking for a solid hour, and we're no closer than when we first landed."

She didn't appreciate the exaggeration, but knew what he meant. She had sensed they were in trouble the minute he started acting like a lost sailor navigating by the light of some far-flung star.

"If this next street doesn't put us back on track," Carl said, "I'm afraid we'll have to call it quits."

Patricia never got the chance to protest. Something growled in the dark alleyway ahead of them.

Carl, spinning, drew his weapon, a GLOCK 9mm with its own tiny flashlight. He had donned the shoulder holster right before leaving camp.

"Wait here," he said, moving forward.

Patricia started to call out to him, but didn't.

A few more careful steps and Carl could see into the alleyway. Four sets of eyes shined in his light.

A pair of medium-sized feral dogs was rooting through the trash in the narrow corridor of open shops and stalls. He noticed that, once again, the stores had been broken into, the glass fronts shattered. One of them had been a restaurant, and suddenly the presence of dogs foraging for food made sense. As with most disasters, the earthquake had created its own food chain, with human scavengers second above all the rest.

Carl fired a shot into the air. The dogs startled and scurried away, their nails scrabbling on cobblestones and over toppled bricks.

"Just dogs," he said, and holstered his gun as they resumed their walk.

Even in the dim aura surrounding his flashlight, Patricia could see the deep lines of tension on his face.

"So I take it you want to go back?" she asked.

"Yes, that's definitely on my wish list. Actually, more like my to-do list."

"Okay, so I want to hear about this to-do list of yours," Patricia said. She needed to keep him talking about anything but turning back.

"Well, one of the items includes keeping *you* safe. Because that's what I promised your husband I'd do."

"Duly noted. So what else?"

"Meeting up next week in Jordan with my wife and sons is definitely high on the list."

They came upon large puddles reflecting the moon. In the disaster footage broadcasted back in Tel Aviv, Patricia remembered that the local Syrian law enforcement had fired water cannons to purge hundreds of looters from shuttered shops. But she imagined the water in this part of the city had formed from some other event; the tight, twisty alleyways could hardly play host to water weapons.

Carl, glancing at his digital map, hesitated at a puddle's edge.

"It's not a moat," Patricia said, and she splashed right through it.

Carl crossed with more caution.

"So," Patricia said once he had caught up, "I trust finding Tira's brother is not on your to-do list?"

"I'm sorry, but no. Finding that girl's brother would be wonderful, and I know it would mean the world to you, but that definitely is one for the wish list."

"Sounds like you got this whole list thing down pat."

He didn't offer a retort—because he had stopped walking.

Patricia stopped too. "What's—"

"Shhh!"

Carl scanned with his flashlight all around. Ruinous shadows leapt. Patricia saw a few black dogs, just shades that stretched and ran away, but other than that, the flashlight revealed nothing.

She noticed for the first time that the sound of helicopters had receded in the distance. She could hear her own breath, and Carl's too. She almost expected the church bells to ring.

Then Carl started walking again.

"I guess my whole life is a balance between my wish list and to-do list," he finally said. "And then there's the scared-shitless list."

Patricia laughed. "Oh my God, another list!"

"Yes, and I fear the scared-shitless list is overriding everything else."

"You? Scared shitless? Hard to believe." She was glad to have loosened him up enough that he would admit to being unnerved. "Give me an example of the scared-shitless list."

He shrugged. "Ending up as just another body on the street, piled up but totally alone."

Patricia stopped Carl with a hand on his arm. "But you're not alone."

A figure ran across the beam of his flashlight—a small figure in a red parka.

Carl whirled around but the figure was gone.

"Did you see that?"

"Yes," Patricia said, and she took off running.

All the passages and cross passages seemed to double back, circle around, and yet twist a slightly different way each time.

Her flashlight, and Carl's light behind her, both crisscrossed, catching flickers of red parka as the figure dashed down one passageway after another, splashing through the puddles like a child.

"You need to stop!" Carl said as he caught up and grabbed Patricia's arm.

The red-cloaked figure vanished down an adjoining alley, into deep fog.

Carl had pocketed his flashlight and was gripping his pistol instead, using its tactical light. Patricia was surprised by his reaction. She didn't say anything though; she was already wondering why a child would run rather than greet people who could provide aid.

"Wait—do you hear that?" she asked, holding up a finger and concentrating on a distant sound. "I think it's..."

"Children singing," Carl finished.

Patricia started forward again, but he still held her arm.

"Don't you go running off without me. We either do this together, or we turn back right now. And I mean it."

She nodded. "Fine. Lead the way."

Carl nodded, too, and led with his gun.

Flooded, potholed, the alleyway served as a nave to the narthex of fog. Even with their lights, they could see no more than a few feet in any direction.

Carl decided to trust his ears and follow the singing. "This way," he said, taking Patricia's hand.

They almost ran into a fountain, which stood dry despite the surrounding pool of water.

"Must be a courtyard," Carl said. They made their way around the fountain, and the fog began to dissipate. "I think... I think this is one of Aleppo's numerous—"

"Shh," Patricia said, "listen."

The choir of children suddenly stopped.

Carl lifted his GLOCK.

"Really, Carl? Do we really need a gun?"

"I'm not taking any chances."

They approached the building where the singing seemed to originate, and Carl pushed open the wooden door, thrusting his pistol inside.

"What is it?" Patricia asked.

He put his gun back in his holster and waved her over. "Come see."

In the dim glow of candlelight, Patricia made out at least thirty children seated at one of the many tables. The kids were passing around two giant bowls of fasulye stew, serving themselves before handing the bowl to the next classmate in line.

At the head of the table sat an older man, so short and delicate that, except for the beard and the bald spot, he might have passed for a child.

Carl and Patricia's presence didn't seem to alarm either the kids or the bearded man. They simply glanced up and then went back to their food.

Carl took a few moments to look around. He put his hand on a nearby wall. He walked over to another and hit it with his fists. Then he came back to Patricia.

"I don't like the look of these crossbeams," he whispered. "And those fresh cracks in the plaster... This building could go at any time."

She nodded. Then, with a look of determination, she approached the bearded, balding man at the head of the table.

"Excuse me," she said, "do you speak English?"

Her question elicited a round of laughter from the children. But then the older man tapped his fork on the table, and the kids immediately turned back to their meals.

"I speak perfect English," he said. "Would you like some of our dinner?"

"Thank you, that's very kind. But I'm wondering if we could speak with you for a moment."

"Certainly." He got up from the table and walked with her a few feet away. Not really far enough for a private conversation, but it would have to do.

"Are you the teacher of these children?" Patricia whispered.

"Yes, this is my fourth grade class. My name is Adad. Would you like to join us?"

"Again, that's very nice, but... is this where you teach your class?"

"No. The school was destroyed. We were brought here by a woman who saved us."

"Oh, that's excellent. Someone from the U.N. or...?"

Adad pointed to an old woman across the room. "She is the one who saved us. She is the one."

The woman stood near the room's entrance, beside a wooden column. Patricia and Carl must have walked right past her on their way in. Which, despite the woman's proximity to the door, was understandable, she stood so still, just staring down at the floor. Long black hair hid all but a few pale slices of her wrinkled face.

What caught Patricia's attention now was the old woman's red parka.

She exchanged a confused look with Carl. The woman had to be twice as tall as the child they had chased.

"We were in the middle of a lesson when she rushed into the room and told us all to leave," Adad said. "She told us the earth would shake and... swallow all the lovelies, is what she said. So we followed her outside, and that's when everything around us started falling."

Adad teared up and it took him a few moments before he could continue. "We heard the screams of my friends and... other students and.... That woman, she brought us here and she gave us this food. We are all alive because of her."

Patricia glanced at the old woman, who still stared at the ground. She had heard this kind of story before. Sometimes a pet would sense something coming and would forewarn its owner, or sometimes a person would save a bunch of lives from an imminent disaster that no one could have seen coming.

"You are fortunate," Patricia said.

Carl agreed. "But that'll all end if you don't leave here immediately."

Adad cocked his head and frowned.

"My friend's right," Patricia said, "this building doesn't look safe. If there's another quake or aftershock... Please, you have to come with us to the Red Cross."

Adad shook his head. "I will only go when she says we should go. Please, speak with her. Ask her when we should leave this place."

Adad took his seat at the table with the kids, and Patricia looked over at Carl, who motioned for her to follow through with the request.

She looked again at the old woman, at the black veil of hair covering her face. Black, in spite of her age. The woman neither lifted her head nor moved a muscle as Patricia approached.

"Excuse me, but... do you speak English?"

The woman nodded.

"Okay, excellent. My name is Patricia, and I'm from the Red Cross. What is your name?"

"Sabeen," the woman said to the floor.

"Well, Sabeen, Adad over here tells us you saved all of these children. Is that true?"

"Why wouldn't it be true? Do you not believe what someone tells you?" Sabeen scurried to a different part of the room.

Impulsively Patricia reached out to stop her, but pulled back at the last second. Physical contact between a Western woman and a Middle

Eastern woman would have ended the conversation more conclusively than Sabeen's sidestepping.

Patricia looked over at Carl, and he took a step toward her, obviously thinking he could help. She held up her hand. She could handle this.

Confidently, assertively, she strode across the room. "Sabeen, I definitely believe you saved the lives of these children."

The woman in the parka said nothing as she stared at the floor.

"But I need you to help me save them again. We need to lead them to the Red Cross, where they'll be safe."

Sabeen looked up at Patricia, right into her eyes, and deeper. Patricia tried not to look away, tried not to be intimidated, and then Sabeen suddenly turned away from her, as if someone had spoken her name.

Patricia turned, too, and saw nothing, just the flickers of candlelight and shadow play.

Sabeen nodded a couple times, as if agreeing with something, then she tried to turn back—once, twice, but both times she stopped and listened; her imaginary friend had more to say.

The third time, she turned back uninterrupted. "How can we trust *you*, when you don't even hear the music in everyday life?"

"I don't... I don't know what that means."

Like anyone else, Patricia had dealt with her fair share of mentally unstable people: like the man in army fatigues in Bethesda who had chased all the parents and kids out of the park with his rant about worldwide conspiracies; or the patient in Dr. Hartman's waiting room who had torn pages out of a magazine and shoved them into her mouth, to "eat away all the hurt in the world."

Both Hartman's patient and the man in fatigues had shared the same vacant stare. Sabeen shared it as well. Patricia did her best to ignore it.

"Maybe I'm just not getting it," she said, "but no matter what, I promise you can trust me—"

Gently, Sabeen touched Patricia's wrist. In a soft, even tone, she said, "Ever since Scotty died, you have stopped hearing the music."

"Look," Carl butted in, breaking Sabeen's hold on Patricia. "We're just here to help—"

Patricia put a hand on his shoulder. "It's all right, Carl. I have it under control."

She stepped around him and led Sabeen by the arm to the darkest corner of the canteen. Only a few kids glanced up from the table, but then dug right back into their fasulye stew. They all ate very quietly.

"How did you know about my son?" Patricia asked.

"Because. He's here, in the dark of the light. I hear him. He sings."

Patricia checked once more, but if somehow the candlelight and shadow embodied her son, she couldn't pick up on it.

"He wants me to ask you something. He wants to know why you have not given his glove to Ryan."

Patricia had already begun to rationalize how Sabeen could have known about Scotty, how she could have guessed. But this last revelation hit her hard.

On his death bed, Patricia's son had asked her to give his Little League mitt to his best friend, Ryan. Patricia had promised. But she changed her mind, after he died. The leather held his scent, and was scuffed from all the pitches he had caught, as if this weren't an empty glove but her flesh and blood.

Carl saw the tears spilling out of Patricia's eyes, and once again moved toward her. She waved him away.

"How do you know about the baseball glove?" she asked Sabeen, who had regressed to staring at the floor.

"Tears so fill your eyes that you cannot see your own son. He is there and wants to be with you." The woman's bony old claw latched onto Patricia's arm. "He wants to return to you, but you refuse to open the door so he can walk back!"

"What are you talking about—what door?!"

Sabeen pulled her close. "A baby," she whispered, cupping Patricia's abdomen as if feeling for a kick. "Give him new life and you will hear it, the music once more."

CHAPTER 25

EVERYTHING ABOUT IT HAD BEEN STAGED. And now the curtain began to fall on Carl's exercise in manipulation, his stage play, utilizing not actors, but real people reading from a script, in a setting that could only convince his audience of one that everything around her was real.

"Promise me you will listen for the music," Sabeen said as Patricia and the last child filed out of the building.

"Yes, I promise."

The psychic took her hand. "The door that your son is waiting to walk through: it will only open if you allow the music to fill your heart."

She said each word exactly as the envoy had planned it. Almost as if he were inside her, working the old woman's vocal cords.

"Those precise words must echo in Patricia's head as you lead her back to me," Wolfenson had told Carl days ago, when they had met to work out the details of this elaborate con.

Carl had wanted to ask why the exact wording mattered, but he didn't bother. At a certain point he had decided to simply follow orders. Or at least appear to.

Sabeen performed her blessing to release the children and gave each child a chunk of bread. And while Adad collected all their belongings, Carl used his satellite phone to call his men. This action, like everything else, was for show. He almost felt like his arm wasn't his own.

Three vans already stood by at the bottom of the hill, and had been for hours, prepped and ready to transport the children to the Red Cross. The path there, through the narrow, twisting cobblestone streets, had already been mapped out.

All according to plan.

Except for what happened next.

Patricia was leading the schoolchildren through the city, holding a boy and a girl's hand, telling them all that they were going to a better place.

And then she started to sing.

Carl recognized the old Arabic tune: "The Chicken Song." He and his own boys had sung it hundreds of times.

Now, without hesitation, all the children he had hired struck up a choir with her, and they started skipping and harmonizing and singing as one.

None of it was in the script.

Right before his eyes, Carl's carefully orchestrated drama had transformed into a real-life fairy tale. Patricia and the children seemed to be traipsing through an enchanted forest instead of climbing over old masonry ripped apart by the earth's tectonics.

At the end of the first song, while the children were giggling and laughing and quieting down, Patricia segued into a traditional Arabic lullaby called "Sleep." The children accompanied her even more boldly than before, and the noise of distant helicopters morphed into a beat.

Carl turned off his flashlight, and the foreboding darkness gave way to moonbeams, twinkling in shattered glass like shiny jewels embedded in a path to another world.

Along the way, he and Patricia locked eyes only once. Somehow she had become transformed since hearing Sabeen's words. She radiated with confidence and energy, no longer the pathetic victim of a dark deception that had stretched across an ocean and two continents, and incalculable time.

He watched as Patricia danced back and forth in the moonlight, singing and drifting ahead of the children like an angel leading them to a better place.

Then, when Carl wasn't looking, someone slammed shut the book of fairy tales. The singing, the high spirits, the spontaneous beauty that had corrupted his script—it was over, it was done.

He couldn't pinpoint exactly when the enchantment had faded. Sometime between loading the children into the vans and his radio transmission to his operative at the Red Cross. But Carl could pinpoint with great accuracy when he had discovered the disenchantment for himself: when he saw Patricia staring out the window, not at all like someone who had just saved the lives of twenty-three children.

"Excuse me," he said, sitting down next to her in the front seat of the van. "Is this the same woman I just saw a few minutes ago?

Where's the bubbly spirit, the song on her lips... the sparkle in her eyes?"

In the window, Carl could see Patricia's reflection as she looked out at the silhouettes of the ruinous night.

"I guess it's gone," she said. "I know you must be disappointed. Especially because the bus is full, so it's not as if you can change seats."

Carl was speechless. He hadn't anticipated her being quite so cold.

When he didn't say anything for a while, Patricia realized how she must have sounded and turned to face him. "Sorry. I'm just tired."

"Well, we've had quite the evening."

The driver eased their vehicle out into the street, and the other two vans in the caravan followed suit. It wouldn't be long before they arrived at the Red Cross.

"Patricia, something tells me you're not just tired. If you don't mind me asking... are you all right?"

She tried to answer Carl's question immediately, but got off to a false start. She had to stop three times before finally coming up with an appropriate response.

"I guess so. But I have a feeling I won't know for sure... maybe for a while. Does that make any sense? I don't know, I guess I'm still processing it all."

She fell silent again and turned to stare out the window, as if she could salvage some insight to her confusion from all the wreckage.

When the plan had first been outlined to Carl, Dr. Fincher mentioned the probability of Patricia slipping into a state of contemplation. He said it was normal, and encouraged. But even though Fincher believed small minds could be easily read, Carl knew no one was one hundred percent predictable. He couldn't afford to let Patricia brood in silence. Not without some hint as to her state of mind. The envoy had too much riding on this plan to be so inattentive. What Wolfenson didn't realize was that Carl depended on it as well.

"Hmm," he said, "why don't we start with how you feel?"

Patricia immediately turned to him, as if she had been waiting for that exact question.

"I feel like somehow I was supposed to always come here... to this exact spot... to this night. And not just to experience it, but to embrace it, so I could change the direction of my life."

She didn't even glance at the children as she said it, but Carl behaved as if she were referring to their great rescue mission.

"I think I understand. Something brought you here—"

"Yes."

"—to save the lives of these children. I can see why anyone would believe that was a turning point in their life."

She sat up in the seat, now fully engaged. "But it wasn't just the children. Sure, they helped. But it was so much more than that."

Carl pretended to be confused, then concerned. "Patricia, what exactly did that old woman say to you back there?"

She almost answered, but then thought better of it.

Carl figured she didn't want to repeat the words Sabeen had said, lest she jinx the prophecy and somehow ruin the magic. Or, he thought, she was afraid Carl would laugh, afraid he might try to debunk whatever the crazy woman had uttered by candlelight.

"I'm comfortable telling you only that I feel like I'm on a different path," she said. "For the first time in a long time, I feel like I have a direction."

Carl acted as if her confession affected him deeply. He tried to speak, but then stammered. His effort eventually ended in silence. When he tried again, he loaded his words with emotion.

"It makes me feel good that something wonderful can come out of such a truly awful disaster. And I'm really proud that I was here for you... and that we did this together."

"Thank you, Carl. Thank you for everything you've done."

She reached out and touched his face.

He knew more than a few things about a woman's touch, and what it meant. There were many variables, including the context of the gesture, the setting, the placement of the touch, and the length. It could express comfort with your company, or, of course, desire. It could even be an act of aggression, an attempt to make another person jealous.

Patricia's touch, whether subconsciously or by design, was so brief it sent a clear message—she might as well have spoken it aloud: whatever connection they had shared that night, it had ended with the rest of the fairy tale.

———

THE THREE VANS PULLED UP in front of the Red Cross tents. Over a dozen physicians waited to examine the children as they disembarked. Carl had hired these doctors the moment the earthquake hit. They had been flown in hours ago, and had been put on standby for this very moment.

Carl walked up and down the examination area. He personally wanted to oversee the operation and make sure each child was carefully attended to. As it turned out, the checkups were necessary. Two of the kids suffered from serious medical issues: one from undiagnosed asthma, and the other from walking pneumonia, a condition she had developed prior to the earthquake; she certainly had not contracted it while working for Carl. Left unattended, those two children might have died. He felt absolved knowing that his effort would dramatically improve these children's lives.

"Stage manager"—those two words had been flashing in his head the entire night. The envoy had given him the job title, as if bestowing him with a princely crown.

"You will be our stage manager in Aleppo, Carl. Totally in charge of convincing Patricia to ignore her brain and think with her heart."

Carl's personal wealth, combined with the companies in which he had a controlling interest, totaled nearly a billion dollars. And for over two decades, he had worked to coordinate the envoy's arrival. Certainly that effort alone should have guaranteed him a meaningful seat as the grand plan was being spitballed into existence. Yet somehow, in the Angel of Light's estimation, he amounted to no more than stage manager, tasked to supervise the workings of a fictional drama.

After the doctors finished the medical examinations, Carl directed the children toward half a dozen trailers, parked near the main medical tent. His men had driven them in from Jordan so the kids could wait in relative comfort for their families.

While Carl waited too, he couldn't escape the thought that, once again, the envoy had used innocent children to achieve his goals. It was bad enough that the Syrian kids served as props, or set dressing. The Angel of Light's use of Patricia's dead son, Scotty, was especially sickening.

Clearly, Wolfenson knew there was seldom better leverage than children. Often in lives filled with disappointment and crushed ambitions, parents end up transferring all of their hopes and dreams to their kids. So what better way to control someone than to have a foot on their daughter's neck, or have their son's soul drowning in the belly of a demon?

After a while, the guards appeared, escorting a parade of adults to the children's trailers. Each family would receive not only food and money, but a safe place to stay if their home had been destroyed. And, of course, each child would be no worse off than when Carl had taken them. He only wished he had been treated the same way.

Patricia, he thought, suddenly glancing around.

In his quest to look after the Syrian children, he had somehow lost sight of her. And he couldn't help but be astounded, not only because he had misjudged her—he had just assumed Patricia would take as much interest in the children as he had—but also because he was shocked how much he had lost sight of his own priorities. His entire future depended on this woman. How could he have let her disappear?

Carl checked the trailers. He checked the vans. He did a thorough search of the medical tent.

No sign of Patricia.

He dispatched a couple of men to hunt for her in the refugee camp. Maybe she had gone there to find the young girl, Tira, who had sent them on the rescue mission in the first place. Little did Patricia know, the girl didn't even live in the city. Carl had arranged for Tira and her father to fly in from Lebanon, with instructions on what to do. Most likely, the father and daughter were flying home that very minute, all the richer.

A caravan of vehicles arrived at the temporary hospital, and when Carl turned to check out the commotion, he finally caught sight of Patricia.

She emerged from the supply tent with a bounce in her step. At first, Carl thought she was moving toward him, but she headed for the caravan instead.

The first vehicle, a Humvee, pulled up behind one of the vans Carl had used to transport the Syrian children. The passenger door flew open and Envoy John Wolfenson stepped out. Immediately Patricia threw herself into his arms.

They kissed.

With the passion of lovers who haven't seen each other for years. Or, Carl thought, with the freshness of two people who had never before touched lips.

The display of affection proved that his plan had succeeded. And yet Carl couldn't explain how.

How was it possible that Patricia believed she could fly halfway across the world and repair a relationship while sifting through the rubble and shattered glass of a devastated city? How could she believe there was any chance of finding something she had lost years ago amidst the piles of dead bodies or in the eyes of survivors whose dreams and loved ones had been crushed by falling stone?

The envoy had been certain his plan would work, citing the dubious human desire to find new possibilities or a different approach to the grim, unavoidable fate staring them in the face. Wolfenson claimed that even the old scar of a child's death could become an asset rather than an obstacle, if repackaged and staged in the right light. Once again the envoy had proven how well he understood human nature: Patricia was clinging to her husband like she never wanted to lose him again.

Admittedly, Carl had been foolish to assume he could outmaneuver the Angel of Light. But he still had no choice. The envoy was holding Ami hostage in his own body. And the envoy had given Carl a list of names, two columns written in pencil, as if each name could be erased when the job was done.

"Sir," someone said, "the envoy demands to speak with you."

Carl didn't recognize the voice, and, when he turned around, he barely recognized the man.

It was Reitz. But he looked... younger. More than that, he had a new scar on his windpipe—from a bullet wound. As if he had been shot that night and had magically healed.

"Excuse me," Carl said, "what did you say?"

"I said, the envoy—"

"No, I heard you. You don't have to repeat yourself. But some subtitles might help. Specifically for the word *demands*."

Reitz just stared at him.

Without all of his personal experiences with the man, Carl might have assumed his employee had numbed himself with opiates. But he knew Reitz, and he knew there was zero possibility of drugs.

Possession gap, Carl thought.

As a licensed pilot, he knew that if you could fly one plane, you could probably fly any other, but not without spending some time getting to know the controls. Carl had seen enough possessions to know that demons endured a similar learning curve, and it always caused a lapse in intellect and social skills.

Reitz said, "I'm sorry, Mr. Saracen, please forgive me. The envoy would like to speak with you." He started to move, obviously expecting Carl to follow him. Only after a few yards did he realize he was by himself.

Reitz came walking back. Patiently, showing no sign of anger, fear, embarrassment... nothing.

"Sir, is there something wrong?"

"Yes, there is." Carl got right in his face, the face of a man he had known for years—a face which he no longer recognized. "Tell me, soldier, tell me right now. What happened to you out in the field?"

Reitz froze, as if his mask had just fallen off at the most important moment during a masquerade ball. "Sir, I don't know what you're talking about—"

"I asked you what are the conditions in the field, soldier?!"

"Everything is 10k, sir."

"10k?"

"Yes, sir."

Carl backed off and fell silent for a few moments, pretending to be contrite. "Thank you, Reitz. I guess I'm getting paranoid in my old age."

"I understand, sir." The guard waited a respectable beat before continuing. "The envoy said the matter's very urgent."

Carl nodded, and this time he followed Reitz. He had gotten what he wanted—confirmation that a man whom he trusted, with whom he had been through thick and thin, was now at the end of someone else's leash.

As they walked toward the main Red Cross tent, Carl thought about a job back in Baghdad, when his security firm had been hired to escort

U.S. officials between the Green Zone and the airport. One day, Carl was behind the wheel of a Humvee, convoying a high-level White House official and her support staff. Reitz, riding shotgun, had just gotten off the sat phone with their air support.

"What's the status?" Carl had asked.

Reitz tried to tell him everything was clear for the next 10k, meaning six miles. But his dry mouth and frayed nerves mangled the message: "Everything is 10k, sir."

Not a second afterward, one of the transport units ahead of them exploded and flew off the road. Gunfire rained down on every single vehicle in the caravan.

The siege had lasted nearly four hours, and he and Reitz barely escaped. But they did escape. And it led to a special relationship between them.

Over the years since then, when they got in the middle of a threatening but unnervingly quiet situation, one of them would inevitably say, "Everything is 10k." Saying it aloud had become their lucky rabbit foot, and an inside joke.

But a demon who had just recently commandeered Reitz's body, and who was pushing buttons in a blind panic, wouldn't know that. Carl had come to learn that the devil and the rest of his legion didn't believe in the concept of luck. And none of them seemed to have a really keen sense of humor.

CHAPTER 26

S HE KNEW DOCTORS SOMETIMES said completely vacuous things.

"Your child appears to be a real fighter."

"We've done all we can."

"We'll just have to wait and see."

During her son's hospitalization, Patricia had heard most of them, if not all. She had begun to think the problem was that the doctors always talked to her in Scotty's room. She thought perhaps they were afraid he might overhear. That he might give up the ghost.

Eventually she realized that wasn't the case: doctors were equally as capable of conveying a message in other ways. A grim look, a heavy sigh, a perfectly timed lowering of the head.

Patricia's husband was getting that grim look now, from two doctors volunteering under the banner of the Red Cross. The doctors hadn't gotten to the heavy sigh yet, but she knew it was just around the bend.

"Why can't any of you say anything?" John said, barely able to keep his voice down despite all the patients sleeping in the main medical tent around him. On the cots nearest him lay the nineteen patients he had saved.

If Patricia knew one thing about her husband, she knew he had always been a talker. His entire professional life revolved around meetings where the whole point was to converse. If a diplomat from another country came to discuss a border dispute, and the man's main mode of communication consisted of staring at John with a grim face, and, later, delivering a heavy sigh, Patricia's husband would send for indigestion medicine.

"I know for sure that none of these victims have much time," he told the doctors. "So let's at least start with one of you telling me what we're up against!"

"Sir," said Pavil, the younger of the two; he had an Indian accent. "You must understand that we are having trouble saying to you what we both have sadly observed..."

Earlier, Patricia had overheard some nurses talking about Pavil. He had recently earned his medical license in India, but before beginning his residency in the States, he was traveling through the Middle East. When he heard about the earthquake, he immediately grabbed a night train from Damascus.

The young doctor said, "It's because your courageous effort to bring these people to us that makes it so difficult for any of us to tell you the harsh news."

John lowered his voice. "Are you saying that a few of them will die?"

"I'm sorry, sir, I said... *harsh news*. There's nothing we can do... for any of them."

As it turns out, the heavy sigh came from Patricia. John stared at Pavil, then looked at his wife, as if to make sure he had heard correctly.

Finally John turned back to both of the doctors. "Maybe you two are tired. I bet you've been working around the clock. Because the last time I checked, every one of the nineteen people we dug out of the rubble were still breathing."

Pavil bowed his head. "Unfortunately, sir, as I said, there is nothing that we can do."

Carl stood a few feet away, waiting for the envoy's response. He wished he had a video camera to capture it all. So far, Wolfenson had not disappointed. But Carl was sure he was just warming up.

"When I brought in these helpless people, I figured what I might get from one of you doctors was... false hope. And I thought that would be the worst thing in the world. But clearly I was wrong. In this tent, apparently false hope isn't even on the menu. Because it appears somehow I delivered my patients to a morgue."

Patricia touched John's arm. He didn't ignore the gesture the way people often do when they are losing their temper and someone tries to soothe them. In fact, he gently and lovingly tapped Patricia's hand as it rested on his sleeve.

Carl had tears in his eyes. Not from anything Wolfenson had said, and not from the physical affection between him and his wife. It was just, one of the nineteen patients lay a few feet away, and the bodily gasses and involuntarily secretions were getting to him.

At least one goal of this whole charade was undoubtedly for Wolfenson to close the deal with Patricia. But other than that, Carl was stumped. He had spent the previous hour examining all of the nineteen bloody, battered, disfigured people the envoy had brought in, and if John had asked for his opinion instead of Pavil's, Carl would not have given him a grim expression. He would have said it outright—these people belonged in caskets.

The envoy was clearly working another angle, but for the life of him Carl couldn't figure out what it was.

"Don't worry, honey," John told Patricia, "I'm all right. I just want to make sure I've got the facts straight. If there was something I could have done, and should have done, then I will spend the rest of my life thinking about it."

He took his wife's hand off his arm and stepped away, leaving her a safe distance behind him as he confronted the two doctors.

"And believe me, gentlemen, when I tell you I will spend the rest of my life thinking about tonight, I also mean I will spend the rest of my life making sure you both think about it right along with me."

The other doctor, who had yet to speak, took a couple steps toward John. He pushed Pavil behind him as if to shield the young doctor from any collateral damage.

"Everyone keeps calling you *sir*," he said. "I don't know why, and frankly I don't care."

Oh boy, Carl thought, bracing himself for the fireworks. He didn't know the doctor's name, but he knew the man was a retired OB/GYN from Chicago; he had come to the country with his sister to see some of ancient Petra. When the earthquake hit, he drove his rental car over four hundred miles to lend a hand.

Earlier in the evening, he and Carl had met outside the main tent. OB/GYN from Chicago, a two-pack-a-day smoker who hadn't lit up in two days, had tried to bum a cigarette. Carl had nothing to offer him because he didn't smoke.

"You're apparently confused about the *menu* here, so let me see if I can help," the doctor went on. "My colleague tried to show you some courtesy, but you'll only be getting one serving of that dish tonight. So let me prepare it for you a different way, but this time without any garnish—all the people you brought in here are going to die. Period. Now please remove all your patients immediately because we need the tent space. And just so you don't think you're the only one going crazy, I'll back your assessment that this isn't much of a hospital. I've been here for over two days and have felt like an undertaker pretty much the whole time."

OB/GYN from Chicago turned and walked away before the envoy could reply. Pavil offered John and Patricia an embarrassed look before wandering off as well.

As Carl watched, astonished, Wolfenson's chest began to heave like he was trying his best to hold down an eruption of grief. He lost the battle, and the muscles in his face practically wrung the tears from his eyes. Patricia tried to grab him, hold him, but he gently pulled away. On the second try, she was able to rope him into her arms.

Hushing him, patting his back, she wondered how she ever could have believed that this man was not her husband. If she was giving herself the benefit of the doubt, perhaps the person she had known for years had simply evolved, and somehow she had missed all the signs. That's if she was giving herself the benefit of the doubt, which she really didn't deserve.

"Honey, I'm so proud of you for trying," she said. "What you did, pulling these people out of the wreckage and then fighting for their lives... I can't tell you how proud I am."

Despite Carl's best efforts to control everything, the last twenty-four hours had sprung too many surprises. His completely indulged paranoia told him there were tea leaves to be read if he only stopped and shook out the strainer. This latest bombshell rendered all of his intelligence reports useless.

Never in a million years could he have predicted that the Angel of Light would respond to a dressing down from a nicotine-deprived OB/GYN by seeking solace in the arms of his wife. It was as if Carl had started the night watching one movie, but when he left and came back with some popcorn, he somehow ended up in the wrong theater, watching a similar movie with the same actors, but completely different performances.

Whatever was going on, the scene made Carl uncomfortable—John was blubbering like a five year-old who had skinned his knee, and Patricia was babying him like a doting mother. So Carl tried to slip away in the same direction as the doctors.

"Wait," Wolfenson said.

Carl stopped and turned around, feeling ridiculous for even trying to make a clean exit. "Mr. Envoy..."

Wolfenson held up a finger and turned to Patricia. "Honey, thank you for your support. But I've got to somehow pull it together."

He wiped the tears from his face, gracefully and yet altogether manly. Carl wasn't sure how he managed to pull it off. The real Wolfenson, even on his best day, would never have been able to look so cinematic.

"I don't care what the doctors here have to say. I'm not going to give up."

"John, what do you mean?"

Instead of answering, Wolfenson turned to Carl. "I need you to swing into action. I need you to step up like you've always done before. Can you do that?"

"Yes, sir, absolutely."

"Excellent." He pulled out the sat phone Carl had given him and started dialing a number. "I'm calling the Interior Minister of Israel. In the meantime, I need you to arrange transportation for these patients to the airport. We're all flying to Tel Aviv. From there, I need you to co-ordinate an emergency med evac to Balshem Medical Center in Jerusalem. They treated me well there during my recovery. Can you do that for me?"

Carl's eyes had drifted over to one of the nineteen patients, a young girl, maybe ten years old. He had to base her age on her height, because any other telling mark had been obfuscated by wounds. Her head looked like a lumpy dermoid cyst, with bloody, matted hair, crooked teeth, and fully exposed tissues and nerves. Her one eye stared fixedly, glassy as a marble, and somehow the bare stump of her arm no longer bled.

Carl looked over at Patricia before answering, but she only had eyes for John. So he turned back to the envoy, who had just put the phone to his ear.

"Sir, are you sure you really want to attempt transporting these patients to Tel Aviv?"

While the phone rang, Wolfenson took a moment to meet Carl's eyes. "We absolutely have no choice. We must do everything we can for these poor souls, or none of us will be able to live with ourselves."

Carl nodded. "Of course, sir. I'll make it happen immediately."

But Wolfenson was no longer looking at him. And Patricia had turned her attention on one of the nineteen.

Carl nodded again and then started up the main aisle of the tent toward the exit. "Brilliant," he said to himself.

What the hell had happened to the "victory lap" in devastated Aleppo? The level jump that would catapult John Wolfenson to the upper echelon of power and fame—providing the platform for the next major step in the envoy's plan?

Apparently someone had called an audible at the Aleppo line of scrimmage, and now the plan somehow was to fly nineteen corpses into Israel.

And where the hell was Fincher?

Carl had been abandoned and shut out in the dark. Not only that, he was being asked to use his influence and his company's reputation to get them past the strictest, most draconian customs department in the world.

He was being asked to risk it all.

The only good news seemed to be, he could count on staying alive at least until they cleared security at Ben Gurion International. But after that, Carl was absolutely certain he was a dead man.

In fact, that's probably where Fincher was: somewhere near the Gaza Strip, choosing the spot for a shallow grave, perhaps even digging the hole himself.

Carl emerged from the medical tent into the smoky night air. At least the helicopters had stopped circling overhead. Maybe he could count on a few minutes of relative silence, so he could clear his head and think of a plan... a napkin plan.

They were the worst kind. Typically it meant you were in some off-the-grid dive, surrounded by at least a few people you had just met, discussing a major operation in a locale you had never been to, and working on more than a few contingency scenarios because your plan had loopholes big enough that even a Russian satellite could spot them. And yet, after that twelfth cup of coffee, you managed to convince yourself everything would work out because you were using a black Sharpie to capture all the details on some table napkins.

"Absolutely brilliant," Carl said.

But it was the best he could hope for against something the Angel of Light had been plotting for years. Maybe even hundreds of years. A napkin plan against something inked into animal skin.

THE STORY CONTINUES in *DEMON DAYS - BOOK FOUR*

ACKNOWLEDGEMENTS

D.L. SNELL

Thanks to Dr. Kim Paffenroth for the Latin, and both Zeinah Abunuwar and Ahmad Al-Shakarji for the Arabic. And thanks to Krakenten for the invaluable lesson in firearms. Also, I would like to acknowledge all the fans of the first book: without you... well, without you we'd still go on writing, but it would be a lonely, lonely business.

RICHARD FINNEY

I want to express my appreciation for the feedback and invaluable support of Jay Frasco Emily Finney was so very helpful with her research. Of course none of this would have been possible without the support of David and the rest of the fine people at Ape Entertainment. And a special thanks to Danuta Skulski, who read the first half of this book overnight. Her enthusiasm for the story and her desire to read the rest of the book kept me writing.

ABOUT THE AUTHORS

RICHARD FINNEY is a Los Angeles based writer and film producer.

Visit his website -- richardfinney.blogspot.com

D.L. SNELL is a novelist, a member of the Horror Writers Association, and a freelance editor for Permuted Press. He has sold short stories to anthologies such as Pocket Books' *Blood Lite* series, and his first novel *Roses of Blood on Barbwire Vines* pits zombies against vampires. Author Nicholas Grabowsky has called Snell's work "damn good writing."